NDIDI AGUWA

FEARLESS

The Battle Begins

To Jimmy,
Don't be afraid to be fearless.

ARCHWAY
PUBLISHING

Archway Publishing books may be ordered through booksellers or by contacting:

Archway Publishing
1663 Liberty Drive
Bloomington, IN 47403
www.archwaypublishing.com
1 (888) 242-5904

Because of the dynamic nature of the Internet, any web addresses or
links contained in this book may have changed since publication and
may no longer be valid. The views expressed in this work are solely those
of the author and do not necessarily reflect the views of the publisher,
and the publisher hereby disclaims any responsibility for them.

Any people depicted in stock imagery provided by Getty Images are
models, and such images are being used for illustrative purposes only.
Certain stock imagery © Getty Images.

ISBN: 978-1-4808-6606-5 (sc)
ISBN: 978-1-4808-6607-2 (hc)
ISBN: 978-1-4808-6605-8 (e)

Library of Congress Control Number: 2018909024

Print information available on the last page.

Archway Publishing rev. date: 08/10/2018

To my cousin, Yagazie Aguwa and to every teen
writer who dreams of being published.

CHAPTER ONE

Zing!

The last lightning bolt of the night strikes, setting my hair on edge and sending a shock through my body. My skin tingles like it is numb, and the Fire in my body shoots through my veins. My heart sinks. The sensation is kind of addicting. The thunderstorm is over, so I won't feel the electrifying rush anymore. All I can hear now is the *pitter-patter* noises of the light rain on my window.

The thunderstorm was distracting me from my habit. Everybody has their own, whether it be listening to music before a game or meditating before taking an exam. Mine is looking at a picture of my family—when we were all together—before going to bed.

The dark wooden frame is worn from my thumb rubbing against it for over a year. The picture, however, is pristine. My eleven sisters and I are in the middle, and our mom and dad stand on either side of us. The six eldest sit in white lawn chairs in the front, while the six youngest stand behind them. Lucky me. I missed out on being one of the oldest. Instead, I get to be referred to as 'the oldest of the youngest'. Because of that, the number seven is my least favorite number.

I set the frame down on my nightstand. I suppose I should look out of place in the picture because I *feel* out of place, but I don't. My mother passed down her bright red hair, ghastly pale skin, and intense hazel eyes to me, along with two of my sisters. Also, her height. Yay, I'm five-foot-ten and towered over everyone until the ninth grade. Add that to my alleged anger issues and you have a girl that is most definitely not winning "Most Popular" in school yearbooks.

Sometimes I wish wielding the element Fire would make me more fearless. Unfortunately, because of it I'm the opposite. I constantly feel like if I lose my cool, I'll torch everyone in sight. I'm like a walking, ticking bomb. And it's only a matter of time before I detonate.

The wooden door creaks open and my roommate, Natalie Wilde, enters the room. We're pretty close, but she looks very different from me with shoulder-length, dark brown hair, eerie green eyes, and skin the color of coffee beans.

"How come you do that every day?" she asks.

"It's a ritual," I say. "I've gotten used to doing it every night."

Natalie walks over to her bunk bed and begins to tend to her many plants. Earthens are hardcore gardeners. She has them surrounding her bed, on the window sill, peeking out of the closet ... if I had allergies, I'd go crazy. But all the flowers do have a nice scent. It's the kind of thing that can pick you up on a bad day.

I touch the teardrop-shaped necklace hanging around my neck. Since I'm the Fire Keeper, I hold the Firestone. It's the power source of all Fire Wielders. If it were to be destroyed, all Fire Wielders would lose their powers ... and die soon after. It's set in stone, and on the back, there's an odd etching. I'm not quite sure what it is, and neither is Natalie. There's a single flame with a lightning bolt on top. Towards the bottom, there's a tiny F etched in the stone. F must mean fire. So is it just another Fire symbol?

Natalie's necklace flashes emerald green in the fluorescent lighting. She guards one of the four Elemental stones, like me, as she's the Earth Keeper, but the Earthstone is an emerald. Hers has a weird etching on the back of it, as well, but hers is a tree with a small E in the bottom left corner. We're not sure why our mothers were allowed to give us the tremendous responsibility of guarding life sources. You'd think they'd get sensible adults, but, nevertheless, we accept out duties all the same. Still, no one is giving us answers, and the Water and Air Keepers are nowhere to be found.

When I first arrived here at Lalande Academy, I set *condolas*, which are special Elemental candles, up all over my freshman dorm room so I could practice wielding my Element upon Dean Martins's suggestion. I go around the room, lighting all ten of them with my hand. I feel a weird thrill whenever I use my powers for some reason. Maybe it's because not everyone in this world can make fire appear at will. Okay. Time to clear all thoughts. Standing in the center of the room, I shake my head to make myself calm and focus on all ten *condola* flames at once. Then I pull them towards me, slowly, very slowly, until they are one. I then add more fire to the ball. It's an exercise that helps me see the difference in every fire ever created. I have to match the right flames with the *condolas* they came from.

Even though I do this once a week, Natalie still looks freaked out. So to cause her even more stress, I separate it correctly into several flames, send them back to the *condolas*, and then flick them around her head. Then I bring them back to me, laughing so hard I can't breathe.

"McKenna, that's not part of your routine!" she shrieks.

"I know, but it was fun making you scared." I toss the fireball in my hands. *"Votoki rupay amsdokir."* That means *I like making you scared* in Kevanese. All Elementals are born with it hardwired into their brain, because Kevanese is the language of magic. As a result, it's impossible for non-Elementals to decipher. Sometimes I'll start speaking it and won't even know I've switched. In fact, many Elemental conversations at Lalande are a mix between English and Kevanese.

"Whatever."

I kill the fire, allowing myself to absorb the flames into my body. The red glow from the Firestone around my neck pulses wildly, as if it's as exhilarated as I am.

It happens in an instant, almost so quickly I miss it. My necklace throbs like a heartbeat, and a wet, watery, running sensation flows through my body. Then it pounds again, and an airy, windy sensation comes over me. My hair lifts off my shoulders.

I glance at Natalie, who seems to be experiencing the same thing as me.

That's weird. That's never happened before.

My necklace violently vibrates like it's possessed. I don't even have time to glance at Natalie in alarm before the lights go out and an indescribable feeling of terror takes over me. Natalie and I scream to the high heavens as a feeling of death and pain fills the room, choking us.

Then the feeling goes away, and the only thing I can see is our necklaces glowing red and green.

I wipe the warm tears from my cheeks and shakily snap up a small flame. I use it to guide me to the door so I can turn on the lights. I sense a short circuit and, using my metal affinity, fix the problem through the walls by feeling the crossed pieces through the wall and uncrossing them.

The lights flick on.

My heart is racing. What has the power to do this kind of thing? And why? I don't think witches and warlocks, whether they are regular or light, have the power to do it. Regular sorcerers can't control the mind, and light sorcerers aren't extraordinarily powerful. The only plausible answer would be a Phantom—a sort of dark sorcerer. But there aren't any Phantoms at our school.

Already in my pajamas, I crawl into my bed and look at Natalie. "We have to tell Dean Martins. Him or Dean Papadopoulos."

"No, we don't!" she cries.

I roll my eyes. "Nat, I felt like I was dying back there. This kind of thing could happen to someone else."

"So?"

I fight the urge to leap across the room and throttle her. She may be an Earthen, but sometimes she acts so clueless that she gets on my nerves.

I pull back my thin orange covers and stand up. I bump my head on the top bunk bed, but I don't even care. "Fine. You don't have to tell Dean, but I will." I fumble for my flip-flops and slide them on my calloused feet. I'm not putting anyone else in danger by staying silent. Natalie's behavior is odd, though. She's usually a do-gooder. She's the one who nags at me to do the right thing, not the other way around.

"*Sin!*" Natalie screams, saying no in our language. It is a guttural, primitive scream that rebounds all over the room. I look at her in alarm and nearly scream myself. Her eyes are a flat black with flecks of purple in them. She snaps at the ground, pointing a finger, and thick, leafy, brown vines sprout out of the ground, out of nowhere. They wrap and wind and twist themselves around me, like snakes preparing to constrict their food.

I try to scream, but I can't; the vines coil around my throat and cut me off. I try to breathe, but the vines will not allow me. I can't breathe. I can only stare at Natalie as she waves her arms around. Why would Natalie try to choke me? "*Parcer,*" I whisper, begging my best friend to release me.

And then she snaps out of it.

The vines immediately snake back into the ground, disappearing as if there is somebody pulling them in an imaginary hole.

Rubbing my neck, I stare wide-eyed at Natalie as my legs give way and I sink to the floor. My heart beats triple time as I try to catch my breath. My best friend is a monster. *My best friend is a monster.* She reaches out for me, and I flinch. What if she tries to kill me again?

"McKenna, wait." She rushes over to me and grabs my arm.

"Don't touch me!" I yell, shaking her arm off and backing away from her. I start heading for the door, letting the built up electricity inside me crackle at my fingertips so she won't get too close. "I'll fry you if I have to!"

"No, no, no ..." she says over and over, shaking her head and not even bothering to wipe away her tears. The clear drops create winding paths as her head moves. "Just hear me out."

Who is this girl standing behind me? Where is my best friend? "No. What is there to hear?"

"Wait. McKenna. *Plaisi.*"

And something in her voice stops me in my tracks.

"What?" I say. This better be good. My neck still hurts.

"It wasn't me." Natalie says, closing her eyes. "It was something else."

"Oh, really?" I ask snidely. "It wasn't you? Because I'm pretty sure it was Natalie Gaea Wilde that tried to use vines to strangle me to death." Now I'm annoyed about the whole thing.

"That's not what I meant," Natalie sighs and runs her fingers through her short hair. "Something took over me when our necklaces started vibrating. It felt like my soul was being locked away in a box and I couldn't get out. I could hear a girl's voice say, 'If you struggle, it's going to make things harder', and then I could feel my powers being used for evil."

Brown vines. "The vines were brown," I say softly. "That's a bad thing, isn't it?"

"See?" She twirls her pendant around on her neck.

The silence after that is deafening; it seems to swallow up the whole room in its entirety. The temperature in the room increases a little, making me more comfortable. The choking feeling in the air seems to loosen a little, and I step in front of our mirror and examine my neck. The skin there is regaining its usual fair color, but now I'm sporting thick, pink indentations.

I can practically hear her heart pumping her element, Earth, back and forth, back and forth, as I wearily slide into my bed. I wonder if the light her power gives off has turned back to green.

I wonder, I wonder. I wonder if Natalie will agree to tell Dean Martins tomorrow. I wonder what I will dream tonight, *if* I do.

I wonder if I'll ever see my mother and sisters again. Heaven knows I'd do anything to find them.

Anything.

*"**Do you even** know what you're doing, Emma?" A girl whines from the passenger seat. "Let me drive. I'm way more familiar with Cortlandt." Strands of her pale blond hair fall in her face, but without her moving a finger, they get pushed out of the way. I notice a puckered scar over her right eyebrow.*

"Pa féi tima desnir, sin," the driver says stubbornly, her annoyance bringing out a Texan accent even in another language. She, too, is a blond, but her hair is the color of goldenrod. Paired with her bright blue eyes, flawless, freckle-free skin, and deep dimples, she's easily the most beautiful girl anyone has ever seen. I'm instantly jealous. And since she spoke in Kevanese, saying "For the last time, no", *all three of them must be Elementals. "I'm not letting anyone drive who has the ability to vervoy. You could accidentally flip out of here and then there'd be no one driving this car. You think I want to die today?"*

"She's got a point, Samantha," the girl in the back agrees. A violet stripe in the front draws attention to her raven black hair, which is a shock against her ghostly pale skin. She trains her matching purple eyes on the girl in the passenger seat. Watching them is almost like watching a movie. The point-of-view angles keep changing.

"Whatever." Samantha's gray eyes roll. Emma drives over a depression in the road, and the car jolts.

"And furthermore," Emma raises a finger. "I got my license before either of you, so I have the most experience out of all of us."

"Again, true," the black haired girl concedes.

"Shut up, Raven. Do any of you even know where we're going?"

"No, Sam," Emma says derisively. "I just hopped in the car without any idea on how to get to Lalande Academy. GPS, hello."

Samantha slouches in her worn leather seat. The Camry is old and clunky, but secretly, Samantha loves it. Somehow I know that, which makes things even weirder. Emma smiles and hums to beat of the wipers. Swish, swish. Swish, swish. Samantha knows this song. She wants to sing along but doesn't know if she should. After a little while, though, she gives in. She has a very nice voice—the voice of a Siren, Emma sometimes says.

"See?" Emma says. "A little rain can make anyone happy."

"Um, Emma, rain usually makes people sad. It ruins plans." Raven frowns.

"Not if you're a Water User."

"Well, not everyone is a Water User."

Raven and Samantha sleep lightly soon after, but they never fully wake up for another hour. When she thinks no one is looking, Emma turns off the wipers. She sees things even better when she looks at them through water. She opens the windows to let the rain in. The droplets feel cool and refreshing on her skin.

"Are we there yet?" Samantha asks. "And can you close the windows? I'm getting soaked."

"Almost." Emma sighs and closes the windows. And that's when I realize why the girls are so important.

There's the Waterstone around Emma's neck.

And there's the Airstone around Samantha's neck.

CHAPTER TWO

"You okay?" Natalie is right in my face as I crack open my eyes the next morning.

"*Plaisi*, Natalie." I yawn, which promptly gets her to move out of my side of the room. "Personal space. Why wouldn't I be okay?"

"You always wake up at the crack of dawn," she says, tapping her foot rapidly and raising her eyebrows. "And we're almost late for an assembly. They announced it ten minutes ago."

Late? If Dean Martins catches us, he'll give us hell. I thrust back the covers and leap out of bed, hitting my head on the underside of the top bunk. At this point in time, I don't even care. "Crap!"

I race into the girls' dorm bathroom and take a two minute shower, shuddering as the water makes contact with my skin. Steam billows off of me, fogging up the bathroom window and mirrors. I throw on a lavender shirt and jeans. Then I slide on my black Converse All Stars and race out of our dorm, Natalie trailing behind.

It seems that we aren't the only ones running late, because a lot of the junior girls are coming out of their rooms, yawning. Half of them are in their pajamas.

I look for my friend Amelie Avanti, but she doesn't seem to be in the hallway. "Have you seen Amelie?" I ask Natalie as we fight our way down the hall. She shakes her head. Elbows and bodies slam into me as the hallway gets even more crowded. There shouldn't be this many people on the second junior floor. I guess more girls decided to stay for the summer than I'd realized.

"Move it, brat," Alexis Avanti, Amelie's twin, nearly knocks me over. She hates me with every iota of her being, and I reciprocate. "Get the hell out of my way." She pushes me away from Natalie and I end up bumping into Paola Pasatino.

"Oh, go screw yourself," I snap, but Alexis has moved ahead and doesn't hear me. This is child's play coming from her. Usually she'd have a nasty line from her arsenal locked and loaded into her pistol, ready to fire at me. She must be really tired, then, because she just missed a great opportunity to put me down. I've half a mind to flick some sparks onto her new designer top by Lily Who-Gives-A-Crap, or some other fashion icon we could never afford, but I'm not that mean.

Paola is sort of a joke at the school. She has multiple piercings on her ear, one on her eyebrow, tongue, lip, nose, and allegedly her belly button. She's biologically a light witch, but she can see multiple outcomes for the future, which is under the regular witch category. Mario's on-again, off-again girlfriend, she prides herself on being edgy and different.

"Sorry," I mumble, lowering my gaze to my shoes. Avoid eye contact at all costs.

I can practically hear her grinning as she says, "No problem, McKenna." I feel bad for her because, except for her roommate, no one really is friends with her. Everyone pretty much steers clear. She's clingy, like lint.

Thankfully, Natalie reappears, grabbing my arm and saying, "Come on, they're about to start." She drags me down the stairs, out of the dorm building, Maiyrn House, and we race to the auditorium building, pushing past a large pack of seniors.

We burst into the auditorium at top speed, ignoring the stares of the seven hundred other high schoolers staying for the summer as we climb a set of bleachers. We sit down next to Celestia Zhou, an Asian-American Fire Wielder. Her layered jet-black hair swings as she turns to face us. Is that a roll of measuring tape around her neck? Yes. Yes it is. She and I became friends when I sort of rescued her from Alexis and Cara's verbal firing squad soon after I arrived here two years ago.

"Has it started yet?" I ask her.

"No," she answers. She turns around quickly, and then whispers, "Check your six. Or, maybe not. You know, if you don't want to look desperate or anything." Natalie turns around to look, smirks, and also tells me not to.

Obviously, when someone tells you not to look, you do, so I whip my head around and come face to face with Mark O'Reilly, a fellow Fire Wielder and a friend of mine. He is sixteen years old, just like me. He has light brown, wavy hair, sparkling hazel eyes, what might be the sharpest jaw line ever, and feathery eyelashes. My heart races, and not because we ran.

"Hey," he says, grinning.

"Hey," I say back. We used to be way less awkward than this, but for the past couple of weeks, we've cut down on the chit-chat and amped up the blushing. Hence the 'hey's.

His twin, Liam, also says hey. They look pretty similar, but everyone can tell them apart because Liam has pale blue eyes and a birthmark on his left temple, and Mark's hair is a shade darker. He elbows Mark before saying, "Mark and I were just talking about the assembly. Know what it's for?"

I tilt my head in the direction of the stage. "Not sure. Probably to remind us to do our community service hours by mid-August or return our overdue books to the library or—"

"—or to introduce those new girls down there," Natalie cuts in.

"Which girls?" Liam asks instantly, craning his neck to catch a glimpse of them. Celestia rolls her eyes and lightly thwacks him on the knee.

"Who are they?" Mark says at the same time, and then pauses. "Bet Liam wants to know, now that his girl radar has just kicked in."

"What are you talking about?" Liam playfully kicks his twin in the leg. "You're the one with girl radar. Not me. Although," he adds sneakily, "He only uses it to find one person—"

Mark slugs him on the shoulder before Liam can get any farther. But I'm intrigued. Who does Mark pay special attention to? Me?

But why would it be me? What a stupid thought. If there's anything I've learned these past two years, it's that Mark and I are friends, nothing more. And, although he is attractive, I'll never admit that he is the reason my heart races for no good reason.

Liam flashes me a grin that, if I didn't know better, would say was flirtatious. But I know that his attention is directed at the stage, and I turn to look. Goldilocks-blonde tresses, near white hair, and that unforgettable purple stripe.

There, on the stage, are Emma, Samantha, and Raven.

"**Let's get started,** shall we?" Dean Martins, on the stage below, calls out. He doesn't have a microphone; instead he uses magic to amplify his voice.

"What are they doing here?" I whisper urgently to Natalie and Celestia. They both shrug. Whoops. They don't know about my dream.

"They're new," Celestia says, looking at me curiously. "Why? You know them?"

"No ..." I hesitate, and then give in. "They were in my dream last night. They were on their way here, but I didn't really think much of it."

"Do you know their names?" Natalie asks.

I nod and start to tell her, but am cut off by Dean Martins. "We have three very special new students here: Emma Richards,

Samantha Mazer, and Raven Blackwood." He points to Emma, Sam, and Raven respectively. "Emma and Samantha are the Water and Air Keepers, respectively, and Raven is a Phantom. They're all going to be juniors."

The crowd breaks out into loud whispers, not even caring that the other two Keepers have been identified. Even I grow suspicious of Raven. I know it's unfair, but in Elemental history, Phantoms have been nothing but evil traitors. Plus, it might have been a Phantom who possessed Natalie yesterday.

"Settle down, guys." Dean makes calm-down motions with his hands, and the noise subsides a little. "Nothing's wrong with Raven, and no, she isn't evil. We've done background checks like we always do for unattended students that show up here. They're all clear. She's lived with Sam for a while, and separated from her twin sister for sixteen years. They will live here on campus like all of you for the remainder of the summer, and in the fall, they will be attending school here. Make sure to give them a warm welcome. You know how important a Keeper's job is. All right. You guys can go back to what you were doing."

The noise starts up again, and elbows and bags are being thrust in my face. I bend down and tie my shoe as Natalie says, "We should go meet them in the commons room."

"Why?" I ask. I want to go back to sleep.

We leave the auditorium, and finally I can spot Amelie Avanti through the groups of people clustered on the quad. She is talking to Alexis. Alexis flips me the bird, and I glare back. Alexis and Amelie are polar opposites. Alexis has dirty blond hair that won't hold a curl, eyes the color of blue steel, and a hooked nose that she won't stop complaining about. But while Alexis is your average blonde cheerleader—who unfortunately is *not* brainless—Amelie is dark haired and violet eyed, kind of like Raven. She suffers from severe acne, but only in the winter. Amelie is the nicest person you'll ever have the fortune of coming across.

"Well, if they're going to be our roommates—at least Emma and Samantha are—then we're going to have to—"

"Wait, what?" I stop walking and turn to face her. "Emma and Samantha are rooming with us?"

Natalie nods and waves at our friend Cole Gangret.

"Who told you that?"

"I just know," she replies as Emma, Samantha, and Raven exit the auditorium. A swarm of people surrounds them. "It makes sense to have the Keepers all together since we're going to be working together in the future. Wait here."

Natalie uses her sharp shoulders to edge her way through the crowd. The force she uses is purely Earthen power; as a regular human, she couldn't make it through the swarm of eager students. "I'm going to have to borrow them for a while," she says as angry glances are thrown her way. Her voice is muffled as she edges deeper. I can't see her now, but there's a scuffle going on in the middle of the circle. She's definitely the cause.

She emerges quickly, dragging Emma and Samantha out by their wrists. Raven seems to have disappeared. They don't even look fazed by her absence. Up close, their clothes are wrinkled. They look like … school uniforms? Blue and gray plaid skirts, white polos with a weird logo. I tilt my head at Emma, and she blushes.

"We escaped right after school on the last day, and her aunt didn't have spare clothes for us," she says timidly, contrasting the confidence emanating from her in the dream. "Do I look horrible? We've been traveling for days."

"No, you look fine," I assure her. I don't add that she'd probably look fine if she was rocking garbage-bag chic.

"Ready to go? You're rooming with us," Natalie says, letting go of their hands. They nod silently, glancing at all of us in awe, like we're the dawn of the new day. Or something.

Someone wolf-whistles, and a guy shouts, "Yo, Emma! Let me show you around!" His friends laugh hysterically, like he told them a really funny joke.

"Where, your dorm room?" the guy next to him says, smirking.

The guy, who I recognize as Mario Espinoza, walks up to and puts an arm around Emma's waist. Emma looks really uncomfortable. Her cheeks take on a deep pink color.

"Whoa, whoa!" I say, holding out my hand. Mario, who is an Earthen, looks alarmed. "What do you think you're doing?"

He regains his composure. "Just trying to be a good friend." Emma tries to wriggle out of his embrace, but he doesn't let her. Figures. Earthens are really strong.

"Get your hands off her!" Sam pushes Mario's chest.

His eyes narrow. "Don't touch me."

"You're one to talk." She raises her hands again, but this time she pushes him with a huge blast of air. He's thrown backwards and hits the ground with a thud. "Stay away from Emma, you greasy, slimy, half-witted, before-picture-lookin' douche!"

"Oh, that's it," he growls, cracking his knuckles and making me cringe. I hate that sound.

I start to feel uneasy when Mario creates rocks and holds them in his hands. "You're not really going to do that, are you?"

He snickers. "People don't disrespect me without paying for it." He gestures to his friends, and they follow his lead, conjuring up their various elements. It's now that I remember that Mario and his friends are our school's "thugs". There aren't any staff members outside right now, at least, none that I can see.

"Run!" I shout.

Our heavy footfalls mixed with theirs reverberate through the air as Samantha, Emma, Natalie, and I race across the quad towards Maiyrn. I can run way faster than this, but I don't want to leave Natalie and the newbies behind. The boys are not far behind us, and when I look back, more people have joined them. Why, I'm not sure. Probably more of Mario's friends. My brain is telling me to do something drastic.

But how can I? Mario and his friends are juniors. They're in my grade. I go to school with those people. Plus, they're Elementals, just like me. People. Using Fire isn't all about blowing things up and setting things aflame. It's about control, especially since our powers could cause damage and destruction. Wielding the most powerful Element means one has to be extremely careful in cases like this. Choosing the right thing is critical.

My stomach begins to feel icy and upset. I know what this feeling is. It's fear. I try to be fearless, but I can't. My powers will grow out of control and I can't do anything about it.

My keycard is in my pocket, but I'm notorious for fumbling with objects. And I know for a fact that the locks on the doors, even with my metal affinity help, will not unlock fast enough to escape the mob.

So instead of blasting them into incinerated bits, I thrust out my hand without thinking and create a Firewall.

Chapter Three

In my defense, I was trying to protect us from the mob. Maybe Dean Martins doesn't know what Black Friday is, because, in the real world, we would have been trampled.

I shift uncomfortably in my seat, shying away from his penetrating glare. It's unusual for one to be able to look at one person and every person in the room at the same and yet, Dean M manages to do it. Emma, who sits next to me, elbows me and gives me a questioning look. I raise my eyebrows, clueless.

It's the five of us in there: Emma, Natalie, Samantha, Dean, and me. Raven is still MIA, but I doubt anyone notices. Or, for that matter, cares. Mario and his friends met with the dean before us, and they came out with smug looks on their faces. They must have successfully convinced him they weren't doing anything wrong.

Absentmindedly, I start to create a fireball when Dean Martins says, "You know, we have a policy about use of magic or powers on campus. It's in the Lalande manual."

The Lalande manual. I try to search my memory to find out where I had thrown that book, which was really cheap photocopy paper stapled together. I figured since Natalie's been here for longer than I had, she'd be able to help me with all of the rules. So I threw it out when I arrived.

But that was two years ago. It's probably a book or toilet paper or whatever they make out of recycled paper.

"Sorry," I shrug sheepishly. "I just remembered that Wal-Mart man that got trampled and died and I didn't want to follow suit."

Emma's laugh is loud and delicate. Dean averts his eyes to glare at her, and she shoves her grin deep inside of herself. I sneak a glance at her, though, and her eyes are still smiling.

"There are other ways to stop aggressive fans, you know. Words are one of them." His crossed arms add to the statement.

Silence. Fans. Ha. Whatever they were, they sure weren't fans. Mario wanted our heads. The other people probably hate the newbies because they associate themselves with Raven. Natalie is fidgeting in her seat and opening and closing her mouth like she wants to say something. Samantha beats her to it.

"Dean, that guy threatened us!" she says, flying out of her seat and slamming her hands onto Dean's desk. "He grabbed Emma, which was *totally* inappropriate, and when I defended her, they started chasing us!" Samantha is fuming, which seems a bit odd for an Air Manipulator. They're supposed to be the cool, calm, and collected ones.

One of Dean's eyebrows raises the tiniest bit. Samantha sees it and continues with, "I think …" she turns to me. "McKenna, is it?" I nod.

She faces forward again. "I think McKenna was completely justified in setting up the Firewall. The injuries that the other students got are nothing major."

Dean sits forward, a frown on his face. He clasps his hands over his varnished wooden desk. "Are you saying that severe *burns* are nothing major?" The question is transparent wrapping paper. The threat inside is visible for everybody to see.

"They weren't severe, Dean Martins. They were barely first-degree." Samantha says, like, *don't be silly.* "I'm just saying that if she needs to defend herself, she should be able to. And, perhaps create another one of those policies about harassment. People need to respect other people. Respect *us*."

Samantha is pushing it, we all know. The creases in Dean Martins' forehead grow more and more pronounced with each of Samantha's words.

"I will take that request into consideration," Dean says, sighing with resignation. He is fifty-seven years old, but sometimes he seems ageless with his neatly combed brown hair, thoughtful brown eyes, and decent early-morning stubble. Elementals tend to live longer than humans, and thus aging slows down in their forties.

His office matches his style. The inside is decorated to look like a log cabin interior. Wooden walls, thatched chairs. There is even a fireplace with an actual fire burning in it, even though New York in July is unforgivably sweltering for most people. I find the heat comfortable. Emma, Natalie, and Samantha don't seem to feel the same way: the three of them glisten with sweat. So, yeah. The fireplace was a fail.

In an instant, I realize that I am still holding my growing fireball. By now, it has gotten so big that my hands are engulfed in it, so I twist in my seat and toss it into the fireplace. The fire grows bigger.

Dean is smiling at me as I turn back to face forward. "Emma, Samantha, you two should train with McKenna and Natalie. Dean Papadopoulos trains them every evening. It'll help you gain complete control over your powers. How does that sound?"

Simultaneously, Emma, Samantha, Natalie, and I crane our necks to look at each other. "That sounds good." Emma says, wringing her hands in her lap.

"Yeah," Sam agrees.

Natalie doesn't like the idea, I can tell. It's as if he told her to go play hopscotch on a bunch of Legos. After a moment, Sam does too, and I'm not sure why. I'm fine with training with them. I've gotten used to it being just Dean P, Natalie, and me, but adding two more can't hurt. Plus, it'll give us a chance to get to know the new girls more, and between my dream and the past hour we've known them, they—along with Raven—seem like very interesting girls.

A smug smile is now tacked upon his face as he says, "Then it's settled. Every day after dinner is when you'll train. An hour and a half long should do the trick. You'll start tomorrow."

His relaxed position gives me the "okay" to stand up. The others follow my lead, fanning themselves and stretching their limbs.

Samantha, who is closest to the door, sets her hand on the doorknob as Dean Martins yanks one of his many wooden drawers and says, "Wait!"

We all turn to look at him. What next?

"Sorry, sorry." His narrow face is flustered as he rummages through the drawer. "I don't usually forget. Emma, Samantha, here." He pulls out two lanyards. A golden room key dangles from each one. "You both are rooming with McKenna and Natalie. They'll show you where the room is."

Emma and Samantha accept the room keys, and, with that, we dismiss ourselves from the office.

"So," Mark says next to me after we run into him on the quad. "I noticed that you all have etchings on the back of your necklaces. Do they symbolize anything?"

Emma shrugs, and Samantha says, "I don't know."

"I don't know, either." I reply, toying with my own. "My mom told my dad to give it to me when she disappeared. All I know is that this is the Firestone, and I'm supposed to protect it. No one ever said anything about the symbols."

"I think all of our Elemental parents did, right?" Natalie offers. "Give it to us, I mean. I've read a lot about ancient Elemental symbols. There were ones to represent the four Elements that looked just like these. Some were infused with magic to protect the wearer of the jewelry. Though I'm not quite sure why they gave them to us so young."

Protection. Her words hang in the air, making me wonder if I was wrong all these years in thinking my mother and sisters abandoned Dad and me. Maybe they didn't. Maybe it was the opposite. Maybe she had no choice but to run away. Something could have forced her to.

"We should go find our parents. It's the least we can do for them." Emma says with certain finality.

"Bad idea," Mark, Natalie, and I say at the same time.

"Why not?" Emma asks.

"Because," Natalie rolls her eyes. "we obviously don't know where they are. Secondly, even if we did, Acerbity tracks our movements. They would find us and slaughter us before we even reached our parents. And thirdly, Acerbity is most likely the reason our parents went missing. So, they might be holding them hostage, waiting for us to look for them, and when we find them, Acerbity will jump out of the shadows, say, 'Boo!' for good measure, and kill us all."

Emma and Samantha look at Natalie like she's grown another head.

"What is Acerbity?" Samantha says. "How can bitterness attack us?"

They don't know who Acerbity is? Where the hell did they come from, under a rock?

"You don't know who Acerbity is?" Mark says incredulously. "Are you serious?" He stops in his tracks.

Sam nods slowly. "Uh, no, we don't, and yes, we're being serious. It's not like anybody told us in the two hours we've been here."

By now, we've reached the entrance to the girls' dorm, Maiyrn House. We stop walking, because neither Mark nor any other boy can't even go near it.

"You girls should ask Dean Papadopoulos tomorrow when you begin training. It'll do you two no good being in the dark about them."

He flashes me a grin and, with that, strides away to the boys' dorm, Piann House.

For a moment, I'm paralyzed. So much for my original plan of not thinking about him in that way. My face flushes red as I turn back to the girls. I know they watched our sort of private exchange. Okay, it wasn't private at all.

"McKenna?" Emma inquires mischievously. "Is there something you're not telling us?"

Natalie and Samantha exchange impish looks.

"Hmph." I sniff. "No." I glance down at my watch for a distraction, any distraction. "Don't be silly. Shouldn't we get you guys settled now? It's getting late." I begin to walk up the stairs, though I know no one's following me.

Emma's laughter rings out. It's clear and refreshing, like Water. It should be comforting, but it makes me want to throttle her now. "Okay then, McKenna. Whatever you say."

Emma and Samantha's bags are already inside the dorm room, I notice as we enter the room. Natalie and I smile as they—well, at least Emma—gasp in awe at the size of the dorm room. "Your— *our* room is so *big!*" Emma cries. She pulls her suitcase over to the vacant top bunk bed right over Natalie, sets it down, and climbs gracefully up to the bed.

"What did you expect? Something small and cramped?" I snort and sit on my bed. "This is supposed to fit four people."

Emma clacks her long nails against the top of the other dresser. "Why are there so many students at this time of the year? You guys don't break for summer?"

"We do," Natalie says, "but most parents keep their kids in Elemental boarding schools year-round—save for other vacations—because it's much safer. There's been a spike in attacks against Elementals recently. Parents can also visit during the year."

Emma fidgets with her pleated skirt, and I remember their situation. "So ... what made you come to Lalande?"

She and Sam exchange cautious glances before Sam finally speaks. "On the last day of school, as we were leaving the building, men and women in black clothes began following Emma, Raven, and I. It quickly became clear to the three of us that they wanted to kidnap us, so we had to run away. We managed to lose them for a bit, and Emma stole a car—"

I laugh out loud. Somehow the idea of Emma being a carjacker is too funny to take seriously. "Emma? Stealing cars? Sorry, I don't see it."

Emma giggles. "It all happened really fast. But hey, a girl's got to do what a girl's got to do, right? Anyway, we tried to go to New Jersey, but friends of the bad guys blocked us off. I channeled my inner *Fast & Furious* and got us the hell out of the city. Raven said she'd heard of a boarding school for kids like us, but she didn't know where. Sam has a family friend in Poughkeepsie, about an hour and thirty minutes north of the city, so we went to stay with her for a while. She knew what school Raven was talking about and directed us here." She shrugs. "That's our story."

I'm kind of in awe right now. The three of them are like a superhero origin story come to life. They seem fearless.

Except maybe for the fact that Emma looks kind of traumatized about the whole thing and Sam is as quiet as a mime in a soundproof room. I'm guessing they had to go through a lot in the city, and they must have left some people behind.

Samantha opens her suitcase and uses her Air Manipulator powers to guide her neatly folded clothes into the empty drawers next to mine.

"Nice powers," I say. "That would've come in handy when I had to clean my room back home."

"I'll pay you to do that for me right now," Emma laughs.

Natalie starts to pace back and forth. "Guys, joke all you like, but you need to realize we need to get right down to business here. If we're to train together, we have to know what kinds of things you can do. Like, for example, other than your Element, do you have another power?"

Samantha frowns. "What other power is there?" she says, *lete-tam*—flying—herself up to the only vacant bed in the oversized dorm, right above me.

"For example, in addition to Fire, McKenna can create light, electricity, and metal. I can create organic food and anything related to Earth, and I can heal almost anything. So, what can you do?"

"Oh." Emma gets it now. "I have power over ice and water vapor."

Samantha nods slowly. "Yeah … I have the power of *dimpahan*, which is like telepathy but you hear the thoughts instead of reading minds. I can perform *vervortade*, you know, teleportation, and I can create other gases."

Emma sits Indian-style and gazes wistfully at the ceiling. "Lucky duckling." Samantha gives her a look.

"What? I like ducklings!"

She's crazy.

"Be serious, Emma," Natalie huffs, sitting on her own bed. "We need to get to know each other so we can join forces effectively."

Join forces? Joining forces isn't the problem. At least, not with them. It's Raven that I'm worrying about.

"You don't need to worry about Raven," Samantha says, staring at me.

Damn, I forgot. Air Manipulators can hear thoughts. That's going to get annoying real quick.

"What about me?" A jolt pushes its way through my body, causing me to shiver. Raven, who mysteriously disappeared before the mob formed, is back.

"Hey, where were you?" Samantha asks. Natalie and I inch back a little on our beds, wary of the floating Phantom before us.

"Eh." Raven shrugs, her ghastly pale arms behind her back. She looks odd with her messy uniform hanging awkwardly on her frail body. "In the void. Out and about. Nothing pleasant."

"Obviously." Samantha's gray eyes roll. "Hanging in the void is creepy."

"What's the void?" I ask.

Raven turns to me, a half-smile on her face. "The void," she says, "is the second dimension."

"Cool," I say.

"Not cool," Raven corrects me. "At least for people like you, who thrive on light. There's nothing even remotely cheerful about it. All you do is move at lightning speed through pitch-black darkness. And it's cold, too. It's better than getting beaten up by people who are anti-Phantom, though." As she says that, I notice a small burn on her bare forearm.

"Oh." My surprise must be written all over my face. Well, she does have a point. It's not like she can defend herself, because then she'd look like the monster they make her out to be. "Did someone do that to you?"

She shrugs, crossing her arms. "The hallways here are crowded. I may have bumped into a Fire Wielder or two."

There is silence, for a moment, silence that is as uncomfortable as an itchy wool sweater. *Bumped. Yeah, right.* I can't help but stare at Raven, who is strange but striking in a way. Her luminous skin is pale and almost see-through, a striking contrast next to her raven-black hair. And who could forget the lone violet stripe?

"Are you rooming with us?" Natalie asks warily.

Raven shakes her head ruefully. "Nah," she says. "Not enough space. Dean Papadopoulos put me with Cara Regeh and those twins, Amelie and Alexis Avanti."

I groan. "Not Alexis," I say. "New people should not be subjected to living with *that.*" Nobody should ever have the unfortunate luck of having Alexis as her roommate. I feel so bad for Amelie. Cara's pretty snotty herself. It's going to be like the Bermuda Triangle in there. Or a Death Trap. Either way, Amelie is going to be screwed.

"Why?"

"They're all terrible witches." Natalie frowns, contorting her calm façade. "Especially Alexis. And her twin, Amelie, is just as bad."

"Wait, what?" Natalie is talking about one of my best and only friends here, Amelie Avanti, Alexis's twin. "Amelie is not bad! You're mixing them up."

"Your eyesight must be really bad, then, because Amelie is exactly like her twin."

"*Sin, wamefído sine.*" *No, she isn't.* My hands ball up into fists and I can feel myself start to heat up. "You know what she is? She's a light witch, for goodness sakes. *A light witch.* You think she's going to go on some kind of rampage and kill everyone with a weak *mistemintea*—telekinesis—spell?" I pause for a second to get my temper under control.

"Not like that, McKenna," Natalie frowns. "They don't have a good grasp on their powers. That's what I meant."

"Oh." My face must be flaming red right now.

Count to three. *Cun, deucé, fasol.* Count backwards. *Fasol, deucé, cun.*

"And besides," I say quietly. "She's not the one we should be worrying about." My eyes dart to Raven before I can stop myself.

Wrong move, I say silently to myself as Raven narrows her eyes.

"You know what?" Raven says to Samantha. "I can tell that I'm not wanted here. I'm going to go back to my dorm room."

And she trains those haunting amethyst eyes at me. "You're right, though, McKenna. Amelie isn't the one you guys should be worrying about."

With that parting message, she disappears with a flash of blinding violet light.

Chapter Four

The hallway is quiet as the four of us walk towards the elevators the next day. No one is gossiping by her room door, no one is getting a drink from one of the water fountains. That's a bit odd for this time of the day. Socializing should be at its prime right now, but the hallway is a ghost town.

Natalie pushes the call button for the elevator, tapping her foot impatiently as we wait for it to come back up. As we step inside it, Samantha asks, "Is it always this quiet?"

"No," I say, pushing the button that will take us down into the basement. *B for basement.* "Usually, at this time, most girls would be in the hallways or the commons rooms. I don't know what's going on."

"Did we miss an announcement?" Emma asks worriedly.

I shake my head. "We would have heard it."

Dean Ioanna Papadopoulos is waiting for us when the elevator doors open. She doesn't look more than thirty years old. She said she was born in Greece to a Fire Wielder and an Air Manipulator, making her a witch. Her heritage makes her extremely adept at the martial arts, including karate. She's tough, but nice, in a sense. She is tremendously beautiful and single, with dark brown hair, eerie gray eyes, and even has a hint of a Greek accent, to boot. Many of the boys ogle her when they think she's not looking. Her most striking feature, however, is a puckered red scar stretching from her temple to her left cheek. It's her only flaw on her otherwise perfect olive skin, making her look like the tough person she is inside. She was sliced by a crazy Acerbitian with a knife made out of obsidian, which is lethal to Elementals, and even though they were able to heal her, the scar is still there.

"Welcome back, girls," she smiles. "I see you've brought the Water and Air Keeper with you today. *Wamevo* Dean Papadopoulos." Dean shakes both of their hands. "It's a pleasure to meet you both. Follow me."

She leads us to the huge training room that takes up most of the basement. All the students in the school could fit in here with tons of extra room. The lighting down here is dim, which is great because it's easier to concentrate with minimal lighting. There's not much in here, except for a lot of dust and mildew. A couple of folding tables and chairs are heaped together by the back wall.

"Have a seat." Dean gestures to the floor. Natalie and I sit, used to this drill. Emma and Samantha look at us for a second before lowering themselves onto the concrete floor. "The first part of training is pretty easy. I have confidence you'll catch on to the whole thing fairly quickly. The first thing we do is close our eyes and clear our minds. If you want to have complete control over your powers, it is imperative that you remain calm."

I shut my eyes and focus on my breathing. In, out, in out. There's a whole lot of nothingness in my head, which is good. Every time I feel myself drifting, I pull myself back.

"Okay," Dean says, and I open my eyes. "Now that we're calm, I want you to create a ball of something. Like, flames, or a rock, or in my case, an orb." She snaps her fingers, and a violet colored sphere forms in her hand. She holds it up for us to see.

I hold a hand in front of me and conjure up flames. They lick my palm, but since I'm a Fire Wielder, they can't burn me. I look over at the others. Natalie, of course, is holding a rock. Emma has some floating water, and she seems to be making shapes out of it.

Samantha … I don't know what those cloud things are supposed to be. Wait a minute … it's a mini-tornado. Since air isn't a tangible thing, it's bound to look weird in a compressed state.

"Now, make it bigger."

I expand my flames and cup them with both hands. My three roommates do the same.

"Try making a weapon out of your element," Dean suggests, demonstrating with her orb. She turns it into a small knife.

"Will it actually work?" Samantha asks. "Like, can you use it in a fight?"

"That's up to you."

A flaming sword would look really cool. Plus, it'd get the job done quickly. I stretch the fireball out and coax it into a sword shape. Then I grasp the handle—which feels kind of weird because the fire is moving around in my hand—and wave it around. It makes smoke patterns in the air.

"Here," Natalie says. "Try slicing my rock." She tosses it at me. Without thinking, I thrust my hand forward, and my sword splits her stone in two. The halves drop to the ground, smoking.

"It *does* work," Emma says in awe. She tosses her water ball back and forth between her hands, and soon, it freezes. "A ball of ice could work, too, right? I don't think anything else made of ice would work."

Dean nods. "If you hit someone's head with that, you could cause some serious damage." She nods at Natalie, who quickly fashions a bow and arrow out of wood and who knows what else.

Samantha stands up and snaps her fingers. Instantly, the air is filled with a weird gas, and I can't breathe. My eyes tingle from whatever it is she put in the room, so I close them. I can hear everyone else choking, too. I use my shirt to cover my nose, which makes the situation better.

She snaps her fingers again, and the gas goes away. Dean Papadopoulos shoots her an odd glance, looking comical with the bottom half of her face masked by the white ruffles on her blouse. "What was that?"

"I had to do something else," Samantha says, sitting back down. She's paler than normal. "Creating a tornado would only cause trouble for everyone down here. Don't worry; the gas wasn't poisonous. I can't do it often because it gives me migraines."

I stare at the new girl. Who is she and where did she come from? The Samantha that stood on that stage is a quiet person. She had her nose inside a novel until it was time to go to training. But this version, Samantha 2.0? She's lethal. She could cause a lot of damage in the blink of an eye. Sure, I could blast someone with fire, or Emma could freeze someone from the inside, or Natalie could choke someone with vines—I say that from experience—but Samantha? All she'd have to do is flick her wrist to fill this room with carbon monoxide.

I think I'll call her Sam from now on. A girl like that needs a nickname.

"Let's work on your fighting skills," Dean suggests after an hour. "Stand up."

We comply.

"There's nothing to teach you, really. When it comes to fighting with another Elemental, all you have to do is keep your strengths in mind. For example, one of Natalie's strengths is blocking. In a fight, she'd go into defensive mode and work from there. You must also keep a sharp eye out for your opponent's weaknesses. So how about we have McKenna go against Emma first? Try not to kill each other. And remember, watch your opponent's movements, not their eyes. Sight can be deceptive."

I face Emma, who is currently smiling. What's her deal? She's been here for less than a day and has already talked enough for the four of us. She probably isn't going to take any of this seriously. We hold up our hands, watching the other, daring her to make the first move.

Then, out of nowhere, Emma pulls her hand up and a slab of ice zooms towards me, but I melt it easily with some fire. I send a jet her way, but she smothers it just as easily. It goes like this for a while, back and forth with no progress. Eventually, Dean claps her hands together.

"This is what you would call a stalemate," she says. "Actually, no. Emma has the advantage here because McKenna can't do anything to her without harming her. So McKenna, why don't you try fighting me instead?"

Emma gives me a fleeting look before going to stand next to Sam. Dean P brushes imaginary dirt off her pinstriped trousers. I've never seen a witch fight before, but then there's a first time for everything. Dean never battled Natalie or me. We were always pitted against each other. She waves a hand over herself, and the air around her turns purple. She's protecting herself. And with a wave of her hand, she does the same to me and the other Keepers. Finally, she thrusts her hands into the air, and the basement is good to go.

"This will protect us when we fight, so we can go full force. I probably should have done this to you and Emma."

"Probably."

It feels wrong to fight an adult with my powers, much less one of the heads of my school. Nevertheless, I shoot out a bolt of lightning in her direction. She's not quick enough to dodge it, but that's okay, because her protection spell absorbs the shock. She puts her two fists together, the air around them turning violet, and magic pushes me into the wall. It doesn't hurt.

Dean P cancels the gravity, and now nothing's beneath my feet. I try to right myself in the air, but I only succeed in flipping upside down. While I'm scrambling to regain control of the situation, she restores it, and I'm plummeting to the ground. Nothing's happened to me, but I'm still mystified. She uses those precious seconds to cast a *julagi*, or weakening spell.

I can't win. She keeps using her witch powers on me, throwing my aim off and giving me no chance whatsoever. The only way I could win if I set the whole room on fire ... of course! True, in any other situation, doing so would kill every non-Fire Wielder in the area, but this is different.

When I stomp my foot, little flames spring up at my feet. *Come on, McKenna. You can do this. Go big or go home.* I make them bigger, bigger, bigger, until the huge basement room is engulfed in fire. Sparks lick at my skin. The glow from the fire illuminates everyone's faces, washing them in yellow light. Every part of me feels like when my foot falls asleep, buzzing and tingling. I always feel like this when I use my magic.

"Excellent, McKenna," Dean Papadopoulos smiles, her brown hair floating around her face. "You reached full power."

Heat rolls down my back. I did it! Usually, I have to be seriously angry to reach my maximum power level. But I did it! I'm stronger than I've been before.

My arms start to tingle even more, and when I look down, faint golden lines of Fire tattoos start to appear. My eyes grow wide in disbelief. *This can't be happening. I'm not mad. Why are they showing up?* I hide my hands behind my back so nobody can see. Breathe, McKenna. Make them go away. Pull. Pull them back in. The stinging feeling begins to recede, and I breathe a sigh of relief.

Excellent.

I kill the flames after a minute. The rush of all that Fire magic makes my head throb. Emma and Sam look at me in awe.

"All right!" Dean P claps her hands together. "Who's next?"

Emma leaps up from her spot on the ground. "Can I go?" When Dean nods, she pumps her fist. The air instantly gets twenty degrees colder.

"Don't get too excited, Em, or we'll freeze to death," Sam jokes.

"You're hilarious."

Dean and Emma go at each other like they're bitter enemies. Maybe it's because she's more pumped up than the Energizer bunny, or she's extremely nimble, but Emma is way harder for Dean to catch. She pushes off the wall just as Dean tries to slow her down. She drops to the floor as an orb zooms toward her face. And when she's not defending herself, she's icing the floor so Dean can slip and freezing various parts of her body.

Emma copies my grand finale and summons a huge wave out of nowhere, sending it Dean's way. It slams her into the wall and splashes all around the room, picking us up and moving us around. I frown as she makes the flood evaporate, wringing water from my hair.

"Great job, Emma," Dean grins at the chipper Water Keeper. "You did very well for your first day of training."

"Thanks," Emma breathes. "That was awesome!"

"Emma's really good," I whisper in Natalie's ear.

"Too good," she responds. "She's been here one day and already she's better than you."

I decide not to take offense to that.

Chapter Five

My hands continue to tingle as we say good night to Dean Papadopoulos. I feel this way after every session. It's as if we're exercising, only it's our powers we're trying to get in shape, not our bodies. I kind of wish we didn't have to stop today. If it were up to me, we'd practice through the night.

Emma's pupils are dilated. "That was intense." She does a little hop in place. "I feel alive!"

The elevator is buzzing with energy. Sam is hovering about a half inch off the ground. Natalie is actually smiling. I guess practicing with their powers after being fairly dormant for two days gives them a rush, too.

Our floor is even quieter than before, if that's possible. We're the only girls in the halls, and everyone must be sleeping because I can't hear a peep coming from any of the rooms.

"What is going *on*?" I mutter, unlocking our room door. "It's never this silent."

Emma climbs up the ladder and flings herself onto her bed, sighing loudly. "It's been a great day."

"Why do you say that?" Sam perches next to her.

"No reason." She pauses for a second. "I saw this person."

"Ah *ha*." Natalie rolls up her sleeves, getting ready to deal with her plants. "This person was a guy, wasn't it?"

Emma nods. "A cute guy. No, scratch that. A hot guy. He kind of looks like that boy McKenna likes. What's his name? Oh, yeah. Mark."

She must be talking about his twin. "You mean Liam?"

"That's his name?"

"He's Mark's twin brother."

"That makes sense." She picks at a loose thread hanging from her shirt. "Liam's better looking, though. No offense."

"None taken." Because I know it's not true, anyway.

She turns to Sam, who is looking back and forth between us in amusement. "What about you, Sammy? Have you met anybody yet?"

Sam rolls her eyes. "Oh please, Emma. I've been with you the whole time we've been here, which is less than twenty-four hours. How would I have met any 'cute guys'?"

"I don't know. You're a very mysterious person. And besides, I saw Liam when I was walking with—"

BOOM!

A deafening explosion outside makes our room quiver, knocking me off my feet. Everything on my nightstand tumbles to the ground, including my picture frame. I hear the glass shatter, but I don't have time to think about that. Natalie's still on her feet, but she looks shaken. "What was that?" Emma whispers.

The ground shakes for a couple more seconds, and then stops. Silence. Then an identical explosion occurs, but this time it doesn't come from close to our dorm building.

Acerbity has struck again.

"You don't know what Acerbity is? Well, now you know. Basement. Now." Natalie says, pointing to the door.

"Shouldn't we leave the building?" Sam says, flabbergasted. I am, too, but not for the same reason. Why would Sam want to leave? Acerbity is waiting for us right outside the building. Everyone knows that if we go outside, we'll all be slaughtered. Actually, I kind of want to go outside so I can fight back. That would be cool. They'd know we aren't afraid any more.

"The basement is protected. Besides, this explosion wasn't an accident. Acerbity is here. So let's go. *Now*."

"What do you mean, it wasn't an accident?"

Natalie shoves us out of our dorm room. All the juniors remember the drill, because the hallway is crowded with girls trying to get out. It's like déjà vu. Thick smoke taints the air, making any girl who isn't a Fire Wielder cough. "I mean, you can't tell me it was a coincidence an identical explosion went off over near the boys dorm. Plus, even if it was an accident, explosions don't just happen like that." She snaps her fingers. "McKenna would have sensed a fire going on."

That is true. The only fire I sense is the one caused by the explosion, and it's not even that big, anyway. It'll be easy to control. *And this has happened before. So why is everyone acting so surprised?*

"I thought the school was protected," Sam whispers. A couple of girls look over at us.

I put a finger to my lips. "It is. Well, the school building is, anyway. Anything else, like the quad, is fair game. That's why they're able to plant bombs but not charge the school."

"So why don't they just sit outside our school and shoot us down as we walk outside? Or better yet, why don't we expand the protection spell to include the stuff outside?"

"This way," Cara Regeh calls from the front of the pack. She's usually the one leading us down the stairs, as she does now, bypassing the elevators. Within seconds, we're joined by the senior girls. The sound of our heavy footsteps reverberates through the air. One flight, two flights … the sophomores and freshmen must have already gone down. I have to hold back a laugh as I think about how much chaos there probably was in the underclassmen dorms. I miss those hallways. They're so welcoming, most likely Lalande's attempt at comforting the youngsters while they're away from home.

"Okay, here's the deal," I say softly. "One, Acerbity knows that us students are outside all the time, and we're way more powerful than Acerbity. So they can't do that without, you know, dying. And two, it's impossible to put a protection spell on something intangible, like the space around a building. Okay?"

Sam nods, but I can tell there are a million more questions she wants to ask.

We reach the basement room. The sound of students talking bleeds through the thick door. All around me, girls take a moment to catch their breath. Hot air is blown near my ear, leaving me utterly repulsed. Not because the air is hot, but because some of the girls were about to go to bed without brushing their teeth.

"Hurry up and open the damn door," snaps a tired senior. "Before we get blown to bits."

I almost remind her that the whole school building is protected and the bomb was outside, and Fire Wielders can't be blown to bits, but she's an Earthen and looks exhausted, so it doesn't really matter.

It looks like everyone is just about here. The younger students are cowering, the older students are whispering, the teachers and staff are barking instructions at anyone who will listen. I spot Celestia with her friends. She waves at me, and I smile back. Some of my guy friends are scattered around the room.

Dean Papadopoulos jogs up to us. She's still dressed for work, even though it's close to midnight. It occurs to me just now that I'm in my training clothes. I quickly cross my arms over my chest. "Keepers! You're okay. Good. You have your stones, right?"

We hold up our necklaces.

"Great," she sighs with relief. "Remember, this is the safest place on campus. Hang onto the stones and you'll be fine. Walk around, chat with friends ... although my advice is to follow the kids in the corners of the room and try to get some sleep."

Just as she says that, Mario Espinoza and Theo Walters sneak up on an unsuspecting, snoozing sophomore with a bottle of whipped cream. Theo freezes his shoelaces together, places his hand in a bowl of what I hope is warm water, and Mario squeezes whipped cream into the boy's other hand. Then they sneak away, laughing like hyenas. I snort. They are *so* immature.

"Or," Dean says slowly, "You could stay awake. It's your choice, really."

"Ooh! There's the guy I was talking about!" Emma chirps after Dean P leaves to chew out our juvenile classmates. I look to where her finger is pointing, and, lo and behold, it's Liam. He's looking in our direction, then away, then back again, this time with a smirk on his face. And then he reaches to the side and pulls his twin out of the group of people next to him.

Oh no. Now Mark glances at us. How is it possible that every time I see him he manages to look even more attractive than before? He's wearing a baggy sweatshirt and plaid pajama bottoms, but that doesn't matter. My heart has been replaced with a bass drum, and it's pounding hard. Liam's talking to him now. They're walking towards us. *Quick, what should I do?* I smooth down my hair. It's probably a big curly poof. Emma's doing the same thing, and it makes her hair look even glossier.

Natalie gives me a jab in the side. I give her a sharp look. This has become our ritual whenever we see Mark.

Mark and I say hi to each other and avoid each other's eyes.

Liam waves his hands around. "There are other people here too, you know."

Mark blushes, and judging by the look Natalie gives me, I do too. Sam gazes at all of us, looking extremely confused. "Aren't you going to introduce us?" Of course she'd be worried about that. She seems to have the most manners out of all of us.

"Oh, right," Natalie says, taking charge. "I forgot you met Mark but not Liam. Sam, Emma, this is Liam O'Reilly, Mark's brother. Liam, meet Samantha Mazer and Emma Richards."

I lean in to whisper loudly to Sam. "Mark's middle name is Cornelius, in case you were wondering. Feel free to make fun of him for it anytime. We all do."

"Very funny, Sparky." Mark uses one of his nicknames for me. He knows I hate both of them—the other one is Mickey, as in Mickey Mouse—so he uses them all the time.

"Cornelius, you say?" Christopher Smith saunters up to us at the same time, quickly followed by his best friend Jackson Chrysler. "Remind me to hold that over you." He drapes his arm on his friend's shoulders. "Who are these two lovely ladies?"

"Nice try, Chris," Natalie gives him the side eye. "Dean introduced them at the assembly."

He holds up his hands. "Don't shoot."

Chris is the kind of guy who knows that a lot of girls think he's hot, but doesn't let it go to his head. He's well over six feet with wavy dark brown hair, a lean build, and dazzling almond shaped brown eyes. Jackson, on the other hand, has shaggy blonde hair and robin's egg blue eyes hidden behind cool black glasses. It's a rare occurrence for Air Manipulators to have vision problems, but it happens sometimes. He's a shy, intellectual guy, and Chris's wingman. The two of them and the twins hang out a lot, even though Chris and Jackson are seniors. Most girls around here call them The Four, as in 'The Four Hot Guys No One Can Have'. I know, right? Lame.

"Emma Richards, reporting for duty." She sticks her hand out, and Chris shakes it. "And you are …?"

"Chris Smith, reporting for duty." He gestures to Jackson. "This is Jackson the Car Dealer."

Sam's brow furrows. "Huh?"

Jackson shrugs, giving her one of his rare smiles. "My last name is Chrysler."

"Oh. Cool."

"We call Chris Christmas," Liam adds, "Because when you say his name fast, it sounds like the holiday."

"You guys really like your nicknames," Emma says wistfully.

"So does anyone know what happened?" I yawn. It's really, really late, and I just want to go to bed. Even though I'm not cold, I rub my arms.

Sam fiddles with her Airstone. "Um, I heard Dean Martins talking to Dean Loicher. They were talking about Acerbity setting off bombs. The security guards got most of the soldiers, and the rest escaped." By heard, she must mean eavesdropped on their thoughts. Or she has superhuman hearing. I don't hang out with a lot of Air Manipulators, so I don't know. But here at Lalande, either one could be the case.

Emma sighs in relief. "So everyone's okay?"

Her friend fidgets. "Well, that's the thing. Five students died."

There's silence as her words sink in.

What?

Died?

Five students. Five teenagers. They're dead. For the first time since the attacks started, people have died. Not because of Acerbity. Because of us Keepers. They must have gotten word that Emma and Samantha were offered asylum here. Everyone looks shocked. Fire seems to descend to the deepest part of me. I really, really hope I don't know them.

"Who?" Mark says.

"Dean Loicher said their names were Emerald Niram, Stefan Ayeth, Kelski Wilson, Piper Sticel, and Ashley Evan." She pauses. "Ashley's a guy."

"Are you sure?" When she nods, his face falls. "I knew him. I'm kind of friends with him. Well, I was."

Natalie rests her hand on his shoulder. Chris's devil-may-care attitude has vanished, leaving him looking like Eeyore.

It strikes me now that the school isn't as safe as I once thought it was. Sure, this has happened before, but no one died. But now that fatalities have been thrown into the mix ... Acerbity's getting closer, too close for comfort. What if more people had died? What if I had been one of those five? What if the other Keepers had? Actually, no. If they killed us, the necklaces would have been destroyed. We're safe. For now. It's the Elemental Stones they want, not us.

So why do they keep attacking the school? They just keep losing members.

"So what are we going to do?" Mark asks, crossing his arms.

"Honestly?" Sam shrugs. "I don't even know. Wait it out, help fix what was damaged. It's not like we can go out there and fight Acerbity." She looks at me. "That's how you say the name, right?"

I nod.

"True," Jackson nods. "It irks me, though, that we can't do anything about it. What good are these powers if we can't use them to defend ourselves?"

"We *can* do something," Emma argues. "We *can* fight back."

Chris laughs in spite of himself. "Emma, we can't fight back. You want us to die?"

"We have powers. They don't."

"And they have obsidian, which is lethal to Elementals," Natalie says. "No one knows why it's bad for us, but we do know they're really good at making all kinds of weapons with it. Of course, since it's a type of glass, it's very brittle, so they have to fortify all obsidian weapons with magic to keep it from, say, shattering before it leaves the barrel of a gun."

Emma balls her fists. "Well, doing nothing is *quite* possibly the stupidest thing I've ever heard. We have the advantage. They have weapons made out of some dumb rock, and you're telling me you're just going to lie low because they'll kill you if you don't?" She shakes her head in disbelief. "Only cowards do that."

Ouch.

"Being brave doesn't mean doing something just so you don't look fearful," Jackson says. "Sometimes stepping back is the best thing to do. Just because we have powers doesn't mean we're invincible. A bullet to the head will kill non-Fire Wielders just like any human."

Mark has a conflicting look on his face, like he's fighting himself. He wants to take Emma's side, but he's worried that would make him look bad.

I know this because I'm doing the same thing for the same reason.

Finally, Emma sighs. "Okay, okay. Whatever you say. It was nice talking to you guys." She makes an about face and walks away from the group. Her tread is stiff and pointed, as if she's trying to make holes in the concrete floor. Emma truly does have a flair for the dramatic. I watch her go for a couple of seconds. Should I go after her?

I should. "I'll talk to her."

Sam places a cold hand on my arm. "She's not so easily swayed. I should go instead. You know, 'cause I know her."

I shake my head. "Believe it or not, I was actually the peacemaker in my family. Besides, you didn't exactly take her side of the argument. Maybe a neutral party will get our ice princess to warm up."

A couple of people call my name as I follow Emma, but I wave them off. She's heading for a corner of the room, the only one not occupied by sleeping underclassmen. As soon as I slump onto the ground next to her, she turns her head away and shields herself with a wall of ice.

Rolling my eyes, I press my hands onto it, and after a moment it starts to melt. When all the ice has become water, she collects it in her hands and makes it disappear. Drama queen status confirmed.

She sniffs as her eyes begin to water. "My father is missing, and the thought of not looking for him because it *might be* dangerous makes me want to scream. So if you're here to give me another lecture on the importance of hiding, I don't want to hear it."

"No, no," I assure her. I exhale heavily. "I ... feel the same way as you do. You know, Natalie didn't tell you this isn't the first time Acerbity has attacked the school."

"It's not?"

"Of course! It happens about twice a year. This is where we usually go when it happens. It's just ... this is the first time kids have died because of it. And it's not like we can abandon the school and hide elsewhere. This is the safest place for us. The closest Elemental school is in Virginia." I bite my lip. "I think everyone's afraid of instilling the idea of retaliation because of it. They're afraid more people will be hurt."

Emma nods like she understands. "But more people will get hurt, whether we fight back or not."

I point a finger at her, getting riled up. "Exactly! They keep avoiding that fact. They say they don't want to wake the sleeping giant, but they forgot the giant never went to bed."

"So how can we fight back?" she asks, blue eyes shining.

"I'm not sure," I admit. "But let's brainstorm together sometime. Maybe we can come up with something."

"Great!" Then she frowns. "I just wish we weren't the only ones who felt this way."

Mark's face pops into my head. Trying not to blush, I say, "I think I know someone who does."

Emma's right. I'm tired of bending over backwards for these wayward people. I want to blast each and every Acerbitian in the face with fire. When they slap us, I want to slap back. I don't want to turn the other cheek. Why should we be ashamed of our heritage? We have amazing powers. We're agile, smart, beautiful creatures. *Elementals*. We need to fight back.

But how?

Chapter Six

"An artist. A football player. An actor. A gymnast. A musician. Two days ago, we lost five students to an explosion caused by Acerbity. They all had so much talent, so much potential. And they were taken away from us. They won't be able to graduate from high school. They won't be able to pursue their dreams. Their friends and family have volunteered to tell us a little more about them." Dean Martins solemnly gestures for Gaby Toki, the first speaker, to step up on the podium.

"Emerald Niram won so many awards for her work. She was truly an amazing artist, and a talented Air Manipulator. She'd already applied to St. Rose for their art and design program, and was so excited about it, she wanted to skip senior year and go straight to college." Gaby steps down, and Brendan Alego steps up.

"Stefan Ayeth was quite possibly the best football player Lalande Academy has ever seen. Even though he was only a sophomore, he had incredible skills on the field. Coach Palmer always played him on the first team as quarterback, that's how good he was. Colleges looked twice at him, not caring he was only fifteen years old." Brendan makes way for Alicia Wilson.

"My brother, Kelski Wilson, always dreamed of being on the big screen. Some of you saw him in the movies *Rule Breaking* and *DeNial*. So at least before he—" She swallows hard, blinking furiously. "He got to live out his dream, even though it was only for a little while."

Piper's sister Paisley takes Alicia's place. "Piper Sticel was ... was my twin sister. She was a great gymnast. The best. And she was the best sister. She was so anxious for the Olympic trials ... and now she won't even be able to try out."

This assembly is seriously dismal. Even if a person hated one of the kids who died, everyone's in agreement on one thing—their deaths were unjust. And even though I didn't know any of them, I still feel bad. Chris feels even worse about it. The only people he's talked to since the attack are Jackson and Natalie. In fact, I'm not sure why he agreed to give Ashley Evan's eulogy, even though it's been a week.

"Ashley Evan was a new friend of mine. He—" Chris pauses. "He was ..." Natalie shifts in the seat next to me, looking worried. *Is Chris going to cry?* Chris looks down, and then back up with a face as dark as a thundercloud. "He didn't deserve this. None of the five students did. He was a normal guy with a dream. He wanted to start a band next year, in college. But because of Acerbity, because of those *assholes*, he can't." He's clenching his jaw like he wants it sealed shut. He doesn't notice Dean Martins giving him a dirty look. Chris is probably holding the podium as lightly as possible so he doesn't break it.

"Thank you, Chris," Dean says crisply, but Chris isn't done.

"We need to stop this. Right now. We need to stop letting Acerbity attack us. No more 'turn the other cheek' rhetoric. No more 'let's lie low' crap. Don't pretend you don't know what happened to Ashley, Piper, Kelski, Stefan, and Emerald. If this is what happens when we don't act, then what will happen if we do? I'll tell you one thing. If we don't fight back, then they'll have died in vain. Everyone who has perished at the hands of Acerbity will have died in vain. Let's stop being a bunch of cowards. *Elemental* cowards." He laughs without humor. "We have Earth, Water, Fire, Air, and magic under our control, and we don't want to use our powers to defend ourselves. Can you believe it? Because I can't." He turns his eyes upward, addressing the five. "Rest in peace, guys."

"Okay, okay," Dean Martins says, practically pushing him off the stage. "That's quite enough." He finishes the assembly by adding remarks onto the five statements, and tells us to visit the front of the campus chapel, where a makeshift memorial has been put together.

My legs are stiff when I stand up, forcing me to stretch before I'm able to go find Sam and Emma. So when Natalie says, "Ooh, I want to smack him so hard!" I nearly fall over.

"What do you mean, you want to smack him? That was a great speech."

She raises an eyebrow. "No, it wasn't. It was terrible. McKenna, we've already talked about this with Emma. It isn't safe for us to go chasing after Acerbity when they have obsidian. You've seen what it can do."

She's talking about Misly Laper, the sophomore who was stabbed by an Acerbitian spy while she was walking to class last year. The spy happened to be her best friend, an Elemental who inexplicably turned to the dark side. She survived, barely, but her mom eventually started homeschooling her because she refused to return.

Chris lopes over, effectively ending our conversation. His face is brighter than it was before, though he's still has a ghost of a frown on his lips. "How's that for a eulogy?"

Natalie must have decided she *will* smack him, because she thwacks the back of his head. "Christopher Henry Smith. What the hell was that? Huh? What the *hell* was that?"

He rubs his head. "Ouch! What was that for?"

"That," she says through her teeth, "was for saying the stupidest thing Elementally *and* humanly possible at an assembly mourning your dead friend. Why would you ever think that was a good idea?"

"Because it's true," Chris says. "I've been thinking about what Emma said, and I realized she was right."

"He's got a point, Nat," I add.

Natalie's eyes get all squinty. "Are you on my side or his? You just don't go around saying things like that. And in front of the whole school? Ugh!" She storms off.

My heart nosedives into my stomach. Why doesn't she understand? Why does she insist on being cowardly in the face of danger? A spear seems to pierce my heart. And anger as hot as the sun starts to burn inside me.

"Do you do that on purpose?" I scowl at Chris as we trudge out of the auditorium.

"Do what?"

"Piss her off. Sometimes she comes back into the dorm boiling mad, and when I ask her what's wrong, she just says, 'Chris.'"

He eyes are wide, and he holds his hands up. "No. I don't mean to. Oddly enough, she can get pretty sensitive. Sometimes I'll say stuff and not even think about it, but it'll get her really mad."

"Like?"

"Like I'm going to tell you." He laughs, successfully angering me even more. "That's between me and her."

"Well, watch what you say around her if you care about her feelings! Remember, she still can get hurt. Just because she's an Earthen doesn't mean she's an unfeeling, sociopathic person. If you're really concerned about Natalie Wilde, you'll do well to stay on her good side. Everybody knows that."

He snorts. "Like you're doing a great job of that. She's mad at you, too, you know. And why are you being so friendly all of a sudden? Well, not exactly friendly. You're talking to me, not giving me dirty looks. I mean, first you were Icy Isabelle, but now you're Friendly Francine. You always seemed to hate my guts. I thought you'd be on her side, being her best friend and all." He stops in front of Piann.

Oh, God. The cheese is real. "I'm actually Merciless McKenna. And I'm on the side that wants to fight back."

There are two places I go when I want to think. One is my room, obviously, but the other one isn't so evident. The car garage became a haven for me when I first came here as a freshman. I had a bad case of homesickness, and Natalie and I hadn't really clicked yet, so I wandered around campus looking for something to do. I saw a teacher of mine, Mr. Brisburne, holding a worn wooden tool box. I followed him to the garage, and he introduced me to Geoffrey, Kenneth, Dendhi, Šan, and Kendall, students working on car, bike, and motorcycle projects there. Then he said I could hang out there whenever I wanted—outside of class, of course.

It's dark inside when I yank open the door to the small building. It used to be the greenhouse before a new one was built four years ago. Geoffrey and Kendall said he rallied for it to turn into a repair shop. The windows on the ceiling are still there, allowing faint moonlight to shine down into the garage. The beams of silvery light make the car shop look eerily beautiful.

Of course, no one's in here. *Duh.* Everyone went back to their dorms after the assembly, so I have the whole place to myself. Plus, it's nighttime. I clap twice and the lights flick on, washing the cars and bikes in yellowish-white light.

Kenneth Afanadu's 1998 Ford Taurus is still in one of the two lifts, which should be odd but isn't. He's one of the fastest kids in the shop, but he's been working on fixing the engine for six months now. Other people have been telling him to drop the project, but he's determined to see it through. I have a feeling Dendhi and Kendall are secretly sabotaging it to see how much patience he has.

Amelie has a learner's permit, but she's only allowed to ride her motorcycle if Mr. Brisburne accompanies her. Recently she told me her front fork was acting up, so I decided to take it on as a project. I quickly discovered her springs were broken and I had to take it apart. The pieces are underneath a checked blanket in the corner from when I left off last time. As I walk over to the heap, a wrench flies through the air, nearly giving me a heart attack.

"Who-who's there?" My voice trembles as I whip up some fire and hold it in my hands. I'll blast someone if I have to.

"McKenna? Is that you?" I sigh in relief as Mr. Brisburne's bald head pops up from underneath a station wagon.

"What are you doing here?" I ask. "I thought all teachers were on their vacation."

He holds up the wrench. "I had to fix my car. I didn't want to go to a human repair shop and pay money, and Dean Martins gave me the okay."

"How come it was so dark?"

He waves a flashlight around. "All those lights make my eyes hurt. I'm getting older, you know. Why are *you* here? Shouldn't you be at the funeral?"

I shrug. "It already happened, and plus, I didn't know any of the kids who died."

"So you had to know them to go?"

"No, I just … I don't like funerals. I'll only go to one if I have to. And I didn't. So I didn't."

For the next half hour we don't say anything. I focus on replacing the springs in Amelie's fork, and Mr. Brisburne tinkers with the belly of his car. Chris's words about fighting back still nag me like mosquitoes even though I try to swat them away.

Finally, I've had enough. I'll ask Mr. Brisburne. He's a sensible enough teacher. Whatever he says I should do, I'll do it.

"Hey, um, Mr. Brisburne?"

He glances up from the hood of his car. "Yes?"

"Can I ask you something?"

"What's up?"

I clear my throat. How do I word this? "What would you do if you want to do something, and everybody else tells you not to, but you think they're wrong?"

He thinks this over for a minute. "I would go with my gut," he says finally. "I would trust my gut feeling. It's best not to second guess yourself when others tell you to. If you're sure it's the right thing, do what your heart tells you to."

My heart's telling me to fight back. I'm sure of it. The only problem is, I'm going to need help. Chris, Emma, and I—and possibly Mark—can't do this on our own. We're going to need help.

And I know just where to look.

Chapter Seven

Paisley Sticel, Piper Sticel's twin sister, commits suicide the next day. Raven was eager to tell me that when her parents were supposed to pick up Piper's things today. When they entered the twins' dorm this morning, Paisley's body greeted them, which was hanging from the ceiling by a long scarf. When I heard the news, I felt even worse about the whole thing. *Is this my fault?*

Needless to say, we had another assembly today, this time on suicide prevention. And because Paisley reacted to her sister's death this way, all people linked to the victims of the Acerbity attack were put on suicide watch.

Including Chris.

Amelie flops onto her bed, groaning loudly. We just came back from doing community service (a.k.a. cleaning up the quad), which took way longer than it should've because Alexis and her friends saw us working and decided it was high time to do spring cleaning—in the summer. They "forgot" to put their crap in bags and "forgot" their stuff all over the quad. Trash rained down from Maiyrn like bootleg, oversized confetti.

"Sometimes I hate Alexis," Amelie says. "But then I remember she's my twin and isn't all that bad."

I laugh as I pull my hair out of the tight ponytail it was in. "Not all that bad? Remember when she replaced Elloa Esjér's shampoo with green hair dye? Alexis locked in the color and Elloa had to look like Medusa for weeks. Or when she cast a transmutation spell on Skylar DriGregia's new white pants, making it look like she leaked on her period? And how about Adhe Frist? He—"

"Okay, okay!" she giggles, holding up her hands. "She *has* done some really mean things. And I guess I should have been concerned when she kept knocking back liquid neon and cobalt that week." The elements on the periodic table, in their liquid states, amplify the magic of sorcerers. They make spells more powerful, since hexes are pretty weak on their own. For example, mixing cobalt and neon will strengthen a color spell, like the one Alexis cast three weeks ago.

"But Alexis doesn't do things like that for no reason. She works hard to get what she wants, and she'll do whatever she has to do to get her way. Elloa is an actress, remember? Alexis did that to her so she wouldn't be able to try out for last year's fall play. Skylar DriGregia was going to win 'best dressed' in freshman year, and Alexis wanted that title. I'm not defending what she did, though. It's just … she's a very determined person."

I shrug. "All I'm saying is that you should try talking to her. Maybe she'll stop for you. But let's not talk about Alexis right now. I've got maybe three hours before training and I don't want to waste them on your sister. What was it you wanted me to do?"

"Oh, right." She leaps up and grabs her new camera, which was perched on her mahogany dresser. "I'm making little videos of each Element for photography club. I thought you and the other Keepers were a good choice. All you have to do is state your name, say you're the Fire Keeper, and demonstrate what you can do with your Element."

"Got it. But don't you think we should take this downstairs? I don't want to cause another explosion." I don't add that my mere existence has caused enough harm already.

She nods. "Good point. Let's go."

We race down the stairs since the elevator is being fixed. The old smell of the building puts a smile on my face every time. The house I grew up in may be an hour away from here, but I've grown to call this worn, cracked dorm home, with its wide hallways, hand scanners as locks, and comfy common rooms with tons of entertainment. The only bad thing about going to school here is that there's no service in our area—and a lot of us think Dean Martins used magic to make that happen. Because of that, most people just leave their phones in their rooms. Elementals aren't supposed to use social media, for obvious reasons. I don't even have a cell phone. Goes with the territory, I guess, when you're one of twelve. Money created by magic has no value, and my parents never had a lot of it.

A minute later, we're standing in front of a tree. "Aaaaaaand ... go."

"My name is McKenna Donaldson. I'm the Fire Keeper and a student at Lalande Academy." I raise my hands and display my Fire capabilities, though I'm careful not to set the tree behind me on fire. I've gotten pretty good at juggling fireballs and creating metal weaponry on the spot, so that's what I showcase.

When she's finished, Amelie gives me a big grin. "Okay, that's all I need. Thanks so much. I'm totally going to get a bunch of extra credit for the semester."

"Who's going to see this, by the way?" I ask as we head back inside. "Besides your club members, of course." I didn't check a mirror before she recorded me, and the last thing I need is to give Alexis another reason to tease me. And *no*, my worries have absolutely nothing to do with Mark O'Reilly.

Amelie pauses for a moment, a thoughtful yet faraway look in her violet eyes, and in that moment, I'm taken aback by how much she looks like Raven. She and Alexis are fraternal, that's true, but with her long, pitch-black hair and odd irises, she could easily pass for the Phantom's twin.

Amelie lets out a breath. "I don't know."

The three Keepers and I get out of the elevator onto our floor after another somber training session. We missed yesterday's because Dean Papadopoulos had to attend the funeral. It's very quiet as the junior girls shuffle sleepily in and out of the three bathrooms on our floor, and all I want to do is fall on my bed and into a deep sleep. Right before Emma unlocks our room door, a hand grabs my arm. I turn around and instantly recognize those navy blue eyes.

"Where have you guys been?" Siobhan Cambiasso, Paola's roommate whispers worriedly. Her golden brown hair, which reaches the back of her knees, is a complete mess, her black framed glasses are slightly askew, and her nightgown is wrinkled like the pads of one's fingers after a shower.

"Down in the basement," I reply, questioning her with my eyes. "What's wrong?"

She pulls on my arm. "Come with me."

Siobhan drags me to her dorm room and closes the door. Paola is leaning on the side of her bed, pale, sweaty, and breathing heavily. Instantly, I'm worried. I may not like her, but I'm not the kind of person to hope a person gets hurt.

"What's wrong with her?" I ask, rushing to Paola's side. I press my hand to the side of her face. No fever. "Is she sick?"

"I'm … not …" Paola croaks. "Sick."

I look at Siobhan. I'm not buying it. "She's not sick," she confirms. "She gets like this every time a vision or possible future outcome hits her. It's very draining."

I give her a look that says *so?* She's wasting my time, then, if there's nothing wrong with her roommate. Siobhan ignores me and picks up an unopened bottle of water from her nightstand, studying it closely. "This'll have to do," she says. She holds it with both hands and closes her eyes. Immediately, the air around the bottle begins to glow violet as the bottle is lifted in the air. It spins once, twice, before settling back in her hands. The water inside has turned a medium brown color.

"Drink," Siobhan orders her roommate.

Paola takes the bottle gingerly and sips. Her eyelashes flutter. "Mm. Earl Grey."

"The problem is what she saw," Siobhan whispers, growing paler by the second. Turning to her roommate, she asks, "Are you up for explaining?"

Paola gulps and nods. "I saw you," she says flatly. Her brown eyes have turned glassy. "I saw you, and Emma, and Natalie, and Samantha. All four of you were dead. At the hands of Acerbity. They subsequently took the Elemental Stones, destroyed them, and wiped out our race."

Pictures swirl around her head. I spot my bright red hair. I'm face down on the ground in a pool of my own blood. Emma is on her back, glassy blue eyes raised to the sky. Natalie is curled up on her side with a look of agony on her face. Samantha is so faint I can barely see her. A hooded figure stands in the background.

Us four. Dead. It can't be true. My throat grows dry and, though I want to run and hide, I can't. My feet seem to be rooted to the dormitory floor.

Annihilation.

Death.

Extinction.

"I also saw you four joined up with Acerbity." The picture disappears in a puff of smoke and another one appears. This time, the four of us are alive and well, but men and women in black clothing and weapons stand behind us. The hooded person appears again, but this time his face is visible. A triumphant smile is plastered on his face. His eyes are a cold blue. They cut through my soul and leave a scorching mark behind. I press my hand to my mouth as warm tears threaten to leak. "Rather than kill us all quickly, Acerbity decided to possess you with dark witches on their side and use you four to round up as many Elementals as possible so we could be brutally murdered.

"The last one I saw was you defeating Acerbity and freeing the Elementals. Apparently, they're still alive."

"Where?" Siobhan demands. *"Where?"*

"I don't know! It's in a dark place, a big one." Paola holds her head in her hands. "Think, think."

My stomach drops to my feet. Could it be downstairs? "The basement room?"

Paola is shaking her head before I even finish. "No, no. This was underground, I think," she says, "in a big metropolitan area. I'm guessing New York City, but it wouldn't be the subway."

"Anything else?" her roommate asks.

"I'm getting the arts. A museum. Something like that."

Either the Museum of Modern Art or the Metropolitan Museum of Art. Two of the places I love to visit.

Paola looks at me helplessly from the floor, her pupils dilating and expanding rapidly. I shudder inwardly at her face, fighting the urge to scream, and rub my hands together. *"Grietzi."* Thank you. "I ... I have to go."

"No problem." She and Siobhan answer simultaneously.

I stride out of the room and stop right in front of my dorm. My palm gets scanned as I make my resolution. *No one must know.*

No one can ever, ever know.

Emma's head is bent over a notebook, Samantha's in a novel, and Natalie is looking outside the window when I come in. They all turn towards me when they hear the creak.

"So? Who is she?" Emma inquires, her pen poised over the paper. "And why is her hair so long?"

"Her name is Siobhan Cambiasso. She's one of my friends. Siobhan has a condition where her hair grows abnormally fast, and since she's a witch, the magic in her body makes the process even faster. Cutting it is pretty much useless, so she just lets it grow."

Emma has an incredulous look on her face. "She's like a real-life Rapunzel."

"Pretty much."

"What did she want?"

I shrug. "Nothing important." I stride over to my bed, ripping off my Converse high tops and pulling on my sweatpants.

Sam gives me an odd look. I glance quizzically at her, and then I remember. Or, at least, remember that I forgot. She can read minds. She can hear my thoughts. And she heard my resolutions before I came in.

Slowly, she gives me an almost imperceptible nod. *I can. What do you mean, no one can know? Know what?*

I am so surprised that I take a step back and nearly trip o. "Did you just speak into my mind?"

She nods again. *I believe so.*

"I didn't know Air Manipulators could do that," Natalie says thoughtfully. "Nobody really does that here. I thought you guys could only hear thoughts. That was another one of the Unquist mutations, wasn't it?" Sam shrugs, clearly not wanting to talk more about it. Nat's probably the only person on the planet who knows what the Unquist mutations are.

I climb into bed, resigned. I don't want to dream tonight. After what Paola told me, I know it'll pop up in my head and spin my night into a nightmare. I struggle to keep my eyes open. When that doesn't seem to work, I decide to focus on my breathing.

I guess I shouldn't be surprised about Paola's three possible outcomes. I mean, what else could happen other than those things? The fact that Natalie and Sam are on board in them, though, gives me hope. It's a small sliver, no thicker than a piece of paper, but it's there.

But who was that man? What was he doing in all three predictions? Why do I recognize him? And why do I worry about him so?

Before I know it, though, my breathing becomes even and I slip into a fitful sleep.

Chapter Eight

We split up in different directions the next morning. Samantha heads to the library with Jackson. Natalie is determined to spend all day in the greenhouse. But, as I collect my sketchbook and multitude of pencils, headed for the Ashton Art Center, I realize that Emma has no intent on going anywhere.

"So ... what?" I ask her, slinging my bag over my shoulder. "You're just going to stay here?"

"Mm-hmm."

"All day?"

"I've got work." She holds up the notebook she was writing in yesterday. "I'm coming up with ideas on how we can fight back."

"I've got a plan, too," I tell her. "I just don't know how to execute it."

"Really?" A grin stretches across her face like the opening curtain of a theater production. "What is it?"

I automatically look around. Even with, you know, the walls and everything, I still feel like someone might hear us. "We could find the missing Elementals, work with them to unite the Elementals from all over the world, and try to defeat Acerbity once and for all. It would take *years* for it to happen, but it's the best I've got."

"That's a great idea! The only problem is we'd need to find out where they are, get permission to go to them *and* convince them to come back. And that's just the first part of the plan."

I nod. "The convincing part will be the hardest, for sure. I don't know if my mom and sisters will *want* to come back."

Emma gasps. "What did you say?"

My brow furrows. *Is she deaf?* "I don't know if my mom and sisters will want to come back. They disappeared on my fourteenth birthday."

Her blue eyes grow wide. "You're kidding. My dad and sister left two days before my birthday. And Sam's dad left one day before her birthday. We thought it was just a coincidence."

Oh. My. *God.*

"*Quowet naviti nadir?*" I ask frantically. *When is your birthday?*

"December sixth, and Sam's is the fifth. Also formerly coincidental." She clacks her periwinkle nails on the desk. "I'm guessing yours is the fourth?"

I nod. "And Natalie's is the seventh. Her mom and brothers left the same day my mom did." I pause to take a breath. "That can't be happenstance."

"So you're saying our Elemental parents all married humans, had kids within one day of each other, and disappeared on the same day?"

I nod again.

"They must be in the same place."

Even through all this excitement, my fingers still itch to draw. This isn't your everyday longing. This feeling has power. It's like … magic.

You need to go draw, my inner voice says out of nowhere.

"You keep working on that," I say with one leg out the door. "There's someplace I have to be."

Ashton Art Center is a brick beauty. It's a one-story building with rich, rusty red stones and ivy curling on the sides. The inside has a black and white theme. White floors, black walls, black floors, white walls. It's supposed to be pretentious, because all a warlock or witch has to do around here to get some color on these walls is knock back a vial of cobalt and neon. I don't really like pretentious people, and the people who frequent here drink Starbucks fraps, waste their lives on Tumblr, and watch obscure anime, so I stay away from Ashton. Most of the time. But since it's the only place on campus where I'm guaranteed silence—I'm certainly not going to sketch with grease in the car garage—I have to suck it up and march in bravely. Each room is for something completely different, like drawing with oil pastels, painting with watercolors, glassblowing, and clay. I head to the right and find my way to the Sketch room.

Dropping into a seat at the table, I set my sketchbook down at the table and stare at it for about half a century, waiting for inspiration to strike me like a bolt of lightning. I put my pencil on the page, almost mechanically, and let an intense pull drag my hand across the page, creating a drawing. Straight lines and curved lines. Short, stubby lines and long, graceful lines. My hand flicks stylishly as I work on the shading. My hand slows, then stops. It's been almost fifteen minutes since I started.

I gasp as I realize what I drew. It's an exact replica of Claude Monet's 1919 *Water Lilies*. It looks exactly the same, right down to the shading. And before I can even fully contemplate what I've done, words begin to appear on the side.

Detrás este es un pasaje secreto. Dónde está?

It's easy to translate the message, although I'm baffled by the use of one of the most popular languages in the world rather than the spell caster's obvious native Kevanese. I've been taking Spanish since the seventh grade, not to mention I'm fluent in nineteen other languages—another product of magic. Dad says a warlock bestowed the gift on me when I was a newborn, like I was some kind of Disney princess in a movie. I'm not a princess, as far as I know, so it's kind of weird.

Behind this is a secret passage. Where is it?

Claude Monet's *Water Lilies*. Before my mother disappeared, she took me to the Metropolitan Museum of Art. I was in awe of all the paintings, sculptures, and exhibits. One of the ones she kept showing me was, in fact, *Water Lilies*.

"I know you'll come back here one day," Mom had said once, pointing to the light-filled painting.

"You mean, we'll come back here." I'd responded. I was thirteen then. It was a month before my fourteenth birthday.

She shook her head. "No. I won't be with you when you come. You'll be with others. I'll be waiting for you, though. Right here." She extended her hand towards the painting again. She didn't dare touch it.

I was nearly fourteen then and was confused. What did she mean?

Now I know what she meant.

They're hiding, I say to myself. *The painting conceals a secret passage. But how? And why tell me now?*

My thoughts are interrupted by the door opening and Mark's tousled brown head poking into the room. "Oh, hey," he grins. "Can I come in?"

"Sure," I nod. "It's a free country." Mental facepalm. *Free country?* Cliché much? 'Murica. Guns. Burgers. Freedom!

He opens the door all the way and plops down in the seat across from me. I find it very hard to look him in the eyes without blushing, so I stare at his nose instead.

"What's up?" he asks, pulling out his own sketchbook and pencil. I forgot that he's won multiple awards for his artwork, and I got a B- in Studio Art II last month. "You look like you've been thinking hard."

The corners of my lips turn up. "You could say that."

"What are you working on?" he asks.

Can I trust him? We're friends, but are we close enough for me to share this with him? Taking a huge leap of faith, I push my own pad in front of him.

His enchanting hazel eyes flit to the drawing. They widen a little as he recognizes the painting, and confirms it with the signature. "You drew that?" he asks, his eyebrows raised like he's impressed.

I nod. "Yeah. Well, technically, there was this kind of force that took over my hand and drew it. And signed it."

"Like, the ghost of Monet?" he jokes.

"Something like that. Magic can be weird sometimes." I laugh. "What are you working on?"

He shrugs modestly, flipping through the pages of his book. "Nothing at the moment, really," he says, "but I do have something I've been meaning to give you."

"Oh, cool." I say nonchalantly, even though my heart is racing like a horse. A thousand horses, actually. "What is it?"

He pulls a page out of the sketchbook, the ripping paper making a *shikk* sound. "Here." I take the page from him, carefully, like he just handed me a boa constrictor.

It's a drawing. A drawing of me, to be more specific. My breath catches as I recognize his attention to detail. My big eyes. My freckled nose and cheeks. My crazy hair with a mind of its own. In the drawing, my eyes are bright. Teasing, like my smile. The way my head tilts combined with my facial expression makes me look like some sort of enchantress.

I know when he drew this. It was actually just a few days ago. I was walking across the quad with Amelie, laughing at something funny she had just said, when Mark called out, "Hey, McKenna!"

I turned to face him, as did Amelie. We were still laughing as his pencil moved quickly and smoothly across the page. "Got it," he said, waved, and walked off.

"What was that about?" I asked Amelie.

She shrugged. "He probably wanted to draw you."

Now, as I look up, I see a crooked smile on his face, the same one he gave me yesterday morning.

"So *this* is what you were drawing that other day!" is all I can exclaim.

He nods sheepishly. "Yeah. You like it?" His hands twist—nervously—around his sketchbook.

"Definitely! You pay a lot of attention to detail." I smile, ecstatic that, of all people, he drew me. "It looks exactly like me, weird eyes and all. You are *so* talented. I definitely wouldn't be able to do something like this."

"Your eyes aren't weird," he argues, laughing a little. "They're pretty. Nice, I mean. Pretty nice." He adds quickly. "I've seen some of the stuff you do, and it's really great."

"Thanks," I choke out, shocked. Now I can't think straight because *he just told me that he thinks my eyes are pretty.*

A rose colored blush appears on his cheeks as he says, "Well, I guess I'd better get going."

"I'll come with you," I respond, standing up with my belongings. "I'm done here, anyway."

He holds the door open for me and we walk out silently, wrapped up in our own thoughts. I want to tell him about the code, the message, and the hidden meaning. But I can't bring myself to without jeopardizing his belief in me.

Thankfully, though, I don't have to.

"Do you know why you drew that?" he inquires, meaning the Monet.

Nodding my head, I respond, "Yes, but you *cannot* tell anyone." I flip through the pages of my book and hold it out to him.

His eyes move back and forth, examining the drawing and translating the message. Now that I think about it, it'd be weird if he had to read it and didn't take Spanish as a foreign language. "His 1919 *Water Lilies* is hanging up in the Met."

"Yeah. Gallery eight hundred twenty-two. And," I add, "apparently there's a secret passage behind it. How, I don't know."

"Do you know what it leads to, then?" He hands me back my sketchbook.

My mother's words ring in my ears. *I'll be waiting for you, though. Right here.* "My mother and the other Elementals are hiding somewhere beyond the passage."

Mark's eyes grow wide as he looks at me. I nod, even though I almost can't believe it myself. "What? How?" he asks.

I tell him verbatim what my mother said to me two years ago. "I had no idea what she meant then, but it all makes sense now."

"It does make sense." he agrees, then pauses. "So ... what do we do? Tell Dean P?"

"I don't know. Emma is looking into this, and she's all for rescuing them, but ... you know from last night that Natalie and Samantha don't really agree. They think we'll just end up getting killed. You came off as opposed to that idea. Are you, though?"

He hesitates for a second, really thinking about it. *Say yes, say yes, please, please!*

He nods, and I breathe a sigh of relief.

By now we're at the front of Maiyrn. I want to keep discussing this with him, to keep forming ideas. I know we can seriously consider these possibilities.

He seems to be reading my mind when he says, "Do you want to meet up later? You know, to talk more about this."

And even though I know I'm grinning, ear to ear, I manage to say, "That would be great. Do you mind if I bring Emma and Chris, though? I think they have some really good ideas."

He nods, also smiling. "And maybe after that, you and I could get some lunch too? I feel like I don't know you."

My heart races. "Sounds good. Where should we meet?"

He tilts his head, just a little. Time seems to stop around is. It's just us, Mark and I. I find it hard to look anywhere but his eyes, hazel and innocent. "Maybe the library? Twelve o'clock?"

"Okay." I wave and turn towards the building.

"McKenna, wait," his voice stops me in my tracks. I face him again.

"Yeah?"

He pauses for a moment, probably thinking over what he is about to say to me. Then, I assume he changes his mind, because he says, "Never mind."

"Okay ..."

There is a long pause in the air. A goofy grin finds its way onto my face, and after a few seconds, we burst out laughing. Mark has a nice laugh. It seems to start deep within him and projects out, but not too loudly. My sides hurt after a minute of constant giggling.

It feels good to laugh.

Chapter Nine

At noon I round up Chris and Emma, and together we walk over to the library. Mark is waiting for us outside on an old, rusty, iron bench, purifying the metal just by sitting there. When he spots us, he jumps up.

"What's up, man?" Chris gives him a high-five. "You're in on this, too?"

"Yep." Mark lifts his hand in a half wave at Emma. "Hey, Emma. McKenna." The smile he gives me nearly turns my brain to mush. Nearly. But I manage to say hey back, so it's okay.

Winston E. Pentlowe is the kind of library that would make avid readers—like Sam—feel like they've died and gone to book heaven. Rows upon rows of mahogany bookcases stand tall on the carpeted first floor, while oak tables and computers are located on the second. It's so clean the dictionaries probably don't have the definition of 'dust' in them. There's a huge glass chandelier that hangs from the ceiling and goes through the second floor, creating a big hole in the first ceiling. A spiral staircase is located in the front right corner of the library, and after waving to Ms. Unquist, one of the librarians, we use it to go upstairs.

"I've got my notes," Emma says, plopping down into a seat.

"And I've got mine," Chris follows suit.

"And we've got … this." I pull the drawing out of my pocket.

Emma frowns. "What's that?"

"The answer to all our questions."

"It's the location of the Elementals," Mark supplies. "Some weird force possessed McKenna's hand, or something like that, and drew this." He points at the picture. "It's Claude Monet's 1919 *Water Lilies.* The message is in Spanish, but it says that there's a secret passage behind this painting."

"My mom kind of gave me a hint two years ago," I add, swallowing. Should I tell them that bit of private information? *Oh, come on. I told Mark.*

"It's okay. You don't have to tell us." Chris gives me a fleeting smile. He knows about my family through Natalie.

"No, it's okay. She said she'd be waiting for me right there. I didn't get it at first, but now ..." I trail off. I've said enough.

Emma pounds her fist on the table, startling me. "This proves it. My dad and sister are in there. Your Elemental family is in there. The other Keepers are the same way." She quickly explains to the guys the conclusion we came to earlier.

"So ... how do we get them out?" Chris asks.

She exhales heavily, blowing blonde strands of hair out of her face. "I'm not sure, but I think we should figure out who left and why they did."

"How do we find out who left?" asks Mark.

Emma gives him a shrewd grin. "That's what the Internet is for, isn't it?"

Mark, Chris, and I crowd around Emma as she searches countless Elemental websites on a library computer for answers. How they're hidden from the world, I'll never know, but it must take a lot of magic to keep them cloaked, because when humans want to find something, they'll find it somehow.

"Aha!" she exclaims, clicking on an article. "'Two Hundred Elementals Go Missing'. December fifth, twenty-twelve." We scan the article, which is unsurprisingly biased, for names. The author basically blames the leaders for everything bad that'd been happening leading up to their disappearances. I spot my mother and sisters' names. They send sparks down my spine and I have to blink back tears.

"Isn't Derek Regeh the chief Elemental defense coordinator?" Mark taps his fingers on the table.

"He's also Cara Regeh's dad," I note, finally getting myself under control. "That's why she has a stick up her ass. Her dad's famous."

Chris snorts. "Elementally famous, maybe." Then he inhales sharply. "These are all important people. They're the strongest and most powerful of all the Elementals. And I'm guessing they took their kids, too, because there are multiple last names."

Emma shrieks. "A pattern! That's what we need."

"So if these people took their children, why didn't Cara's dad take her?" I say. "Heaven knows no one would have missed her."

"That's a good point." Mark says. "Except ... these aren't all their children."

"Huh?"

"When I lived in Colorado, I became good friends with a guy named Paul Saser. His dad holds the position right below Cara's dad." Mark points to the screen. "That's his dad's name. Charles Saser. His older sister and brother are on here, too. See?" His finger lands next to the names Rebecca and Patrick Saser. "Cara has a younger brother who's a grade below us. And look, Isaac Regeh's name is right underneath his dad's. And I bet there are more cases like that."

"So what's your point?" Chris asks.

"My point is this. Why would the most important people in the Elemental world disappear *on the same day*? And with all their children but one, to boot? And why are the kids that were left behind all the same age? This has got to be more than a coincidence. Something's not right here, and I, for one, suspect Acerbity had something to do with it."

"Where do you want to eat?" Mark asks as we cross the road to the strip mall. Dean Martins gave us the okay to walk go to the Asham Shopping Center, but only after making us swear up and down that we would be careful.

"Do you want to try McDonald's? I mean, it's pretty much the only place to eat around here." I kick aside a rock in my path, suddenly nervous. *Why didn't I think this through? A date? With Mark? To McDonald's? Why did I say that? This date is going to be a complete fail. Is it even a date anymore? McDonald's shouldn't count. Da—*

"Sure. I haven't been to one in forever."

He holds the door open for me when we reach it. I'm immediately blasted by cool air from the AC, which makes Mark and me shiver. As Fire Wielders, you'd think we wouldn't be able to get cold, but that's not the case. We do get cold. Easily.

"What do you want to eat?" I ask him, walking to the back of the line.

He looks up at the menu for a moment, frowns, and says, "I'll just get what you're getting."

"Well then, I hope you like double cheeseburgers. With no pickles."

He grins at me, which makes me grin even bigger. "Oh, so you're that kind of girl?"

"You bet."

"So what do you like to do?" Mark asks me when we sit down with our food. "I know you like to draw, but what else?"

"Hmm." I twirl a fry. "I like to draw, yes. I also like to build and fix stuff."

"What do you mean, build and fix stuff?"

"You know, stuff mechanics do. Work on cars, motorcycles, and bikes. Once and a while I'll try to build a model car from scratch, but Mr. Brisburne always ends up helping me."

Our conversation thins out after that, mostly because we came here to eat, not just talk. And though I feel like I can tell him anything—well, almost—I'm definitely not going to risk him thinking I'm disgusting by talking with my mouth full.

I'm having a really good time hanging out with him, at least until he says, "Emma said something about your Elemental family leaving, and I saw a bunch of girls' names with your last name on the list. I know about your mother, but did your siblings leave, too?"

I nearly choke on my last fry. This is the very subject I was trying to avoid. Telling him about my mother was hard enough. If I tell him about my sisters, too? It'll break me.

I circumvent the impending danger by saying, "Yeah. They did. Now it's your turn. Tell me about yourself."

He looks perplexed by the topic change, but still eventually says, "Well, like you, I like to draw. I like playing sports, too, like football and basketball."

And just like that, the crisis is averted. I tell him I like playing football, too, which I do. Basketball, though? Not so much.

"A lot of guys come together to play pickup games on Wednesdays and Fridays. You should join us sometime," he offers.

I steal a fry from him and smile. "I just might." The look on his face tells me he genuinely wants me to. Electricity courses between us, and everything inside of me lights up.

His eyes shift to the side of my head for a second, and his smile dissolves. "Oh, this is just great."

"What is it?" I look backwards. Alexis Avanti, in all of her designer-apparel glory, has arrived. Even more surprising is the fact that Raven is scowling next to her. Alexis scans the restaurant before her gaze settles on us, her eyes narrowing. And before I can even say, "I'm lovin' it", Alexis and Raven are standing beside our table, effectively ending my first date with Mark.

"Mark! I didn't know you came here often!" Alexis bats her eyes, ignoring me.

His cheeks gain color. "Um, I don't. McKenna thought this would be a good place to have lunch."

"McDonald's for a *date*?" Her eyebrows skyrocket. "Wow, Mida—I mean McKenna. I know you like to roll around in grease and car oil like a pig in the garage, but this is tacky, even for you." She sneers. "And maybe try a little foundation? Or … any sort of makeup? Sure, it'll make you look like a beautified swine with mommy issues, but some is better than none."

Mark begins to open his mouth, most likely to defend me, but I signal to him with my eyes that I can handle it. "Raven, maybe you should take your rabid dog outside. She's getting a little unstable. Plus, McDonald's doesn't allow pets in their buildings."

Raven looks up from her black nails for the first time since this exchange started. "Light will succumb to Darkness in the end. The beautiful will be subjugated by the rest," she says in Kevanese.

Um.

Who's the unstable one?

Mark and I share a glance. Sam's friend is a bit … weird. To say the least.

Alexis, seemingly unsatisfied by her prop, grabs hold of Raven's wrist. "Come on. Let's just get food and go."

"Alexis should really consider using some of her magic to make herself smarter. Maybe then she'll come up better ways to try and humiliate you."

I smile at his joke, but something about her words shook me. *A beautified swine with mommy issues* … Is that how my peers see me? As someone who's mother and sisters left her because she was so intolerable? And why was she about to say Mida-something instead of McKenna? The only Mida- name I know is Midam‾ela, but that name is only given to special Elementals.

"Sometimes I wonder if she's right," I whisper. "Maybe my family hates me. Maybe spending so much time in the garage is making me uglier."

Mark reaches a hand out across the table, but pulls it back before he touches mine. Damn it. I was hoping he'd do it. "No. Don't even try to start beating yourself up. That's like if you were in a fight with her and you turned your fists on yourself. I used to be so self-deprecating, and to be honest, it's one of the worst things you can do to yourself. She's irrelevant and you know it. She's just trying to get under your skin. You're fine the way you are."

Nervously, I reach out a Converse-clad foot and rest it next to his Vans. When he doesn't jerk his foot away like I've just told him I contracted Ebola, I rest easy. Without warning, he moves his leg so his right knee touches mine.

Mark O'Reilly's knee feels very nice.

Chapter Ten

I don't even leave my room the next morning. After everything that's come out, I kind of want to stay in bed all day. The sun is calling me through the window, but I roll over to the wall instead. The room gets lighter, lighter, lighter …

TWANG!

My eyes fly open at the sound of loud music. I roll over to see what's going on and nearly fall out of the bed. Emma, as in Emma *Richards*, is strumming a black and white electric guitar on the other side of the room. She goes off on a crazy cool riff, bopping her head to the music. Her fingers fly across the neck of the guitar like she's played the instrument all her life. If she had an amp, my eardrums would have been decimated.

"Um … Emma? What in God's name are you doing?"

She doesn't hear me. The music is too loud. I flick my hand in her direction and let a bit of electricity shoot across the frets, just so she gets a harmless shock. "Ouch!" She stops playing.

"You didn't tell me you played the guitar," I say.

She looks over at me in surprise. "McKenna! You're awake. Oh, yeah, I've been playing for a long time. It's therapy." She begins to play a softer, slower tune that sounds really sad. It's very well crafted, and it sounds almost personal.

"Did you write that one?"

She nods. "I wrote it after my dad and sister left. It's called Stay or Go."

Something about her face makes me say, "You really miss them, don't you?"

Tears form in her eyes. "My mom's great, don't get me wrong, but … she's not an Elemental, you know? Dad and Flarina got me. They knew what it was like to be overly emotional, control water, breathe it in, just constantly be aware of its presence. Everyone looked at me weird for not getting cold, but constantly being too hot. I'd give anything to have them with me again. Every night, no matter how childish it is now, I wish upon a star for them to come back. In fact, anytime I find something to wish on, I wish for them." Deep breath. "I need this mission to work. It'll break me if it doesn't."

Emma's confession shocks me like a blast of icy air. "Does Sam share your sentiments?"

"Not anymore," she says, shaking her head ruefully. "She hates change. She's finally gotten used to the idea that her dad is gone, and that her ignorant mother is all she has left, although her parents divorced like five years ago. Her mom is cynical and skeptic about everything. She doesn't even know her own daughter and ex-husband have powers. Mr. Mazer thought that would be best."

"Wow."

"Yeah. Sam refuses to believe her dad is alive. Everyone that disappeared is dead to her—literally. Finding the Elementals and changing her life even more? Something tells me that's not on the top of her list of things to do."

Things to do. Yeah, that reminds me. We agreed to talk to Dean Papadopoulos at eleven today. I can tell from the sun's position that it's about ten-thirty. Ugh. I have to get out of bed soon.

"Ready to talk to Dean?"

Emma knocks on Dean Papadopoulos's office door. I hear muffled noises—papers being shuffled—and finally Dean's loud, "Come in!" Emma turns the chrome doorknob and enters the room. Mark, Chris, and I are right behind her.

"What's going on, guys?" Dean asks, putting some papers down and clasping her hands on her desk. "Can I help you with anything?"

I sit down in a chair across from her desk. "Yes, actually, you can." Emma, Chris, and Mark follow my lead, taking seats on either side of me.

"We know where the rest of the Elementals are," Emma says, barely able to contain her excitement.

"And we need your help liberating them." Chris adds.

Dean Ioanna Papadopoulos stares at us, her mouth in an 'O' shape. I should have known. We've blown it. Freeing the Elementals was a far-fetched, crackpot, insane idea. If other older, more experienced, valiant men and women have tried and failed, how could we do it?

"Are you out of your minds?" she says, looking at us with a hard expression.

"You can teach us to defend ourselves. We know you can." says Emma in a soft voice. "You can train us so we can be prepared." She gives me a look. This isn't going to be easy.

Dean shakes her head, leaning forward. "No, no, no. This is not a matter of whether I can train you guys or not. This is a matter of, hello, you guys are only sixteen! Hello, you guys are still kids! Hello, you and McKenna are Keepers, which means we need you to stay alive! Hello, in case you haven't noticed, Acerbity is on the prowl and will find you and kill you! They are the predators, and you are the prey. You are not going anywhere!"

Why did I expect her to say anything else? She's a sensible, reasonable adult. "Dean. This isn't a matter of whether we're going or not. We *are* going. We have to. There's no other way. We now know where the Elementals are. My mother and sisters are alive."

"What she means to say is," Mark rests his hand on my arm, stopping my rant. And my heart. "The Elementals are hiding in a secret passage somewhere beyond a painting in the Metropolitan Museum of Art."

"How do you know?"

"We'll get into that later. Let's just say that magic was involved."

She shakes her head. "Magic's always—wait, back up. Did you say the *Met*?"

He nods. "In NYC."

Her eyes grow huge. "The Tunnels! Of course! Everyone thought all the doors were locked, but Olivia would have never allowed that to happen." Then her face drains of color. "Oh, no. The Tunnels. It can't be." She leaps up from her desk and begins to ransack her bookshelf, plucking out books like she's picking fruit and then tossing them to the ground. My heart beats faster at Dean's erratic behavior.

She finally finds the book she's looking for—an old one with a red leather cover and yellowing pages. I have half a mind to warn her not to flip through the pages too quickly or she'll destroy the book.

"Ah. Here it is. 'Felicity Caste created the Tunnels as a refuge for Elementals when persecution of her people inevitably becomes prevalent in the future. However, she warned that even her magic, as powerful as it is, cannot withstand the test of time, and the Tunnels will close forever four hundred years after her birthdate. They will then collapse in on themselves.'"

I feel like I'm about to throw up.

"When's Felicity's birthday?" Chris asks slowly.

"August 20th, 1614."

"So the Tunnels will close up on August 20th of this year. That's five and a half weeks from now."

Emma gasps. "Dean, we have to do this now. Now or never."

Dean rubs her hand on her forehead, sighing. She closes her eyes, taking deep breaths. She's probably thinking about how many milligrams of Tylenol she's supposed to take. She has to say yes. She just has to. Those lives are in danger, and we're the only ones who know.

After a minute, she open her eyes and sits back in her chair. "I'm in. But no one, and I mean *no one* other than the people on the rescue team, can know. It's crucial that this is kept secret. And you'll need about ten people to help. After you interview each person for the team, send them to me so I can wipe their memory of the meeting. Training starts next week. I should be sending professionals out there, but you girls plus Natalie and Samantha are the most powerful people in the world. You're the best ones for the job." She smacks her head. "There's something important I'm forgetting."

"That's okay." Emma pencils in Dean P's name in her notebook. "Now we just need to get Nat and Sam on board, and we can start interviewing people."

Dean's face turns as white as a sheet. "What? You mean Natalie and Samantha don't agree to this?"

"Unfortunately," Mark confirms.

"Minor speed bump." I add.

Dean takes a deep breath. "Oh, Lord. Where's my Tylenol?" She gets up, walks over to a cabinet, and takes out a white bottle.

"Come on, let's go find them," Chris says animatedly, before standing up and leaving.

"We'll be back in ten," Emma calls before racing out the door after him.

Mark and I look at each other after ten minutes of explaining the past days' events. "We should probably go after them and find them before they start breaking rules," Mark laughs. He takes my hand. "*Ladojúc.*" Let's go.

I almost forget to breathe.

After a while, my heart rate goes back down to normal. I'm almost used to the feel of Mark's warm fingers laced between my own. His hand is almost as hot as mine—almost. I have to resist the urge to look at him, take a good look at his face, try to read his expression, figure out what's going on.

I don't know what's going on. I like him, I won't deny it anymore. But we've always acted like we're just good friends, nothing more, and now *this*. Whatever *this* is. Holding hands like a couple—*no, no, get rid of that thought. You're not a couple; no one is dating anyone. For the love of all things holy, McKenna, get it together and get real! Stop it! You. Wish!*

"You okay?" Mark looks at me quizzically.

I realize I may have been staring at him during my mental argument with myself. "I'm good. Fine, actually." He smiles and I return it sheepishly, like a kid being caught with her hand in the cookie jar. Except, no. My hand is currently entwined with his.

I spot Emma and Chris walking our way from my peripheral vision. "There they are," I say, pointing with my free hand. Natalie and Samantha are on either side of them, lost in an intense conversation.

"Emma! Christmas!" Mark says loudly, and they look at us with odd expressions on their faces, like they've never seen us before. Like they've never seen us *together* before.

Nevertheless, they approach us and Natalie says, with a huge smile on her face, "We're on board."

That was fast. "How did that happen? We thought you would be totally against it."

"We were," Sam confirms, "but that was before they told us Mark's theory and the Tunnels closing. We have to find them before anything else happens to our parents." She sighs wistfully. "I'd never thought I'd say this, but he's definitely alive. I know that now. And since he is alive, I need to go find him."

"Good," says Mark as we turn around to walk with them back towards Dean Papadopoulos's office. "Now we can start looking for people to come with us, because it can't just be the six of us. Dean says we need four more."

"Us?" Emma inquires. "Who's *us*? You guys have to get interviewed like everyone else. No one's set in stone except for the four Keepers."

Chris nods. "Really? I mean, I'm fine with that, but ..."

Emma laughs, writing something in her notebook. "Just kidding. You guys are honorary members of the Liberation team. That's something we know for sure."

Samantha clears her throat. "And another thing. What's up with the hand-holding? Are you dating now? Finally, I mean?"

"No!" we say simultaneously. Chris laughs hysterically. I'm sure my face is turning bright crimson. Mark is blushing as well.

"We're not." I say quickly. Does everyone know? Are my feelings written on my face? In black Sharpie?

"No," he corrects. "She wishes we were."

"What the ...," I sputter. "No I don't. *You* wish that." I stare at him indignantly for throwing me under the bus.

Mark gestures to me, and looks at Samantha. "Since you're the Air Manip, you can be the judge of that." This earns him a snort from Chris.

"Come on, you guys," I huff, dragging him along. "We have to hurry up."

The others quickly fall behind, and after looking back to make sure they aren't listening, he says, "You know I didn't mean that. You know, back there. I mean, I do feel a certain way about you."

I shake my head, willing my heart rate to go decrease. "No biggie. You have a very strange sense of humor. But on a serious note,

Mark, remind me to explain myself later. Privately. 'Cause I think I feel the same about you."

He nods. "You're right. Let's talk about this later when it's not so ... crowded."

And for some odd reason, I let go of his hand and we start running, racing each other back to Dean's office.

I win, of course.

CHAPTER ELEVEN

"What are your strongest spells?" Emma asks three days later of Eli Carson, holding her notebook and writing furiously in it.

"I'm really good at *mistemintea* and various attack spells." Eli runs his hand through his brown curls, his eyes glued to his Nikes. Those are good spells that we may need. I look at Samantha for confirmation, and she nods her head in agreement.

"One last question: do you have any fears?" This time Natalie asks the question.

Eli looks very uncomfortable in his seat. He clears his throat, and I feel bad for him. "I'm deathly afraid of spiders."

Samantha's brow furrows. "What do you mean by deathly?"

"I mean, if I see one, I'll probably faint."

Natalie looks stricken as Emma makes a mark in her notebook. Eli's chances of making it onto the liberation team have dropped fantastically. Not quite a minute ago, he sounded like a shoo-in. "Okay, we'll contact you in a couple of days. Thanks for your time. Dean Papadopoulos wants to see all interviewees in her office, so you should head on over there." I shake his hand and shakily, he staggers to the door.

He should probably get that checked out.

After she leaves, Emma crosses Eli's name out. "Nope," she says dramatically. "The Tunnels will probably be filled with arachnids and I sure as heck am not going to be the one dragging his unconscious body through them."

"That really was too bad," Samantha says. "His power range was excellent. And he's really nice. We really could have used him."

I nod in agreement and say, "True. Okay, how many people do we have, Emma?"

She checks the list. "We currently have nine people. Natalie, Sam, you, and me, then Mark and Liam O'Reilly, Christopher Smith, Jackson Chrysler, Amelie Avanti, and me. Katonah Fordham should be here any minute for her interview." She twirls her pen around her fingers. "I hope Dean knows what she's doing, 'cause I find it kind of funny that those that are definitely on the mission are people we know well. Sure, we're all friends and stuff, but will she be able to make a liberation team out of us?"

Right as Emma finishes her statement, Katonah bursts in the room. "Sorry I'm late, guys," she apologizes breathlessly. "I got here as fast as I could. Vianney Rose wanted me to watch her practice her new part in ballet." Katonah is one of the many regular sorcerers here, like Eli. She has dark brown hair, curious eyes that match her hair, has never seen a pimple in her life, and is an amazing chef. She usually smells like whatever she's cooked up in the kitchen. She's an incoming senior like Chris and Jackson.

"It's fine," Natalie says, and gestures to the seat across from us. "Have a seat, please."

Katonah plunks down into the seat. "So, what's this interview about?"

"We're going on a mission, but we need more people on our team. We're interviewing people to see if they're fit to fight." I explain.

"Fight who?"

"Well," Emma interrupts, "we're hoping we won't have to fight anybody, but we're going to rescue the Elementals. We know where they are."

Katonah's eyes grow wide. I smile, fully realizing the extent of our mission. If we succeed, not only will the Elementals be back where they belong, with the rest of us, but everyone on the Liberation Team will be remembered until the end of time. For the past couple of days, Natalie has been fantasizing about having her name printed on the page of a history book.

Paola's vision haunts my thoughts as well. *We could also be killed or be possessed by Acerbity,* I remind myself. Sam knows as well, but we haven't talked about it with each other or with Natalie and Emma.

"Okay. Question one. What kind of Elemental are you? We already know the answer, but we're supposed to ask to make it all official," Natalie asks.

"I am a regular witch."

Emma nods. "Okay. What Elemental powers did your parents possess?"

Katonah shrugs. I remember her saying that she and Vianney Rose were orphans. They were in foster care for four years before they came to the school two years ago. "I don't even know who my parents were. Vi and I are orphans. After I turn eighteen, next month, though, it won't matter, so don't say *I'm sorry* or anything like that."

"Oh. Okay." Natalie is clearly uncomfortable."

"What are your strongest powers?" I ask.

"*Mistemintea,* blocking, disarming ... things like that. I'm pretty good with offensive hexes."

"Are you good at mixing chemical elements?"

Katonah grins, her whole face lighting up. "Ranked first in the class of 2015."

"Do you have any fears?"

Katonah laughs. It's a nice laugh. "When you've lived in an orphanage, you stop being afraid of things. The only thing I'm scared of is losing."

Sam grins, and the weight on my shoulders is lifted slightly. If we accept her, our team will be complete. "Thank you for your time. Make sure you drop by Dean P's office on your way out. We'll contact you about our decision in a few days. Have a nice day."

"Oh, I will." And she gets up and leaves within five seconds.

When you've live in an orphanage, you stop being afraid of things. Knowing Katonah, she's probably telling the truth. Why can't I be like her: strong, tough, and fearless? Why am I, a Fire Wielder, the wuss?

Emma turns to face the rest of us. "I think we have our Liberation team right there, am I right?"

Natalie rolls her eyes, standing up. "Emma, we have to give everyone a chance. It has to be a fair system. Lauma and that guy Kirdi look pretty good."

There's a knock at the door. I look at Emma with a confused expression. Did she invite anyone else? Katonah was supposed to be the last one on our list.

Jasmine Alec opens the door with a burlap satchel slung over her shoulder, her colorful floral print hijab fluttering in the sudden breeze. "I have letter for you," she says, smiling. She reaches into her bag and produces four white envelopes. Jasmine always smiles. She was born in Pakistan and moved to the US at age eleven. She didn't learn English until then, so she has a heavy accent and mixes in Urdu with her choppy sentences. We're always telling her to speak Kevanese so she's more comfortable, but she refuses. She wants to be fluent. To make up for her bad English, she smiles. Constantly.

I take the one with my name on it. "Thanks," I say, but I'm not really paying attention to her. I'm staring at my name. It was obviously handwritten; I can barely make out the sender's chicken scratch. The problem is, though, I don't recognize the handwriting. And even stranger is the fact that the return address says it was mailed from the Metropolitan Museum of Art, which I'm pretty sure is impossible.

Wait … *the Met?*

Emma rips her letter open the moment the door shuts behind Jasmine. She gives herself a paper cut—I can see the blood forming a dot on her index finger, but she either doesn't notice or care. Her blue eyes move back and forth as she reads; her lips mumble the words to herself.

"Well?" Natalie says, almost impatiently.

Emma's face becomes whiter than snow as she finishes reading. "Oh, no." The temperature in the room drops about thirty degrees, and I shiver.

"What is it?" I ask as I hold my palms out, making the room warm again. "Who's it from?"

Emma sinks to the floor. Frost starts to develop around her. "Acerbity," she whispers. She drops the letter on the ground, seemingly locked in a trance. "They're there."

I rip my letter open at high speed. The paper nearly catches fire. That's insignificant, though, and I barely notice as my eyes scan the paper feverishly.

Dearest McKenna Donaldson (or should I say Midam˜ela Caste-Donaldson),

Greetings from the Met! I hear you're planning a trip down here to the Big Apple, and I must say, that's a wonderful idea. Your rescue team is impeccable. Your mode of transportation is exceptional. And your skill set is like no other. What could possibly go wrong?

We're anxiously awaiting your arrival in the Tunnels. This is almost like a dream come true for us. The four Keepers, all in the same place at the same

time, trying to liberate their mommies and daddies. Oh! Let's not forget your sisters, too! All eleven of them. I do wonder sometimes what Meredith was thinking, having twelve children. And with a human, no less.

I digress. Don't bother coming down here, because you're not going to make it out alive. Or, wait. What am I saying? Come down if you like. You all already know your three possible fates.

Wait, what was that? You and Sam Mazer haven't told Emma Richards and Natalie Wilde yet? Oh, boy. That's going to be a headache. Better have some of Dean Papadopoulos's Tylenol handy.

Have a happy road trip,
Acerbity

I read the letter again, and then again. My stomach feels like it's bungee jumping inside my body. Swallowing hard, I fight the urge to scream. They do have my mother. They do have my sisters. Emma Marie is only twelve. She doesn't deserve any of this. My mother doesn't need anything more to worry about.

Tears cloud my vision as I think of my sisters, enduring the probable tortures down there. For once, Saige and Bethany won't be causing double trouble. They're only nineteen. My six older sisters wouldn't be able to take care of my younger sisters. They'd be too busy trying to stay alive.

And someone's watching us here.

We can't go. We're not safe. Now that I'm riled up, my powers will be out of control. I could hurt somebody in there. I could hurt someone here. I need to go to the door. I need to—

Suck it up, McKenna ... Mom always used to say that to me when I cried over spilled milk when I was little. *There are so many people in even worse situations than you are.* I take a deep breath and wait for my heart to stop beating erratically.

When I look up, Emma and Natalie are staring at Sam and me with odd expressions.

"What three possible fates?" Natalie asks.

"Paola," Sam says, not even bothering to lie. "Paola had a vision. That night, when I read McKenna's mind? She was thinking about it. Paola predicted our death, alliance with Acerbity by possession, or victory on our mission. Which seems pretty obvious, but it isn't, not really."

"Our, as in the whole team?" asks Emma. She sounds desperate, which is justified. We're all desperate. "As in, the boys, too?"

I shake my head, wanting to know that myself. Mark. I can't let him die. Not on my watch. "She only saw us four. No one else."

A gust of wind rips my letter out of my hands. I look around in alarm. Sam's hands are raised, guiding the letters to above our heads, and, with a snap of her fingers, they disappear.

"Where'd you send them to?" Natalie asks.

"The dorm room." Sam wipes her hands on her capris. "Dean P is going to be here any moment, and you know she's going to take them away, burn them, or worse, cancel the mission. We have to act like nothing happened, or there will be more problems."

The door opens yet again. Dean Papadopoulos comes in carrying a cup holder and five drinks. "Three camerine shakes, one lava coffee, and an iced tea. Did you make your decision yet?"

"Thanks for the shakes, and no, we haven't," answers Natalie, taking a long sip. "All those people with all their fears. One girl is afraid of blood. I had to cross out her name before she finished talking. Kirdi has great powers, but his ego is a bit overinflated. I need a break."

"I didn't think Kirdi was bad," Emma counters. Condensation forms on her cup, so much that water spills off her iced tea and into her lap. I don't think she notices it.

I hold my lava coffee to my lips so my hands have something to do. *She better not suspect. She* better *not suspect.*

"Are you okay, McKenna?" Dean P looks at me like I just told a joke in Croatian. Which I can do, but that would be weird right now.

"Of course!" I say, almost a little too enthusiastically. "Why wouldn't I be?"

She smiles warmly, convinced. "You're right. You just seemed a little worried."

You have no idea.

CHAPTER TWELVE

The letter sits crumpled on my bed. I don't want to get rid of it. Though the threat is horrible, it is my only connection to my mother and sisters. I don't want to lose them. Again.

As I stare at the letter, thinking, the words vanish.

"What the heck?" Emma says. She clutches her letter in her hand, crystal tears falling, and, not for the first time tonight, I wonder what it says. "The words just *disappeared!*"

I bring my letter to my face, holding it right in front of my eyes. No, no, *no!* Not again. My link to my family has just been severed. More of my ties to them are slipping away like sand through my fingers on a windy beach.

"Okay, everyone just calm the hell down," Natalie tries to sound normal, cool even, but she's gripping the bedpost next to her so hard, the wood starts to splinter and break.

"How can we?" Emma says thickly. Her golden hair is plastered to her face, glistening with salty tears. This is the least beautiful she's ever looked. "My dad and sister are in danger, and you want me to calm down? We have to leave today!"

"Emma. Think about it. This is exactly the reaction Acerbity wants us to have. They'd want us to freak out and rush over there without any training, weapons, anything, like the hot-tempered sixteen-year-olds we're supposed to be. We can't give them the satisfaction, or our lives." Samantha tosses her letter on the floor. "McKenna, can you burn them?"

I shake my head. "I thought you didn't want to burn them!"

"Well, I've changed my mind. Everyone, put yours on the floor. We're not telling anyone about these letters, and we're not thinking about them anymore. Remember, I can hear what you're thinking."

Emma crumples hers up and pitches it on the floor in disgust. It skitters next to Sam's. Natalie follows suit.

I *really* don't want throw it in, but I know I have to. Reluctantly, I add mine to the pile, take a deep breath, and raise my hands. My fingers tingle like a foot that fell asleep before fire shoots from my hands and consumes the papers. Flames lick at the letters, dancing with each other until there's nothing left. "There."

I destroy the flames and stare at the darkness they left behind.

Natalie sighs. "Where *is* she? She's always on time for everything. Doesn't she know this meeting is for something *slightly* significant?"

"Relax, Nat. She'll be here. Something probably held her up," Emma says, twisting her hair up into a ponytail. "This meeting isn't even that important."

"It can't be just *anything*." Natalie ignores Emma. "Emma's here and she's always at least fifteen minutes late. We were supposed to start forty-seven minutes ago." She raises her eyes to the ceiling, as if talking to God himself. "She's probably with Jackson. They've been hanging out a lot lately. Have you noticed that? I have."

I sigh, shifting in my seat. Dean Papadopoulos's office became the Team's official headquarters after she gave us the key to it. We told Sam we were having a meeting at two forty-five today, so where is she?

"I'm here!" Sam appears out of thin air. I can never get used to her *vervortade* powers enabling her to just materialize wherever, whenever. If this were a thousand years ago, she and the other Air Manipulators wouldn't be able to do that, or become invisible. Funny how mutations work. Her hair is windblown, white cheeks flushed rose pink. She looks excited. "Sorry I'm late!"

"*Sorry you're late?!*" Natalie explodes. "We've been here for nearly an hour! Is that all you have to say? What about an explanation?"

"You wouldn't believe it if I told you." Sam is glowing with happiness. I've never seen her like that: looking like she might float away. She always has a dreamy air around her, but it's an effect of her Air powers. This is way different.

Natalie crosses her arms. "Try me." Looking down at Sam's feet, she adds, "Are you floating?"

Sam looks down. "Oh. Oops." She plants herself firmly on the ground before saying, "I kissed Jackson. Wait. No. Jackson kissed me. I don't know."

"What!" Emma shrieks. "You what?!"

She lowers herself into a chair. "I know, right? Since the day I arrived, we've been friends. And I guess that turned into something more. I don't know if this is going to mess us up or something. You know what I mean?"

"Whoa, whoa. Back up. Jackson kissed you? Jackson the senior? Chris's best friend?" Natalie asks, bewildered.

Sam rolls her eyes. "Yes, Natalie. Keep up."

Natalie snaps the pen in her hand. "Great. This is just great." I look at Natalie in surprise. *What the heck?* Why isn't she happy? I haven't really noticed Sam and Jackson, but it's not a big deal. It shouldn't be.

"What's the problem?" I ask. "Isn't that a good thing?"

"No, it's not. Relationships always distract the people in them. You and Jackson won't be able to concentrate on what's important. You'll be too busy 'spending time with each other' or some other bullcrap."

"We're not dating!" Sam exclaims, spinning around in the black office chair. "We just kissed. Is that such a crime?"

Emma places a hand on Natalie's arm. "Come on, Natalie. Don't you take pride in being a rational thinker? Just because they kissed doesn't mean they don't realize what's important."

"Fine." Natalie scowls.

Sam's smile is smug. "So, do you want to confirm the Team members?"

Emma nods. "Okay. I have us four, Mark, Liam, Christopher, *Jackson* ..." She looks pointedly at Sam, who blushes profoundly. "Katonah and Amelie. Any objections?" No one speaks. "Good. The meeting is adjourned." Emma stands up and Sam winks out instantly.

Natalie stands up quickly, shoving papers in her messenger bag. "I'm going to *get* Jackson. Better pray he comes out in one piece." She dashes out, muttering curses under her breath.

"That girl." Emma shakes her head ruefully.

Chapter Thirteen

"**M**cKenna and Chris, you're up!" Dean Papadopoulos barks out my name what feels like the millionth time this afternoon, even though it's probably only the third. "Let's go, people! And be glad we're only using powers this week. Next Monday will be hours of grueling shooting and sword practice!"

I sigh and square up. Chris gives me a small smile before hurling a huge rock at me. I dodge it and shock him with a bolt of lightning. I then send flames at him, but this time he's quick enough and shields himself with a stone.

"Pretend your opponent is Acerbity. Would you stand there, using weak offensive moves, or would you get as many hard blasts in as you could before he or she could blink, hmm? There isn't any playing around in those Tunnels. This isn't a pleasure trip, it's a mission! So act like it's one!"

When Dean gets like this, it's best to ignore her. I turn my attention back to the boulders that are closing in on me, but it's too late. I'm slammed into the wall. His move would have killed me if we weren't protected by Dean's spell. Instead of getting smashed, I just feel a brief bit of pressure on the front of my body. Chris quickly ties me up with a super long vine so I can't walk away.

"That's how you do it, *Sparky*," he says, smirking. "If you were an Acerbitian, I'd've slit your throat."

"Good job, Chris." Dean pats him on the back, and he puffs up his chest.

"*Good job, Chris,*" I mimic, making a face at him. He just laughs and goes over to stand next to Liam. I look over at the others. Liam and Katonah are trying not to laugh, but are failing miserably. Amelie has a weird look on her face, like she feels bad for me. I don't even look at Mark's face. Surely, he must be in hysterics like his brother. Who the heck likes a Fire Wielder who can't fight?

"Take twenty!" Dean announces, signaling a break. Everyone scatters around the room.

I try to untangle myself from Chris's trap, but am unsuccessful. Natalie chortles at my dilemma before smashing the rocks with a curl of her fist and ripping the vines off me. "*Wamekir commen.*" *You're welcome.*

"*Grietzi,*" I pant, resting my hands on my knees. "I got distracted by Dean."

Emma peers at the small group of people. "Where's Sam?"

I point to her left. Sam and Jackson are in deep conversation, their heads bent towards each other. "I never would have guessed," Natalie says flatly. "Seeing as they hate each other and all."

My nose tingles, sensing the tangy odor of magic behind me, and I whirl around. Dean Papadopoulos smiles at me. "Nice job, McKenna. You're doing great so far."

"Thanks. I shouldn't have lost that last one."

"Don't put so much weight on your right foot, especially when you kick. I saw you do that when you fought Katonah. It makes you react slower. Otherwise, you should be fine." Dean nods and strides away.

"Do I put a lot of my weight on my right foot?" I ask Emma and Natalie. "Is it noticeable?"

"Do a kick," Emma suggests, holding her chin in her hand. "Let me see."

I crouch a little and thrust my foot out to the side. My foot connects with something as I kick, and my eyes widen as I see who it is. Oh no. *Mark!* My surprise throws me off balance, and I fall to the ground with him.

Gracefully, of course.

"*Oh my God.* Oh my God, I am so sorry. *So* sorry. That was an accident. A total accident. Are you okay?" I say. My mouth keeps moving even though I want to stop talking. It's like my brain isn't even connected to my larynx. *Shut up! Shut* up!

Emma and Natalie laugh hysterically, looking down at the mess I made. I scowl at them and curse them in my head.

Despite being sprawled on the ground next to me, he smiles. "Are you?"

I nod, swallowing a dozen other things I want to say. *Why am I still on the ground?*

"Well, then I am, too." He heaves himself up and extends his hand to me. I grab it, still shaky. I kicked Mark. I assaulted him with my foot. An appendage of mine menacingly—albeit accidentally—connected with his torso and knocked him to the ground.

"Somehow I predicted that happening," Natalie says, finally calming down. "I just didn't know it'd be as funny as it actually was." I roll my eyes. Some best friend.

"It was kind of funny, McKenna," Mark laughs. "I'm just walking over here, getting ready to ask you a question, and all of a sudden, *wham!* Kicked by your foot! Slow descent to the ground. You're off balance, and you start falling, too. We collapse on the ground. Gracefully, of course."

I can't help but crack up. When he puts it like that …

"See?" Emma says. "It *is* funny."

"So, what did you want to ask me?" I say. Emma and Natalie suddenly become extremely fascinated with a speck on the ceiling.

Mark looks uncomfortable as well. "You know that conversation we were having the other day?"

"I have a vague recollection."

His lip curls upward. "You said we could finish the conversation later. I was thinking … we have fifteen minutes left in the break. You want to go outside for a few minutes?"

Be fearless, McKenna Blaise Donaldson.

I grab hold of his hand. "Let's go."

Walking across the quad with Mark O'Reilly is a testing experience. It tests your ability to put on a game face. It tests your ability to be fearless. It tests your ability to be yourself when you don't want to. It tests your ability to restrain yourself from cracking corny jokes and making painful puns.

"Can I be honest with you for a minute?" Mark says, his cheeks coloring a bit.

"Sure. What's up?" I give his hand a little squeeze.

He runs the other through his hair. "I'm starting to think that you think I'm more courageous than I really am. I'm actually extremely worried about this whole mission thing."

It's all I can do to keep myself from breathing a sigh of relief. I totally thought he was going to say something about our "relationship". God, I hate that word. "Don't worry about it. We're all nervous. But we can do it. I know we can."

He shakes his head quickly. "No, no. That's not what I meant. I'm going to go on the mission, but … I really don't want to do this. The fear I have … it's … it's paralyzing."

A million jagged thoughts fill up my head at once, leaving me with almost no room to process what Mark has just said. "You … don't want to go on the mission?" I drop his hand, suddenly feeling cold.

"McKenna—"

"It never was your intention to help us out, was it? Did you ever actually care? Was this just a ploy to get close to me?" How could I not have seen this coming? Wasn't it Natalie that said guys will say anything just to get a girl?

"I guess I didn't explain thoroughly."

Clenching my jaw is the only thing that's keeping my sudden rage at bay. To think I liked Mark, to think I *trusted* him! Especially with all that information about my family. "What else is there to explain? It's all so clear."

He takes hold of my hands, and when I try to pull away, he doesn't let me. "Please believe me when I say that I want to help you. I want you to be reunited with your family. I also want to rescue my friend's family, too. Remember? When I was in Colorado, my family was close to Paul's. I'm petrified of the idea of going underground into channels that are going to collapse in on themselves in a matter of weeks. But I'm going to do it. I'm doing this for you, and Paul, and everyone else whose relatives are lost in the Tunnels."

"That's what you meant?"

"That's what I meant."

A wave of guilt hits me like a baseball bat to the face. How did I let myself jump to conclusions so quickly? How did I let my emotions get out of check like that? I'm supposed to be controlling my powers, and that includes not getting extremely angry in less time than it takes to blink. Mark did not deserve any of that.

"I'm so sorry, Mark. I shouldn't have assumed the worst. I tend to do that a lot, but I'm supposed to be keeping that in check. Forgive me?" I force myself to look into his eyes.

"Of course. I don't blame you, you know. I would have come to the same conclusion if it were me." He looks down at our hands, which are still joined, and his cheeks take on a muted scarlet color. Sudden nervousness forces my mouth into a cheesy grin.

"I might as well extend that minute of honesty. Um. Ahem. Remember what we were talking about the other day? You know, before we raced the other day?"

I laugh. "You mean the race that I won?"

"*You* won? Is that what you've been telling yourself?" He tentatively puts his arms around my waist, making my heart stop. *Is he going to kiss me? Is he really going to do it, in front of whoever walks by?* "You know what? Never mind. I'll concede that one."

"I knew it!" I sing-song. "But continue, please."

"I recall you saying that you feel the same way about me as I do about you. Is my recollection accurate?"

I nod slowly. I think a Boy Scout tied my stomach into knots. "I did say that, but the operative word was 'think'. I'm not one hundred percent sure how you feel about me, to be honest. I mean, you haven't said much about it."

He looks a bit sheepish. "True, true. Though, to be fair, I don't say much in general."

Feeling a bit bold, I touch my forehead to his. Leftover sweat from practice should make the whole thing gross, but for some reason it doesn't. "So if you're not going to *tell* me, how am I supposed to know?"

The wind blows, warm and soft like feathers. A lock of hair falls in front of his eyes, and before I can stop myself, I reach out and push it back where it belongs. Something changes in his hazel eyes; I can see it instantly. They grow a bit darker, and they dart to my lips just for a second.

Is this what happened to Sam?

He whispers something right before pressing his lips to mine, but his voice is so low, I don't know what he said. That doesn't matter. Even if I had heard him, the kiss would have wiped my memory in the same way it restarts my heart. My breath catches in my throat as I close my eyes and put my hand on the back of his neck. He's tentative at first, as if he's worried I'll pull away, but then he grows more confident.

Everything is still around us, as if the sparrows in the air and the leaves dancing in the wind have stopped to gaze, to marvel at this perfect thing of beauty. And though there are seven billion people in the world, and countless other species, right now, right here, it's a small world, and Mark and I are the population. It's just me, him, and the marginal space in between.

It's magnificent.

I pull away and stare into his eyes, breathing hard from the heady kiss, searching, searching for hints, clues, anything that might tell me what on Earth is happening. All I can see, though, are his gleaming hazel eyes and the flames behind them. Something else, too. Admiration? Fondness? Affection? I don't know.

"McKenna," he breathes, resting his forehead against mine again. He's so close I can feel his racing heart. He's taken on a dazed expression, which makes him look even cuter.

"Yeah?"

"Does that answer your question?"

I can't help but giggle like a little schoolgirl. "Yes. Yes, it did." I want to kiss him again, be able to breathe again.

So I do it. For the first time in my life, I don't contemplate the consequences of what I'm about to do. I just follow through. That first kiss was like a drug. I want to hate him for getting me hooked on it, but I know I can't. Because I'm falling, falling, plummeting down to the ground. And only he can catch me.

Jeez, McKenna, way to sound like an intolerable romantic sap. You two have literally kissed twice, and already you're talking about falling for him like a lead anchor? How ... tasteful of you. Have you considered a career in penning romance novels?

Somewhere, off in the distance, I can hear someone calling our names. Samantha? Emma? We turn to look.

"Where have you guys been?" Sam races towards us, breathing heavily. Seeing the two of us, she says, "*Oh.*" Then she shakes her head. "Training restarted. You and your boyfriend need to get going."

She *whooshes* out.

"Boyfriend?" He says to thin air. Looking at me he says, the beginnings of a grin on his face, "Is that accurate?"

I decide to tease him by saying, "Maybe." He takes my hand as we start walking and, despite my own words, I know it is true.

It *is*, in fact, accurate.

Chapter Fourteen

The weeks go by in a blur. Four weeks, to be exact. We have training every day, from four to six thirty P.M. Training gives us time to bond, and by week two, at our breaks, we sat in a circle and just talked. It's like starting a club at a regular high school. The first week is kind of awkward, but the ice melts by the time you adjust and create a rhythm.

Dean Papadopoulos works us, hard, though. Every day, the Keepers and I tiredly stagger to our room, worn out. Our limbs are always sore after running laps around the track, skill development, and singles and doubles combat.

Natalie warms up to Amelie, eventually. It takes a while, but eventually she stops frowning whenever Amelie spends time in our room.

August twentieth gets closer and closer with each day. I get a weird feeling when we flip the page from July to August on the calendar in our room. Like not all of the Team members will be around to turn the page again from August to September.

I try not to dwell on that.

On August sixteenth, Dean makes an announcement at the end of training: "You're ready."

We all cheer, high-fiving each other. Ready. Finally ready. If Acerbity were to come crashing through the basement doors now, we could take them on. With a jolt, I realize that I could be face to face with my mother and sisters within seventy-two hours. Will they recognize me? Have I changed much? It's been two years, but I'm pretty sure I look the same, only taller. My personality hasn't wavered that much, either.

"You need to remember to lie low when you're heading down there. Since Samantha is the most perceptive, she will drive. No speeding, no tickets for illegal parallel parking, no nothing. Stay under the radar, and remember, your goal is to get the Elementals out of the Tunnels and unlock the Compass Doors as quickly as possible. The window of time is very narrow. What we're doing is highly dangerous, but I know you can do it."

Sam salutes, meaning *yes, ma'am.* Dean Papadopoulos explained to us two weeks ago that the Compass Doors were entrances to the Tunnels that could be reached from the four corners of the earth. Felicity put them in place because she knew that the Elemental population would spread rapidly in the future. If she hadn't created them, Elementals would have to travel to North America to access entrances. Because America wasn't a country when she was alive, she decided to create the Tunnels in a—seemingly—empty continent.

"Wait," Katonah argues. "Shouldn't I drive? I'm the oldest. I've had my license the longest."

"True," Dean admits. "But Sam is much more perceptive. I'm not saying I don't trust you, but you guys need to adhere to the rules and Sam's the only one out of all of you I'm one hundred percent sure will follow them. Okay?"

"Fine," Katonah grumbles.

"Good. Now go and pack. Everything except clothes, though. I have gear that you're going to need."

Mark finds me in the mess of Liberation Team members. "I can't believe we're leaving tomorrow," he says, giving me a hug. "We only have a short amount of time before the Tunnels are destroyed."

"Well, then it's a good thing that we're ready. Who's in charge of food?"

"Natalie's overseeing everything, of course, but I think she delegated Chris."

I turn sideways to avoid knocking into Liam as we walk. "And tools? Please don't tell me that's my job."

"Nope, it's mine," says Katonah, appearing next to us. "I'm in charge of ropes and stuff like that. Not sure what we're going to need them for, seeing as we have our powers, but whatever."

"Maybe we're going to tie Acerbity up. You know, act like we surrender, and then, *whoosh!* Tie them up in the blink of an eye." I make fast tying motions to go with my story.

She frowns. "We're not going to be doing any tying if Dean Martins doesn't let us go, though."

"What?" asks Mark. "Nobody's asked him yet?"

"Nope."

I groan. "Are you serious? I can't believe we waited until the last minute! Whose job was that?"

"Unimportant." Katonah sighs. "Look, it's not going to be easy for us to convince Dean M to let us go. You know he's doing everything to preserve you four Keepers, and running headfirst into the Tunnels is at the bottom of his list. This mission is going to be a bust if Dean P doesn't get his permission, so be prepared to sneak out if we have to."

I nod, and she walks away.

I close my eyes and the Acerbitian letter randomly pops into my head. Well, not randomly. It's been plaguing me since I burned it weeks ago. I haven't told anybody else about it since then, not even Amelie. By talking about it, I would have to talk about my mother and sisters, and I didn't feel ready to do that.

I think I am now.

"I need to tell you something."

"Okayyy," Mark answers slowly, eyebrows furrowed. He follows me out of the basement with a suspicious look on his face.

As we walk across the quad to the music hall, I grow more unsure of myself. Am I doing the right thing, telling him about the fears within the deepest part of my heart? Should I opt out?

Stop. Think. Do not be afraid. It's just Mark. You know, your fighting partner, the guy you would trust with your life. And if you can trust him with your life, can't you then trust him with the knowledge that there were people in your life that aren't there anymore?

I open the door to the music hall and step inside, holding it open for him. It's relatively quiet, although I can hear the faint, distant song of a bow gliding across a cello's strings. We walk down the deserted hallway and I lead the way to the best piano room in the hall. It's a Cable-Nelson, designed by Yamaha, and its sound combined with the room's exceptional acoustics makes it my favorite. That and the fact that we have a Cable-Nelson at home.

I've come here almost every day for the past two weeks. I miss my sisters like crazy, and the piano, at least for me, is a way to connect to them. Sunday night was piano night at my house, at least until my family went from fourteen members to two. We'd all take turns on the piano, because Dad made sure everyone knew how to play, and we'd hold up scoring cards—which were really just whiteboards—to judge the person's performance. Jacqueline, my oldest and most musically inclined sister, almost always won, except when she'd throw the competition and let someone else win.

"So what did you want to tell me?" Mark asks, leaning against the piano.

I wring my hands and bite my lip, nervous. Suddenly, it feels like a scene from the movies where the devil and the angel sit on either shoulder, arguing. *Just do it. Pretend you're about to get in a pool. Don't dip your feet in, do a cannonball!* But the water's so cold! Besides, I hate water. I'm a Fire Wielder, not a Water User. Duh. *Okay, okay, bad analogy. Just do it. Do it. Do it. DO—*

"I don't want to be the Fire Keeper anymore!" The words practically explode out of my mouth, all jumbled together.

"What?" Mark looks hopelessly confused, and rightfully so.

I cross my arms so he can't see my hands shake. "All right, I got off on the wrong foot here. Um … what I *meant* to say was … well …"

"McKenna? Are you okay?"

And of course I ruin the whole thing by bursting into tears.

Now, let me just say right here that I am currently the World's Ugliest Crier. Someone ought to submit my picture to the Guinness Book of World Records. If someone sent my image to Hollywood, directors probably would fall over themselves to claim rights to the next big horror movie. Big, hot teardrops roll down my face, my face gets red, my eyes get puffy, my temples become pale, like islands in a sea of red, and when I try to stop crying, I get the hiccups. There's a reason why I don't cry often.

I don't even know *why* I'm crying. That's the thing. Maybe it's the heavy load on my shoulders, or the sadness that comes from missing someone, or both. Mark looks very uncomfortable—to say the least—but, to his credit, he does pat-slash-rub my back. For some reason I find it funny, but my giggles combined with my hiccups just manage to make me sound like a distressed whale.

Finally, after what feels like a century, my hiccups disappear and I manage to stop sobbing. As I'm wiping my eyes, Mark asks, "Feel better now?"

I laugh. "Yeah. I don't even know why I was crying. You seemed uncomfortable, though. You've never seen a person cry before? Is it all 'be a man' and 'walk it off' in the O'Reilly household?"

Oblivious to my teasing tone, Mark sighs and sits down on the piano bench. "I don't really know what to do when girls cry. I'm not sure whether I should say something, or hug them, or … I don't know. My mom's pretty thick-skinned, and growing up I wasn't around a lot of girls. At least, I'm pretty sure I wasn't. I was kind of taken off guard."

We don't really say anything for a few minutes after that. I regain my composure and rehearse what I'm going to say.

Then Mark breaks the silence with, "So … about that thing you wanted to tell me …"

And before I can give my speech, my mouth starts from the very beginning, all the way back to when my mom and sisters were around. I tell him about my sisters—Jacqueline, Mia, Christine, Saige, Bethany, Shannon, Kristen, Lauren, Joy, Kayleigh, and Emma Marie—what they were like, the events leading up to and after their disappearance, and the threatening letters. I tell him how scared I am that I'll lose control of my powers, and my dream of being fearless, and how much I hate being the Fire Keeper. It's choppy and rambly and random, but it does the job. I don't care if he didn't catch some parts. At least I said it.

To my surprise, though, he nods like he understands everything I say. He smiles, just a bit, and says, "Yep. Life can be a bitch, to some more than others."

"What do you think I should do?"

He shrugs. "Nothing."

What?!

"Um, nothing? I'm in the middle of a *crisis*, Mark! I can't do *nothing!*" I jump up and put my hands on my hips indignantly.

"*So* not what I mean. That came out wrong. Look," he says, patting the space beside him. I sit down reluctantly. "No one is fearless. That's impossible. There's always something you're going to be scared of. That's just life. In fact, being fearless is more of not letting your fears shape you as a person, not letting them cripple you. As Fire Wielders, we're dangerous. That's just how it is. You've got to get over your fears of getting all Incredible Hulk mad and killing people, because we all have that problem. And we can get through it together, but you need to have faith in that." He squeezes my hand gently. "You're more than just your powers. You're stronger than them. And I know that you can control them because you've been doing it your whole life.

"As for not being the Keeper … well, I believe that everything happens for a reason. For some reason, you were born to a Fire Keeper, and you succeeded her. But something's different about you. I don't know what it is. I just feel like you're going to change the world."

Change the world. Could I? Could I alter the course of history? Could I do something that would affect the lives of those around me and last for years? Sounds scary, but kind of incredible too. Maybe I'll even get a mention in a history book. Still, I ask in a small voice, "You really think I can?"

He grins. "You've got it in you."

Then we sit there, basking in the quiet noise of the music hall. Mark opens the piano and drums his fingers on the keys, looking lost in thought. Then, to my surprise, he begins to play.

The opening notes of "River Flows in You" ring out and slash through the quietness in the air. Mark has excellent technique, the movements of his hands fast, but not too fast. He sounds great, so great that I get up to dance around. The familiar melody is a comforting sound.

For a couple of minutes, I am free like a blue jay in the woods. I twirl around in circles, letting my feet take me wherever they want to go. I don't dance to the music, I am the music. I haven't done this in a while, just being carefree and playful. I've been so tense for the past couple of years. So rigid, afraid of going off like a bomb. I convinced myself that I heard the ticking, and time would soon be up. Now, though, I don't worry about anything. Why should I? I am safe as I can be from Acerbity in an Elemental boarding school. I have Natalie, Amelie, Sam, Emma, Celestia, Siobhan, and so many more people. Mark is at my side. There is nothing to fear.

But like everything else in life, including life itself, the song comes to an end and Mark's hands stop producing the well-known, liberating notes of the song. "That was fantastic," I say breathlessly. "You're really good."

"Thanks." He hops up, strides over, and offers his hand to me. "May I have this dance, my lady?"

"You may, Sir Mark."

Even though there is no actual music, Mark and I glide to the beats of our hearts, going wherever we may take us.

Before Mark, I was like a five hundred piece puzzle with one of the pieces missing. I wasn't complete until he came along and helped me find the last piece, the missing piece. That missing piece was confidence. Not necessarily fearlessness, although sometimes the two can be interchanged. He helped me regain my confidence.

Mark, my close friend, my boyfriend, and so, so much more. He did it. He helped me complete myself, and I know he will continue to, every minute of every day of every month of every year.

And I love him for it.

Chapter Fifteen

Packing for the tunnels may sound easy, but everyone knows it's not. Like packing for any trip, there's always the 'what-am-I-going-to-wear' craze, but Dean said that she had special gear for us to wear, so we can cross that off our list. Other problems quickly take that place, though. How much food to take, what's necessary and what's not, what size of pack to take … the list goes on and on. It's enough to make my head want to explode. Thank goodness Natalie is in the mess hall, calling the shots.

"Should I carry other people's things in my bag?" asks Emma, throwing her journal into her small drawstring bag. "I mean, I'm obviously not taking water with me."

"No," Sam says, distracted. "We might have to split up, and if you have someone else's stuff—"

"I see what you mean."

I pick up the *Water Lilies* drawing and stare at it before placing it in my sack. This is it. We're this close to reaching my mother, sisters, and the other Elementals and bringing them back. We will be the ones to do what others couldn't.

"So, McKenna," Emma says sneakily. "Where exactly did you and Mark go after the meeting?"

I look up, startled. "What do you mean, where did we go? Didn't anybody tell you? We went to the music hall."

"Uh-huh. Okay. And I'm supposed to believe there was no romantic dinner or anything."

"Hey, hey. Hold on just a second." I stride over to her side of the room, almost knocking over one of Natalie's stray plants. "Believe me when I say if there was any 'romantic dinner', you girls would be the first to know."

Sam smirks from behind her book. "Glad to hear it."

"And you," I jab my finger in her direction. "You're not getting off easy. Tell us what's really going on between you and Jackson. Are you dating or not?"

She sets down her book with a sigh and crosses her legs. "Dang. All right, fine. Remember when I came to our meeting late a couple weeks ago?"

We nod.

"I told you that we weren't dating, that we only kissed. Well, I lied. He asked me out that day. We were talking, and I lost track of the time. I knew Natalie would be furious, so I didn't tell you the truth. Sorry."

"What's there to be sorry for?" a voice says. Emma and Sam look up and I whip my head around to see Natalie standing in the doorway. She steps inside and closes the door. "Celestia convinced me that I was overreacting. I'm happy for you, Sam. I'm happy for all of you. Including Emma."

"Why me, though?" Emma says after a while, hugging her knees. "I don't have a boyfriend."

Natalie looks up from the plants she's tending to. "Don't pretend. You think no one sees you and Liam circling each other like predators?"

Emma crosses her arms stubbornly. "Hmph. Not true." Even miffed, she conjures a big ball of water and sends it over to hydrate Natalie's flowers. "I'm really happy for you, Sam. You too, McKenna. You and Mark are so cute together!" She flops back on her bed and cuddles a pillow.

"Oh!" Natalie says suddenly. She stands up. "I almost forgot to tell you. Dean Papadopoulos wants all of us to come downstairs immediately."

The rest of us hop up at once. "What's the matter?"

"She wouldn't tell me, she just said leave your bags up here."

We race out of the room and down the stairs. I, of course, beat everyone to the mess hall. Dean stands in the middle of the room, Mark, Liam, and Jackson surrounding her, along with about a dozen adult men and women.

"What's happening?" I say.

Dean sees me and sighs. "Oh, good. You're here. Where are your roommates?"

"They're coming. I outran them." And as I say that, the mess hall door flies open, and there they are. Katonah, Amelie, and Chris are right behind them.

"I—I have some bad news," she says, an uncomfortable expression on her face.

"Is everything okay?" Amelie asks.

Dean clears her throat. "I'm extremely sorry, guys. You ten won't be the ones going on the mission. I'm sending these trained soldiers to go in instead."

I have to fight so hard to keep my mouth from hitting the ground. I think I'm in danger of giving myself lockjaw.

"What?" Several of the others shriek. Emma's voice is the loudest.

"Calm down, let me explain. We've gotten word from spies in the Hudson Valley branch of Acerbity that our enemies are planning to kidnap the four Keepers. Because of that, we are on high alert. No student is to leave the school until the threat has been removed. Especially not you guys. I'm very sorry.

"They'll be leaving tomorrow night, and if all goes according to plan, they should be back on Monday. Don't feel like you've been useless. You provided us with vital information about their whereabouts. You all did everything you could. However, your safety comes first at this school."

I reach out and squeeze Natalie's hand, smothering a humorless laugh when she flinches. She shoots me a sympathetic glance. Well, as sympathetic as Natalie Wilde can be. She knows how much this means to me. I look over at the soldiers, who have grouped together on Dean P's right side. Most of them look uncomfortable. They're wearing regular clothes, not uniforms, but they still look tough and hard-ass. The shortest guy is buff and has about a trillion tattoos. One of the women looks like she could bench all of my Earthen friends at once.

My face falls with my heart. I had grand visions of a heroic and daring rescue mission. I imagined us courageously liberating the Elementals and escaping the Tunnels with seconds to spare. We were going to be lauded as champions.

I guess it was just a dream.

I'm in a daze throughout the whole next day. I feel like I'm looking from the outside in. Dean said not to feel useless, but I can't help it. All this preparation … for nothing? I don't even head over to the car garage to work on Amelie's bike. What's the point? Sure, the mission will probably be successful, but I wanted to do it myself. This was my chance to be a hero. This was my chance to be a role model for other Elementals. If I could be brave, then others can, too.

I only come out of my rooms for meals; otherwise, I stay in bed. I know I'm being all angsty-teenager, but at this point, I *so* do not care. Sam and Emma try to bait me by telling me Mark is outside and he really wants to talk. I don't doubt he came by, but that doesn't make me budge, even though I *would* like to see my boyfriend. They start getting outrageous and tell me that the President is waiting along with Mother Teresa and Albert Einstein. That's when I let my hair catch fire, something I almost never do. They leave me alone after that.

I'm busy counting the tiny bumps on my wall at night while Emma and Sam are chatting quietly when the door flies open. Natalie pokes her head in.

"Finally!" Emma exclaims. "You've been gone all day!"

Natalie ignores her. "Come with me. We need to hurry."

I cock my head. "Is everything okay? Where were you?"

"We're leaving now. Let's go."

"Leaving to go *where*?" I ask.

She looks behind her to make sure no one's listening in the hallway. "Katonah and I mixed up a sleeping tonic and gave it to the soldiers. We have to leave before anyone notices. They're supposed to be leaving in half an hour!"

I leap out of bed before I even know what I'm doing. Just like that, Natalie has flipped a switch inside of me. Energy shoots through my veins like someone injected it with a syringe.

"Let's go girls. Time to be heroes."

"**Go to the** bathrooms. I managed to nab the gear we were going to wear." Katonah points behind her. We race to the restrooms by the kitchen with newfound vigor.

The 'gear' isn't really gear. They're zip-up athletic jackets with short collars, track pants, and sturdy boots with grip. Black, black, and more black. They're essentially running clothes, but they're made with a comfortable material that doesn't make any noise when you move in them. Come to think of it, Dean probably used magic. I know I would have.

Also, did I mention they were black? I hate the color black because it's too dark. I'm not really a fan of dark colors. And they're black. Just putting it out there.

"What's going on?" Amelie asks from her stall.

I fumble with the zipper on my jacket. "Who knows?" I remove the Firestone from my neck and shamelessly shove it into my sports bra. That way, if we're stopped by Acerbity, it'll be harder for them to get to it. I'd punch them all in the face if they tried to take advantage of me.

"Jackson does," Sam calls. "He's been here helping Kat and Nat. He *dimpahanswas* messaged me a minute ago, and said Dean Martins told Dean P to keep a close eye on us Keepers so we don't get kidnapped. Dean P was going to see the soldiers off, but she had to leave because there was a problem on the fifth floor of Maiyrn."

There's a minute of silence before Amelie pipes up with, "That's bad, isn't it? The watching thing, I mean."

"Yeah," Natalie says. "Really bad. It means we have to be really careful if we want to go anywhere."

I swallow hard. The plan Emma and I came up with is sounding better and better with every new threat.

"Okay, everyone," Katonah says after we've all changed into our black gear. "I know you probably weren't expecting this, but we are going to have to leave tonight for the museum. Natalie and I, with the help of Jackson, created a sleep serum that'll keep the soldiers from waking up for about ten hours. Dean Martins spoke to Dean Papadopoulos. He said that a bunch of scouts spotted a group of Acerbity members headed towards the school. They disappeared before they could catch them, but Dean Martins instructed her to keep a closer eye on the four Keepers to make sure they didn't get kidnapped."

I look at Emma, Sam, and Natalie, and somehow we master the four-way glance. All of our expressions convey worry. Kidnapped.

The word sends sparks, shivers, down my spine. Somehow, coming from Sam's mouth, it didn't sound so bad.

"Any objections?" she says, looking around. When no one says anything, she continues. "Okay. I'm going to ransack their rooms for any extra materials we may need. The rest of you can wait in your dorm rooms until—"

"Wait!" a female voice shouts. Raven materializes before us, dressed in the same gear. "Sorry I'm late," she says. Her hair is gathered in a tight ponytail, but the purple lock has come loose.

"Wait ... what?" Sam sputters. "Raven, what are you doing here?"

Raven looks at Katonah, so we all swing our attention back to her. "Dean P called Raven up at the last minute," Katonah explains. "She said Raven has incredible darkness powers, and she believes we need her. Obviously that was before she canceled the mission, but I figured it was still a good idea to call her."

The rest of the Team mutters their consent, but I carefully examine Raven. Something is off. I can feel it. Something is definitely wrong. I just don't know what.

CHAPTER SIXTEEN

Raven travels through the void, telling us she'll meet us at the Met. She'll turn into a shadow, scope out the whole museum, and report to us with something close to a plan. Phantoms are night owls, so sleep isn't a problem for her.

I lay in bed, waiting for the RA to come by our room, using her powers to tell if anyone's missing. We're all holding our breath, trying not to think too much, as if Kaelyn Rwola will burst into the dorm, somehow knowing what we're about to do. I hear her making the rounds, her purposeful walk muffled by the walls.

When she opens her room door and locks it—she stays on our floor, but she's not a student—I jump up. "Let's go!" I open the window and stick my head outside. Mark, Chris, Liam, Amelie, and Jackson are standing among the bushes. I wave at them, and Mark waves back.

"Do you have a rope?" Chris says as quietly as he can.

"We don't need a rope," Natalie says, coming to stand next to me. "It's called *scaling the wall*." She swings herself over the edge and grabs hold of a brick. Before I can open my mouth to stop her, she climbs down the wall in record time. *Earthens.*

Emma gulps. "I, on the other hand, am not going to be doing that. We are four stories up, people! Are you out of your minds? I *refuse* to be a grease spot on that pavement."

"Well, then how are you going to get down?" I raise my eyebrow.

"I'll go with Sam, same as you."

Sam takes our hands and *vervoféi* us outside. Katonah hasn't arrived yet, so while we're waiting for her I sit down on the grass so my breathing goes back down to normal. At any moment, someone could come outside and find us here, effectively ending our mission before it starts.

After five minutes, Katonah appears in front of us. "Sorry I took so long. Kaelyn forgot to come up to our floor, so I had to wait longer."

"That's okay," Liam says. "We need to go now that we're all here."

I wave for everyone to follow me before walking as quietly as I can to the car garage. The freshly cut grass makes almost no noise under our boots. We have to wind around trees, take back routes, and hug the sides of buildings to avoid the security cameras as much as possible. Since I left my keycard in the dorm, I melt the lock inside the door and push it open. "Mr. Brisburne?" I call out. No answer. "Good. Follow me."

"Don't turn on the light," Mark says out of nowhere, making me jump. He's looking at Amelie, who I can see from a patch moonlight has one hand on the light switch. "Someone will see the light and get suspicious."

"Can you make a small flame or something?"

"Sorry," he shrugs. "Security guards might see."

"We'll have to wing it, 'cause all the moonlight is falling at the front of the garage," Katonah takes over. "Besides, McKenna knows this place like the back of her hand. Right?"

"Right," I say. And then promptly trip over a rubber … thing. "Whoops."

I hold my hands out and stumble towards the back of the garage. Thank goodness my metal affinity alerts me to the doorknob. I open the door to where the school vans are located. There's a bit of light for us to see here. "Come on." I wave for the others to follow me and stop in front of a white van. "This is the one."

"Yay!" Emma says drily. "We get to be mistaken for a bunch of pedophiles!"

"It's the only one that can fit all of us, Emma."

"Do you have the keys?" Katonah asks. When I jangle them in the air, she says, "Good. We need to move faster."

I toss them to Sam, who catches them with ease. Quickly but quietly we hop in the van, strap on our seatbelts, and breathe sighs of relief.

"When I count to three, Sam, I want you to start the car. I'll open the garage. It's really loud, and I think someone will hear us. Okay?" Katonah plucks the garage opener from the driver's visors.

Sam nods.

"One ..." Sam puts the key in the ignition.

"Two ..." She takes a deep breath.

"*Three!*" The garage door rattles and groans as Sam's wrist twists to the side. The van roars to life, and after putting it in drive, speeds out of the car garage towards the parking lot.

She peals out of there quickly and hops onto a deserted road. "What's the Met's address, McKenna?" Jackson asks, staring at his phone.

I smile. I know it by heart. "1000 5th Ave, New York, NY 10028."

"Thanks."

The GPS lady's computerized voice rings out loud in the car. *"In three hundred feet, turn right onto U.S. Route 9."*

"An hour and two minutes, ladies and gentlemen," Sam announces. "So sit back, relax, and enjoy the ride."

Mark takes my hand and looks at me. "You ready?"

"I was born ready." I mentally smack my forehead. What is it with me and clichéd responses?

We turn onto the highway, and I peer out the window. The stars are especially bright tonight, looking like the sun exploded and a billion pieces scattered themselves across the night sky. Even after the sunset, the summer heat feels nice on my skin, but the others grow hot, and soon all of the windows, including the back ones, are rolled all the way down.

"You do realize that anyone could see inside the van, right?" I comment. *"Anyone."*

"That's true," Liam says. He rolls up his window, and soon, everyone's windows are back up. Sam turns on the A/C and puts it on the coldest setting, full blast. Everyone sighs with relief. Well, everyone but Mark and I.

I spot Jackson's hand snaking toward the radio controls. And Sam does too, because she swats his hand away. "Hey. Driver controls music."

He mock-pouts. Then he smiles and rests his hand on hers.

"I wonder what the Tunnels will be like," Chris muses from the back. "I bet they're infertile. Bet you can't grow a single plant down there."

"They could be dry and crumbly, too," adds Emma. "Not a drop of water."

"Maybe they're protected from all sorts of magic, period."

"Nah, there's magic." Natalie says. "I was reading up on them the other day. Magic distorts time down there. It's very easy to lose track of it. You'd think you were down there for five minutes, when it was really five hours. Or, you could be down there for two hours and think you were there for two days. It messes with your head."

"That's terrifying, when you think about it. We could think we were down there for ten hours, then come back to the surface and find out it's 2189." I say.

"Let's hope, then, that time stays the same." Katonah taps on the window lightly.

I look at my glow-in-the-dark watch. It's only eleven o'clock. Mark leans in to kiss the side of my head. Then he says, "How do you feel?"

"What?"

"How do you feel about possibly reuniting with your mother and sisters in less than twenty-four hours?"

I squeeze his hand. "I'm actually nervous. I mean, what if they've changed? What if they don't like you?" I stare at him, worried. *What if they don't want to leave?*

"Everyone changes, so you don't have to worry about that. And if they don't like me, I'll deal." He rubs his thumb in slow circles on my knuckles, effectively distracting me. "As for not leaving ... things have changed for the better now. It's safer than it was two years ago. I doubt they'll want to stay. Plus, when we tell them what's going to happen, they're not going to want to stay."

"You're sure?"

"Ninety-nine percent sure."

"Only ninety-nine percent?"

"You can never be one hundred percent sure."

Up front, Sam gasps, interrupting our conversation. "Oh, no." she switches from the left to the right lane.

"Wha—oh, shit." Jackson says.

By now, the red and blue flashing lights can be seen from inside the car. There's a police car right behind us. I turn back to look at Mark in horror as the *COPS* theme song begins to play in my head.

Oh, no is right.

It's only been half an hour, and we've already broken one of Dean Papadopoulos's rules.

Chapter Seventeen

Samantha swears and pulls the van over to the side of the road. "Do you have your license and registration with you?" Natalie inquires from the boot of the vehicle.

"Yeah. They're right here." Sam is getting more worried by the second; I can see from the mirror that her pupils are dilated and the winds behind her eyes blow frantically and violently. "No. no. no. This is not happening. Is this for real? This can't be happening." A slight breeze blows throughout the van.

"Sam. Look at me," Jackson instructs. She complies. "Calm down. It will be all right."

"No, it won't! I've never been pulled over in my life. Sure, I've only been driving for less than a year, but still! My record is clean!" She starts hyperventilating, which is odd, seeing as she's an Air Manipulator.

Jackson puts his hands on her shoulders and patiently waits for her to stop ranting before saying, "Trust me, Sam. It *will* be okay."

Sam allows herself a small smile, and slowly, her breathing goes back to normal. Just in time, too. The police officer walks up to her window and she rolls it down. Though it's very dark outside, I can still see that he looks to be in his late thirties, with something close to a gut. His wrinkled, navy blue uniform has multiple badges on it. His blond hair is thinning, but still is disheveled.

"How do you do, sir?" Sam says in a fake Australian accent. Her voice is calm. You wouldn't have been able to tell she nearly passed out a minute earlier.

"Do you know how fast you were going?" he asks. We all know that Sam was going pretty fast. When she shakes her head, he says, "Eighty miles per hour. The speed limit on the highway is sixty-five. I need to see your license and registration."

Sam hands him the necessary items. "What was so important that you decided to go at a speed way past 10 miles above the limit?"

She says, "I'm terribly sorry, officer. You see, there's a family emergency in the city, and I needed to get there as fast as I could. I should have remembered to abide by the law and keep to a reasonable speed."

The police officer gives her back her driving info, takes out a black flashlight, and shines it in the van. When he sees all of us sitting in it, he does a double take.

"These people are all part of your family?"

"No," she smiles and shakes her head. "They're my mates. They all wanted to come along for moral support."

The officer spots her and Jackson's entwined hands. "He's a friend, too?" Okay, was that necessary?

"He's my boyfriend. His name is Jackson." Jackson lifts his free hand in a half-wave.

"Why are you all wearing the same clothes?"

"Hmm?" Sam gives him a big smile.

The officer seems to contemplate all of it. I cross my fingers. *Please don't investigate. Please don't give us a ticket. Please don't—*

His deep voice cuts through my thoughts. "Well, Samantha Mazer, I'm going to let you off with a warning. Make sure this never happens again, or you will get a ticket."

Sam sighs with relief. "Thank you, officer. Trust me, it definitely won't happen again." She looks back at the rest of us. "Right, guys?"

"Right," we chorus. I release a breath I didn't even know I was holding.

Someone yawns in the back, and everyone's gazes shift towards the sound. Emma stretches and blinks like she's just waking up from a long nap. She rubs her eyes and says, "What ... what's going on?"

The officer's brow furrows, but eventually, he says, "Stay safe, kids," and goes back to his car.

Sam rolls up her window before dropping her Aussie accent and slumping in her seat. "Oh, thank God. I thought my nose was going to grow, I lied so much. Are you even allowed to lie to a police officer?"

"It might be against the law," Katonah sighs. Then, "I wonder why he didn't give us a ticket? If I were a police officer, I sure would have."

Sam's hands tighten on the wheel as she pulls back onto the road. "I'm sorry, okay? I didn't mean to speed. Also, I didn't want to do it, but I spoke into his mind, telling him not to give us a ticket. I made my voice masculine, acted as his conscience, and told him it wasn't right. I shouldn't have done that." She thumps the steering wheel with her fist. "We're supposed to use our powers for good, not for evading justice."

"It's no big deal," Emma and Liam say at the same time. They look at each other and laugh.

"Emma, were you actually asleep?" Mark asks.

"No," she says, as if it were obvious. "I thought it would make us look less suspicious if at least one person was 'sleeping'. If all of us were wide awake, I know he would have sensed something was off.

"That's really smart," Amelie says appreciatively.

"Well, we didn't get a ticket, so that's good," Sam grins. "So your distraction technique probably worked. Still, I'm not budging from sixty-six."

"The speed limit's sixty-five," Natalie reminds her.

"I don't like driving on odd numbers. It freaks me out. For those of you that are wondering, though, we're halfway there."

The oncoming traffic is way thinner than that it would have been during the day. Still, every so often, someone forgets to lower their high beam, and the rest of the people in our van are nearly blinded. Light doesn't bother Mark and me because we're Fire Wielders. We can stare into the sun until the day we die—if we want to—and our vision won't be impaired in the slightest.

"What is it with people and their high beams?" Sam complains. "I can see just fine with my low light on."

She turns on the radio, and Jackson gives her a triumphant smile. He knew all along that he was going to win in the end. The last notes of Meghan Trainor's cringey "All About That Bass" spill into the car.

The familiar set of claps start, and Emma shrieks. "On Top of the World!" she shouts, and starts singing with Imagine Dragons. *"If you love somebody, better tell them while they're here, 'cause they just may run away from you …"*

Emma's enthusiasm is contagious, and soon, everyone is belting out "On Top of the World". Imagine Dragons can no longer be heard. We may not all be good singers, but we have heart, and that's enough. It's always enough.

We reach Manhattan shortly after midnight. I yawn, stretching my arms out. Mark fell asleep fifteen minutes ago. Before waking him, I take a moment to admire how peaceful he looks. He's sort of smiling and he doesn't drool, although he is snoring slightly. His long, brown eyelashes, the kind that every superficial girl envies, brush the skin underneath his eyes. He looks handsomer than I've ever seen him, probably because he isn't stressed.

His eyes flutter, and then open. "Tired?" I ask.

He laughs softly and runs his thumb across my bottom lip, making sparks shoot down my spine. "Not anymore."

The only people who stayed awake the whole time are Sam, Jackson, and me. The others drifted in and out of consciousness at different intervals, but they're all starting to wake up now.

"McKenna, Amelie, can you two take first watch?" Jackson asks.

We nod. I don't like the idea of staying up late, but at least I'll have uninterrupted sleep afterwards.

Sam parks the van a block away from the museum. The loud engine dies, engulfing us in deafening silence.

I unclip my seat belt, open my door, and hop out of the van. Amelie does the same, and at the same time, we slam our doors. I lean on the car and lower myself onto the dark, paved road. Seconds after, she joins me. The air smells of faint exhaust and lingering aromas from the food stands that are usually outside.

"So, we just sit like this, right?" I say.

"Right."

"We sit like this, keep watch, and if anyone, especially Acerbity, threatens us, we take them out with our badass fighting skills."

Amelie laughs softly. "You got that right."

Something is different about the sky. Sure, the black blanket is tinted with brown and orange, but it goes deeper than that. I stare at it, trying to solve the mystery. Then I realize what it is.

"The stars. I'd forgotten you can't see them in the city," I say to her.

She looks up, squints, and raises her eyebrows. "You're right. I've never been to New York City before. Some first visit this is turning out to be."

I smile, thinking back to when I was thirteen. "We used to come here every couple of weekends," I tell her. "My mom and I. It was tradition. We even had a members' pass." I press my hands against my cheeks

"If we get out of here with everyone, maybe you can continue doing it."

I drum the pads of my fingertips on the road. The feeling I got when the calendar turned from July to August still haunts me. In fact, it's stronger now. We're this close to starting the mission. Any number of things can go wrong. I have to worry about guarding the Firestone. How am I supposed to do that on top of everything else? Acerbity will target us from the moment we step foot into the Tunnels. They've got obsidian with them. How am I going to be able to accomplish everything?

Amelie is a great listener and secret keeper. But do I really want to tell her what's going on? Although, the only people on the mission that don't know are Katonah, Liam, and Chris. Sam told Jackson, I'm pretty sure. Lately, I've felt a great urge to give away all of my secrets.

I mentally argue with myself for about thirty seconds before saying, "Can I tell you something?"

"Sure."

I exhale heavily, blowing out of my face the strands that came loose from my ponytail. "Earlier this month, like, the first day of August, I had this feeling."

She nods for me to go on.

"I had this feeling that not everyone on the Liberation team would be alive to turn the calendar page again. I think one of us is going to die in the Tunnels."

Amelie's violet eyes cloud with confusion, then worry. Seconds after that, though, her face is serene. "Isn't that to be expected, though? I mean, we're ten—eleven—teenagers walking into a den of grown Acerbity members, trying to find two hundred plus people that are most likely caged up like dogs. Someone's probably going to be killed. We just have to accept that."

I gape at her. "So then why did you come? Why are you here if you're so sure people will die?" She must be braver than I thought.

I refuse to let myself make up false excuses for others this time. I learned my lesson with Mark.

"Why did you?"

I roll my eyes. "*Óleh*, my family is in there. I want to get them out! You, on the other hand, have nothing to lose here."

"Maybe I do!" She doesn't look at me; instead, she stared out in the streets. "I'm sorry. I'm tired of being that optimistic, cheerful Amelie Avanti. I'm trying to be real. I'm trying to see the world for what it really is. Everybody has to die someday; there's no use in pretending there isn't a high chance of someone getting hurt here. Understand?"

Speechless, I nod. Apparently the conversation is over. I stare at the building itself. Or, at least, I try to. It's gotten so dark, I can barely see it. The street is deserted, which is probably unusual. The streetlights illuminate the road like it's a catwalk for nonexistent models that won't walk the runway. This is the city that never sleeps. So, what, is this street in a coma?

The silence is awkward. Amelie and I have never really argued before. My anger towards her doesn't feel right. My palms start to itch.

"But on a serious note, McKenna, if I die in there, can you and Mark name one of your kids after me?"

I make a sputtering sound, trying not to laugh. "What the hell? Where did that come from? Amelie, we're just—"

"Dating, I know. Didn't we have this argument a month ago? A certain someone used the line 'just friends'."

"You're right."

"And when we have arguments, who always wins?"

I sigh. "You." Amelie is so quirky.

She hugs her knees tightly. "That's right."

I look down the street, checking for Acerbity, but there's still no one in sight. After what feels like a really long period of time, I check my watch. Quarter to one. "Time's up," I yawn.

We hop up, brushing imaginary dust off of our clothes. I sit back in my seat, smiling at the thought of sleeping in a van outside the Metropolitan Museum of Art. If that's not weird, then I don't know what is. Mark has fallen asleep again, his head hanging off to the side. Emma and Liam are whispering urgently across the back seat.

"Liam." I whisper his name.

Liam whips his head around to face me. "Oh, you're back," he says. He shakes Chris, who is snoozing with his head against the window.

"Wha ..." Chris mumbles groggily.

"It's time to go."

Chris unbuckles his seatbelt and stretches. Cracking his knuckles, he slips through the aisle, followed by Liam. The humid August night air creeps in as the door stays open for a second to let them out.

I look back at Emma, who also watched them go. She catches my eye and grins. My heart feels happy and sad at the same time. Emma has become like a sister to me. And now ... there's a chance we may never see each other again. I'm familiar with this situation, or at least the aftermath. I'll definitely miss her, though, if she's the one who dies. For sure.

For sure. I tilt my head, trying to find a good position to sleep in. Nothing is set in stone. There's too much uncertainty in everything. You can never get a guarantee these days, no matter how hard you try. I've thought long and hard about my changing life, and I know one thing is certain.

Lately, I'm not sure of anything.

CHAPTER EIGHTEEN

The Metropolitan Museum of Art is an intimidating building. It's been a while since I've been here, so this hits me hard as we sit in the car, waiting for Raven to call. It's huge. The tourists standing on the steps and around it look like midgets compared to its majestic build. The golden railings gleam in the sunlight, and the massive beige pillars and fancy designs on the façade make it seem swankier than it actually is. An architecture buff would faint at the very sight of the building. Enter a bright blue sky with tufts of white cotton and you have yourself a perfect way.

"So tell me. What exactly are we waiting for?" Katonah asks Emma.

"Raven has to call us so we can go in and enter through the passage," she says. "There can't be people where we *vervoy*. She was initially going to come back over here, but we changed plans while you were sleeping."

Just as she finishes her sentence, the iPhone comes alive. It's the standard combination of rings, and it's atypical for Emma. I would have guessed her to be one of those people who had the number one pop song as her ringtone, like your stereotypical insufferable cheerleader. "That's her!" she exclaims, and hits 'Answer'.

"Hello?" she says.

She presses speaker so everyone can hear. There is a bout of static before Raven's muffled voice reverberates through the car. "Hello?"

"What's going on? Did you find a good place?"

"What? Oh, yeah. It's ... the gallery ... it ... kind of dark in ... very good ..." Her voice comes and goes.

Emma holds the phone closer to her mouth. "You have bad reception over there, so I'm just going to hang up, okay?"

"..."

Pressing end call, she says, "Change of plans. We're not bringing the big box the soldiers packed. Or, rather, we can't bring that box."

Mark's brow furrows. "Why not?"

"Well, it's very heavy, so more than one person would need to carry it, and it wouldn't even make it through security. We can only bring our drawstring bags."

"How are we going to bring them, anyway?" Katonah asks. "They have weapons in them."

Sam grins. "That's where I come in." When she has everyone's attention, she takes a deep breath.

And disappears.

I reach a hand out to wave it around in the empty space she left behind, but when I do, I hit her shoulder. I only have a couple Air Manipulator friends, so every time I see one exhibit his or her powers, it's always cool.

"Invisibility. Of course!" Liam says.

Sam reappears. "Yep. I'm going to need assistance carrying all the bags in there. Who wants to help me?"

Natalie pops off her seatbelt and says, "I will. I'm one of the strongest."

"Good. Everyone, give us your bags." When she and Natalie have them all in their hands, Sam says, "Okay. Let's practice being invisible, Natalie. It's going to feel strange the first time, though, so be prepared for some odd sensations." She drops the bags in her lap.

Rubbing her hands together, she shifts in her seat so she's facing her as much as possible.

"What kind of sensations?" Natalie asks, but it's too late; Sam aims her hands at her just as she finishes her sentence. Natalie disappears in less than a second. "Whoa!" she shouts. "Holy—what did you do to me?"

Sam laughs lightly. "How do you feel?"

"Invisible? Weird? I don't know. I feel like the winds are cloaking me. They're wrapped around me like a blanket. I actually feel really secure. But, I feel wind everywhere, so also violated, too."

Emma laughs out loud, but other than the violated thing, Natalie's description of being invisible has left me intrigued. "Try me," I say.

"Okay," Sam says. "Here we go." She closes her eyes, breathes in deep, and points her hands at me.

Everyone gasps again, clearly unsettled by my disappearance. It does feel as if I've been mummified by all the winds on earth. They swirl around me, lifting my hair and my necklace, which is kind of weird. But, on the plus side, Natalie is visible again.

I grin at her and she gives me a high-five. "Sam, you never told us invisible people can see each other."

"C'mon, guys," Katonah urges. "We have to go."

Sam, Natalie, and I sigh simultaneously. "Fine," Sam mumbles, exasperated. She waves her hand, and quickly, the winds untangle me from their arms and I become visible again.

I rest my hand on the van door. "Let's go, guys. We don't have a lot of time to waste." I open the door. The hot August air hits me hard in the face, but I don't mind.

Stepping out of the car, Sam says, "Natalie. If we're going to be invisible, we have to do it now." Natalie nods, and Sam makes them both disappear with the bags.

"Lead the way."

All eight—no, ten—of us gather on the right side of the van and start walking towards the Met. All sorts of scents register in my nose as we pass by street vendors. Hot dogs and hamburgers and ice cream … my stomach growls, wanting to indulge in the American favorites.

It's fun to watch the people, too: the elderly gossip amongst themselves behind their walkers and alongside their canes; the teenagers that were dragged along by their parents—in a vain attempt to recreate the long-dead concept of 'family fun time'—take selfies and share them with their friends via social media; a little girl, maybe five or six, throws a temper tantrum as her mother wearily drags her along.

It's the city at its finest.

We jog up the stairs, weaving around sitting and standing people. The tourists stare at us as we go. But the real New Yorkers don't even give us a second glance. They've seen it all. Even eight empty-handed teenagers in matching tracksuits don't raise suspicion.

It gets cooler as we enter the museum. As a Fire Wielder, I'm hyper-sensitive to temperature, so I can tell that it goes from about eighty-nine to seventy-one degrees Fahrenheit. The rest of the Team members catch their breath as they look around the building. The arches are gold and cream, the pillars seem to stretch from the ground to forever, and the octagonal information desk is roping in a lot of art enthusiasts. There are a couple of lines for security blocking the entrance. The guards look no nonsense and weary beyond belief.

"Psst."

We turn around.

"No, guys," says the air. It's Sam. "It's me, Sam. Come outside for a second."

I look at Mark, eyebrows raised. He nods and we walk out of the security check line. We gather at one side of the huge staircase in the sun.

"What's the matter?" Katonah asks, crossing her arms.

Sam pauses for a second before materializing. "We can't go through the checkpoint."

Emma nods, like, *Go on.*

"It's just too risky. I've been thinking about it for a bit. Acerbity is in there; we already know that for sure. But they could be watching the door. Some of them could be posing as security guards at the checkpoint. They could have already seen us! We don't know what could happen."

"That is true …" Chris says.

"Ahem," calls Natalie's voice. "Being invisible is fun and all, but do you mind turning me back? Wind feels weird. I don't know how you Air Manipulators stand it."

"Oh, right," Sam says. She waves her hand in Natalie's general direction, and Natalie reappears.

She bends over and rests her hands on her thighs. "Thank God."

"So …" I trail. "How are we going to get through?"

"Hmm? Oh, I'll just make all of us invisible. It's not taxing." And she waves her hand again and at once we can't be seen. Well, we can see each other. In fact, it's as if nothing happened. But we know humans can't see us. So why does it feel like cold, heartless eyes are observing my every move?

I feel a tap on my shoulder and I spin around, spooked. But it's just Natalie, holding my bag. "Here you go."

I take it, relaxing. "Girl, I thought you were an Acerbitian soldier."

"Nope, it's just me. Sorry to disappoint."

"Yeah," I whisper after she's gone. "Just you."

I still get the feeling Acerbity is watching me.

There aren't a lot of people in the gallery, just the security guard, a couple of cameras, and a little old lady. And judging by the way she staggers around even with her cane, she's as blind as a bat. I keep forgetting that we're invisible, so whenever the guard looks our way, I tense up.

Raven can see through the invisibility and steps out of the shadows immediately, and we crowd around the painting. It looks like it always does, gold and green and wonderful. I can tell some of the others want to say something about it, but just because we can't be seen doesn't mean we can't be heard.

Mark grabs my hand, and I grab Amelie's. We all hold hands as Samantha, Jackson, Raven, and Katonah got concentrated looks on their faces. The winds swirl around my waist, my ankles, my head, my arms … and they take me apart. I feel as if every atom of my body as separated itself from the others. I'm floating in pieces in the air, and so is everybody else.

And then we get sucked in.

Chapter Nineteen

I was hoping the Tunnels would be somewhat clean, with minimal insects. A level below a labyrinth, if you will. It's the complete opposite of where we've been trudging through for over an hour since we dropped in. And when I say 'dropped in', I mean it literally. We materialized in the air and fell on the ground in a tangled mess. It *hurt*. These Tunnels are ugly and disgusting. There's mildew and dust everywhere. Mark and I have been holding up a ball of fire the whole time, and Katonah and even Amelie have been able to create illuminated orbs.

Natalie and Chris are disappointed. They were so excited about coming here, had high expectations. This, though? *This?* The ground is uneven and rocky. The walls are rough and dirty and chunks of *stuff* fall from over our heads, sometimes narrowly missing us, sometimes not. There's a constant dripping noise, though I can't figure out where it's coming from. There's hardly any air here, so Sam and Jackson are working hard, providing more oxygen so we can breathe better.

After another half hour passes, Emma becomes the first person to speak since we arrived. "Anyone else here have a pounding headache?"

Come to think of it, there has been a dull ache in my brain for a while now. I guess the stress of not being able to identify the weird form of Chinese water torture put the pain on the back burner.

"It's the time distortion," Natalie says. "It's messing with us. We're not used to it; that's why we're getting migraines."

I use my free hand to rub my forehead. This is getting tedious. I look over at the others. Everyone is clearly tired of walking ... well, everyone except Raven and Mark. Raven doesn't seem affected by the time distortion, though. She has a ghost of a smile on her face. She's walking, too, which is very weird. I'm about to ask her about it when the path gets wider, and soon we come to an intersection. Natalie gasps and spins in a circle.

"The Crossroads," she breathes.

It's nothing special, really. Four other pathways connect to the huge, empty space. They look identical to the one we came from. A creaking sound comes from behind me, and we all turn to look. The pathway we took to come here starts to close up. The walls push together and dirt rains down on the ground.

We're trapped.

"Well." Liam says. "That was unexpected."

After an awkward moment of quiet, I say, "This is where we part ways, huh?"

We soak that in, too.

"Who's going with whom?" Raven asks. I look at Mark, and he smiles back at me. We fight well together. Dean found that out at training one day. It was one of our mock fights, and she put us on teams of two. Whoever we fought, we won.

"Well, we already made the pairs up. Dean did it at training. So Emma and Chris are a pair, as are Sam and Amelie, Mark and McKenna, Jackson and Liam, and Katonah and me." Natalie explains.

Raven nods. "Okay, I guess I'll just go with Amelie and Sam." And with that statement, everyone sighs with relief, even Amelie. Because even though Amelie can change someone's mood to peaceful for hours at a time, other than that and having magical persuasion, she'd be kind of useless in a quick fight.

I pull out Sirius. "Let's go here," I say after it lights up, pointing at the one on the far right.

"Okay," he agrees, and we race through the opening.

After ten minutes of constant running, the other roads start appearing. They branch off this main Tunnel and go to who-knows-where. Dean told me to use my Keeper Sword, Sirius, as a guide. It glows when you hold it in the direction of the Compass Door. It's a key *and* a helpful tool, since getting lost definitely is not on the agenda for today. And is it even today? Or is it tomorrow, or a week later, or even a decade later? Am I twenty-six and don't even know it? Well, I wouldn't be. If it was more than a couple of days, we would be dead.

"McKenna." Mark's voice shakes me from my reverie.

"Yeah?" I whisper.

"Do you hear that?"

I listen for a sound, any sound. But I can't hear anything.

"No." A soft whine. "No, wait. Yeah."

It sounds familiar. It's definitely not a human, no, it sounds more like the baying of an animal. Mark and I look at each other as the sounds get louder and louder. He draws his bow and I reach for my sword. There's the outline of an animal in the darkness—a dog.

Somehow I know.

"Genesis!" I scream, crouching down and ruffling his black and white fur. It's now that I realize that I'm not the only one hugging the Siberian husky. And I'm not the only one that called his name.

"You know Genesis?" Mark asks.

"He was my dog. Last I knew, he was at home with my dad. I know that he would have said something." Then I'm suspicious. "How do you know him?"

"I don't know. I just knew his name and fact that he was part of my life at some point in time. I felt drawn to him."

"How is that even—never mind, we should get going. Details can come later." I sigh, burying my face in my dog's soft coat. "What are you doing here, bud?"

Genesis barks.

Mark reaches into his pocket and pulls out a handful of trail mix, picking out the M&M's. Genesis pokes his nose in Mark's hand, sniffs, and then eats the combination of nuts and raisins.

"Good boy," Mark pats his head.

"We should probably go."

"Probably. Come on, Genesis."

As my dog trots alongside us, I say, "How do you think he got here?"

Mark shrugs. "This place is full of mysteries. Who knows? Maybe Acerbity kidnapped him and let him roam around the Tunnels. Although I'm not sure what that says about them if they've resorted to kidnapping animals."

Genesis barks again, and I get an idea. "What if they sent him to us? What if he's trying to warn us?"

"About Acerbity?" He pauses. "I think you're onto something."

"But … we already know about Acerbity." I chew on my lip. "They wouldn't bring him over here. Like, 'Just a friendly reminder, we're here before you. Just in case you're illiterate and didn't read the letter.'"

When he barks for a third time, I start to get nervous. "You okay, buddy?" Genesis sniffs and tilts his head. And it's then that I hear the footsteps. They're light, almost jovial, like the person is having a good time.

Mark glances at me. He looks ready. *Ready to die,* I think bitterly, remembering Amelie's morbid pep talk. But that's not true. He looks like a true fighter. And if my partner is ready, I have to be ready, too.

And then the figure appears, and it takes me less than two seconds to recognize him. He's the guy from Paola's predictions, and even beyond that, I know I've seen him before. He's wearing his black zip-up jacket and cargo pants and beat-up military boots. His blue eyes gleam like chilling blue icicles. He seems to have caught the wind in his chocolatey hair.

"Well, well. McKenna Donaldson and Mark O'Reilly." The man, *Colin*, says. Somehow, some way, I know his name. He clasps his hands together and grins. It's then I notice the obsidian weapons in holsters and sheaths on his belt. Genesis growls, glaring at the man.

But Colin just laughs. "Fancy meeting you here."

Chapter Twenty

Before I can blink, Colin lunges for me. He grabs my wrist and his obsidian knife at the same time. Stifling a horrified gasp, I aim a jet of fire at the hand with the knife, but he's too experienced for that. He moves his hand casually to the side and the fire misses him.

Mark attempts to grab Colin's leg. For some reason, though, he comes up short and lets out a cry of pain. A silver-gray flash—some kind of sharp stone—cuts through the air. There's more than one of them here. The acrid smell of smoke fills the air.

Everything is happening so fast. I'm not sure who's winning the fight between Mark and the other guy. There may be more, but I can't think about that. I keep evading Colin's black, glossy knife, keep trying to burn him with fire. Flames pop up on the ground, but they're too small to be dangerous. Genesis is barking and running around in circles, not quite sure what to do.

A gunshot pierces the air. Fear spreads inside of me like a bath bomb, slipping effortlessly through my veins. Metal can't hurt us, but other materials can easily be made into bullets.

His fist meets my side; his knife just misses my ear. I choke back a yelp and push him away from me. My hands are hot though, so when they come in contact with his torso, it scorches him.

Burn him while you spurn him. Ooh, that rhymes. I direct all the fire to my foot and kick him where it hurts most. This time he yells, clutching his undercarriage. His knife drops to the ground, and I kick it away.

Good thing I did, because Mark's attacker leaves his post to yank my feet out from underneath me. I hit the ground, hard. My shoulder throbs with pain, but I manage to swing a leg out from under me and catch his hand with another hot foot. My hair, even in its ponytail, has chosen this exact moment to plaster itself all over my face with sweat. Instead of seeing the outlines of our attackers in the darkness, I see my glowing red strands of hair.

Mark reaches a hand out and I take it, gingerly getting to my feet. There's a cut on my face but I'm okay. Shoulder pain, a knot in my side from Colin's punch, and a bunch of other little things plague me, but nothing I can't handle.

Something moves behind Mark's back. "Turn around," I yell quickly, just as Colin tries to carve a line into Mark's back with what little strength he has. Colin almost gets him with his obsidian knife, almost, but Mark is way too quick. He reaches out and flips the perpetrator, who is still guarding his crotch, over onto his back.

A burly arm reaches out and catches me by my neck. I try to pull it away, but it won't budge. I try burning him, but no, he's wearing long sleeves. Thick long sleeves. Fireproof … I detect a hint of magic. A traitor fortified it. I use my foot to kick behind me, hoping to catch something, anything, but before I do, he picks me up off the ground. *I can't breathe. I can't breathe. I can't breathe.* I chant this in my head like I'm in a cult, only I'm the one being sacrificed to the god of asphyxiation.

Spots continue to dance in front of my eyes. Sure, I may be a Fire Wielder, but I still need oxygen to breathe. And this pudgy loaf isn't letting me breathe. Genesis bites the guy's leg, but other than yell in pain, he does nothing. It's déjà vu. I'm back in my room with the vines working their way around me, Natalie staring with her cold green eyes. He quickly gropes around my neck and chest area non-sexually, and even through my jumbled thoughts I can tell he's searching for the Firestone. Thank goodness I hid it back at Lalande.

"The stone. Where is it?" he yells. It hasn't occurred to him that I couldn't tell him, even if I wanted to, because he's restricting me from speaking.

Wait. Even though I can't touch him, I can still set him on fire by aiming for his head. But I hesitate. This guy may work for Acerbity, but he's still a human being. And while I myself am not a human, I'm similar to them. I can't kill him. My thoughts start to become alphabet soup as I start to lose consciousness ... everything is spinning ...

Mark ... Mark ... rescues me. He manages to shake off Colin for a split second, picks up his thrown aside bow, lifts it, and aims at us. Well, not me. I think. It's hard to see through the haze. The arrow whizzes through the air and hits the guy's arm. He releases me with a shout, clutching himself, and I drop to the floor. Colin bounds over with Mark at his heels.

Any tiny sliver of hope of sparing the two men disintegrates. I'm tired, I can barely breathe, and we haven't even completed our mission. Fatigued teenagers, even Acerbity-fighting ones like myself, don't have a lot of patience. So when Colin grins and aims his gun at me, I raise my hands and direct a huge ball of fire at his body.

The flames consume him, licking at his sweaty skin, devouring his evil face, and stripping him of his life. Only his fireproof clothes remain. I don't stop, even after his screams do. A minute passes before Mark says, "McKenna. He's dead."

"You ... think?" I wheeze, sitting up.

"Whoa, whoa, whoa," He cautions, gently nudging me to lie down again. "This is no time for you to be getting up. You almost passed out. You need to rest."

"I'm fine."

"No, you're not."

"Yes, I am."

"No."

"Yes."

"No."

"Are *you* okay? I heard you scream before."

Mark sits down and examines his hand. A bright line of welling scarlet stretches from his pinky to his wrist across his palm. "I've got this hand thing, but other than that, I'm fine."

I force myself to sit up. "I should have a bandage in my pack." Mark hands me the bag with his good hand. I clean the cut with some water before applying rubbing alcohol as gingerly as I can, and he lets out a hiss. "Sorry."

"It's fine," he says through clenched teeth.

"The cut doesn't look too deep. We'll still have to replace the bandage frequently," I say as I wind the cloth around his hand. "Good thing he got your left hand, not your right."

"Thank you." Mark flexes his fingers and winces.

"What about the other guy?" I ask, coughing. "Is he dead? Or was he scared by his friend's death and ran off?"

"Nah, he's here. He's weak, though. Still nursing his hand wound. It'll probably be okay if we leave him here."

The guy moans from wherever he is.

"He has a strong grip."

"He does." He puts his right hand on my shoulder. "You didn't know Colin, right?"

"Not that I'm aware of." I shrug. "Seemed like your average Acerbitian."

He mulls this over for a half a minute. Then, "You know what you told me earlier about wanting to be fearless?" When I nod, he smiles. "You looked fearless during the fight. You looked like you could do anything. Progress."

"Was that before or after I was held up by Pooh Bear over there?"

Mark laughs and presses his lips to mine. It doesn't last for more than a second, but my mouth still buzzes. I can't help but smile. "See?" he says. "Even you can laugh about it. Oh, crap. I just channeled Emma, didn't I?"

"Can we leave now?" I ask after a while. "We don't have time to waste."

"Can you breathe normally?"

My body chooses this exact moment to force me to cough like crazy. "No …"

"No."

Eventually I get better and we can continue. My stride is shaky, I notice as we run. We can't go at top speed because if we did, Genesis wouldn't be able to keep up. I give him some of my trail mix, sans M&M's, as we run … okay, I give him all of it. We're making good progress, so I doubt we'll even need it. And he likes it. Besides, trail mix is the worst thing to have disgraced the Earth with its presence. I shouldn't even be feeding it to the dog. He deserves better.

I tell Mark this, but he just tosses a handful in his mouth and says, "It's actually not that bad."

Boys.

A snake slithers by slowly and I'm not even fazed. We've seen pretty much everything in these Tunnels. So when the huge mutilated creature holding a flashlight makes a surprise appearance via side passage, I don't even blink.

"What is this thing?" Mark mutters, more to himself than me. It stands about seven feet tall with scaly green tinted skin. It has two eyes, though they're more like cat eyes than, I don't know, the regular kind of eyes of a weird creature thing. Yellowish goo dribbles out of its mouth and drips on the ground. Its skin is mottled with spots and warts and cuts and bruises.

"*Kalogen*," I say. Genesis goes over to it, sniffs its leg, and raises his leg to pee on it. We're so focused on the beast's appearance that we can't do anything when he picks up Genesis and eats him.

"What the—!" we shout. The monster looks at us and growls. It takes a step towards us, then another, its long tail swinging.

"You ate my dog!" I yell, anger bubbling up inside me. Funny, I'm not even sad about Genesis being eaten. I'm mad. "You ate my dog, you jerk! Are you crazy? *Are you crazy?* Don't you know I could set you on fire *right now?* Mark here could blast you to pieces. And I think we're gonna have to do that because—" I stop ranting in both English and Kevanese when the monster growls at me. And when I say growls, I mean opens its mouth and screams at me, showering me in goopy saliva that I pray isn't lethal to Elementals. Its breath is so horrible, it makes me want to go jump in a dumpster because I know that'll smell like freaking Febreze compared to this.

"This would be a good time to run, wouldn't it?" I say, wiping my face with my sleeve.

"I think so."

The monster is faster than it looks. It's not as fast as us, obviously, but it comes close. Its big feet make the ground shake beneath us. I look behind us to check it out. Its eyes have turned red. Who could have created this revolting monstrosity?

I blow out my fiery orb and mess up its flashlight so the thing can't see … which means we can't see. Oh God. Mark and I blindly stumble along, feeling our way through the Tunnel. Sirius is back in its flashlight form so the monster doesn't see the glow. A hand reaches out and takes mine, and I groan. I've had enough hands reaching out for me for a long, long time.

But it's just Mark. "Follow me," he whispers. I can barely hear what he said.

He veers off to the left. We've gone into a side passage. The beast zooms by, unaware that we've detoured.

"What's up?" I say quietly, leaning on the wall behind me.

"I thought this would lose him for a second." He sighs, and through the darkness I make out the outline of his body. "I need to tell you something really quickly." I must make a weird sound or something because he says, "No, really, I do. I need to say this before anything happens. I know I'm using up valuable time, but it's important." A hard swallow. "When that guy was choking you, I thought you were going to die. I wanted to help you sooner, but Colin was in the way, so I couldn't."

"It's okay," I say, reaching for his other hand. "You saved me in the end."

He shakes his head. "No. It's not okay. Because when you were caught, I realized something. Or maybe I knew it all along. But it hit me hard, like a baseball bat, and if I died, or if you died, I wouldn't have been able to tell you."

"You also would have been dead. You know. If I died." Pause. "No? Okay, that's my cue to shut up."

Silence. He's trying not to laugh now, I can tell.

"So … are you going to tell me?"

"Huh?"

"You brought me here so you could tell me something. Are you going to say it?"

"Oh, yeah."

More silence. He's nervous. I'm nervous. What is it about dark alleys that make everybody nervous? I bet he has bad news. The monster's spit is poisonous. We're in the wrong place. It's not you, it's—

"I love you. Well, I'm pretty sure I'm in love with you. Wait, no. I'm sure." He pauses, then says it again with conviction. "I love you. And I'm sorry I never told you before."

My head spins around. There is a bubble, a huge one, that expands in my chest. It's warm, and fuzzy, just like my favorite bathrobe. My heart swells and my Fire sings and there is a freaking choir in my body and I have to fight the urge to sing along.

"And I know we've only been dating for a month, but it's something I feel strongly about. This isn't—I hope—me being a stupid teenage guy. I understand if you don't feel the same way; I just wanted to tell you how I—"

Somehow I find his lips in the darkness. This time it's me cutting him off, but in my case, I do it with a kiss. There's that song again, the one where my heart and soul sing in perfect harmony. The shock takes a couple seconds to register, but when it does, he kisses me back, his fingers slipping into my hair.

"Are you crazy? Of course I feel the same way. I love you. We've been friends since freshman year. I feel like I've known you forever."

I think he's smiling, but I can't be too sure. "Glad to know I don't know what I'm talking about. I should probably shut the hell up."

"No," I say, smiling in the dark, "Keep talking."

"In that case, Micky D," he replies, using his new pet name for me, "Remember when I told you that you could never be one hundred percent sure of anything? Well, it turns out I was wrong. I'm a hundred percent sure that I love you. And that percentage is not subject to change."

And he kisses me, and for a brief ten seconds we can lie and pretend everything is all right.

Finding the monster is easy when Mark and I run at full speed. Evidently, the beast is unintelligent. It's been running in one direction the whole time we were in the passage, and it just now stopped to rest. Mark tried taking it out with an arrow, but its skin is too thick. He made it mad, though, and used its sharp nails to slash him across the face. Three gashes, bleeding and sparking, stand out on Mark's face. That stopped me from feeling bad for slicing its head off with Sirius, the awesome Keeper Sword. We can't let that kind of thing roam around the Tunnels. Also, it ate my dog.

I don't notice the wall in front of us until I slam into it. "Dead end," Mark says cheerfully, holding a blood-soaked cloth to his face.

"Thanks. I didn't notice."

I stand up and examine it. "What do we do now? Wait ... this is supposed to be a Compass Door." Sirius is glowing at its brightest now.

"Apparently."

I brush off the dirt, hoping to uncover an actual door. But there's nothing. I run my hand along the wall. No knob, but there's a hole. A key hole.

"Mark! Look!"

He complies. "Do we put the Sword in it?"

"Let's try."

I heft it in the hole. Nothing.

"Try turning it," Mark offers.

I twist it, and fire and light fill the room. Sirius itself starts to glow even brighter. My hair floats around my head in all the uproar. All this happens for a minute or so before he says, "Um ... McKenna? I think you can take it out now."

"Oh. Right."

I yank Sirius out of there, and the light dies and the fire burns out. I lean against the other wall, exhausted. "Well. Half of our mission is complete."

"And we're only half dead."

I reach my hand out and press it against the wall for some leverage. My hand hits a rock, but instead of doing nothing, it moves in.

"What the what?" I look at Mark.

And the floor disappears beneath us.

Chapter Twenty-One

I never expected to go like this. I always thought I'd be, like, one hundred and fifty-six and in a nursing home with my family surrounding my bed. Not sixteen and plummeting to my death in the wretched Tunnels. I'm yelling; heck, we're both yelling, but it's not like that's going to help. And for the first time, I wish I was an Air Manipulator. Controlling the winds would be kind of helpful right about now.

"Ahh!" I scream. I flail my arms, trying to grab something, anything, and come up with nothing.

"Ahh!" I can hear Mark, although his voice is kind of muted.

How deep does this thing go? I feel like we've been falling for hours, when it's really just been seconds. It's so dark; I can't see a thing. It's like Bizarro at Six Flags New England, except the initial drop is eternal. And there aren't exactly any safety restraints.

Any last prayers? None that I can think of, but I'm really sorry about taking two dollars from Dad's wallet last year to buy a pack of gum during summer break. And that time in eighth grade when I—

Just when I think we must be nearing the ground, my free fall is slowed. Mark and I stop shouting at the same time. Hmm. Maybe I am an Air Manipulator.

"Oh, thank God. You guys are *loud*," a voice says.

I force my eyelids to open so I can identify the female that spoke. There's light down here. She sounds familiar. Very familiar.

It can't be. It can't. Same brown hair, same blue eyes, same widow's peak, same smirk ...

"Ahem. Earth to Sleeping Beauty?" Bethany says impatiently. "Are you going to wake up, or what? I know I'm not your prince, and I sure as hell didn't kiss you, but I don't have all day."

"Bethany?"

"Donaldson," she replies. It's her trademark response. I grin. My sister. Well, one of them, at least. She's here. In the Tunnels. And if Bethany is here, the others have to be, too.

I hop off the bed of air and lunge at her. She squeezes me tight, so much I can barely breathe. But I don't care. Instead, with what little room I have, I breathe in the smell of her, of family.

"Hello?" calls another recognizable voice. "Did I suddenly become an Air Manipulator? Is that why I'm invisible?"

"Oh, shut up, Saige."

I turn around and come face to face with Bethany's twin, although she could pass as my twin considering the extreme similarity in our appearances. "I knew you'd be here. You and Beth are like Siamese twins or something. Even Kristen and Lauren aren't that attached, and they're identical."

"Whatever." She goes to stand by Bethany after giving me a quick hug. "Who's this guy? He's pretty hot."

Saige has always been very straightforward. If she thinks someone is stupid, she'll tell them. Mark looks like he doesn't know what to make of any of this. "This 'hot guy'," I say firmly, "is Mark O'Reilly. He's my boyfriend. These are two of my sisters, Saige and Bethany."

"Nice to meet you," he says, extending his hand. My sisters shake it.

"Oh!" Saige exclaims. "I remember you! You and McKenna used to be the best of friends. Well, until you and Liam moved away."

Now I'm confused. "You know him?"

"You don't?" Bethany laughs. "We all know him. You two were like white on rice. Saige and I always used to say you were going to get together when you got older. Guess we were right."

Mark and I exchange puzzled glances. "McKenna and I met two years ago at Lalande Academy."

Now it's the twins that look confused. Then something dawns on Saige's face. "Oh …"

Bethany says, "What's 'oh'?"

"Mom. Memory wiping."

"Cheerio." Another one of Bethany's odd sayings. She says it instead of saying, 'oh', because "o's are Cheerios", according to her.

"She wiped our memories?" I ask.

"She had someone do it."

"You were right," Mark smiles. "We did know each other before."

"I was, wasn't I?" I take his hand and smile back. So we were separated. But not by Acerbity. By Mom. My smile slides off my face after that thought.

"Okay, cut the chit-chat, cut the lovey-dovey romantic gazes," Saige claps her hands. "Let's take you to the others and get something for Mark's face. Bethany's the doctor of the family. She'll fix you right up."

"Relax, guys," says Bethany as we walk. "You're safe down here. Put the weapons away."

I frown. "Are you sure? Really sure?"

"Yes. My goodness. You'd think this was Iraq."

I retract Sirius into its flashlight form and put it in my pocket. Mark slings his bow back on his back. These parts of the Tunnels are nice. It's not as dirty as above, as far as I can tell, there aren't any rodents, and the air here is clean. They've been living the good life down here.

Soon, the Tunnel stops being a Tunnel; it widens out to the ends of wherever. At least, that's what Saige says. Because standing in front of us, daring us to try and get in, are two black iron doors that stretch to the ceiling.

She pulls out a relatively large key and fits it into the keyhole, and after turning it, yanks on the handle. "It opens outward so we have the element of surprise if, somehow, they get down her and try to attack us."

Whatever that means.

"Don't freak out if people stare," Bethany says. "Our community isn't exactly used to having new people, especially not the incumbent Fire Keeper and her boyfriend."

"Wait. You think we want to stay?" My eyebrows shoot up.

"Isn't that why you came?"

"No!"

"We unlocked the Compass Doors," Mark speaks up. "And we fell through by accident. Actually, it's a good thing we fell through. The other part of our mission is to get all of you out of here. The world is safe now. We're not quite sure why you left, but you can come back now. You need to. We need you."

"All two hundred of us?"

"Yes."

"The world still isn't safe."

"It's safer than it was two years ago."

"Acerbity is still running around upstairs."

"They don't have powers. We do."

I can't take it any longer. "Look, guys! The Tunnels are collapsing in on themselves on the twentieth of August. You have to get out of here or you'll *die!*"

Saige and Bethany look at each other warily. "We'll have to talk to one of the leaders," Bethany says.

"Which one?"

"Mom."

I blink. I'm not sure I want to talk to her anymore, but I know I have to. "Take us with you."

"Fine."

The twins have matured a lot. Before they left, they were pulling pranks left and right. Now, at nineteen, they're calm and ready to lead. It kind of scares me. How much have the others changed if Saige and Bethany are tame now?

The Elementals did a great job of making the space habitable. Bethany explains that the Earthens created the small houses lined up in rows and the food, the Water Users help with the bathrooms and irrigation, the Fire Wielders regulate the temperature and oversee food preparation alongside the Earthens, and the Air Manipulators supply the whole place with fresh, well, air. People are milling about around us in boring clothing, and the only person I sort of recognize is a boy who looks like Cara Regeh.

"So you're an Air Manipulator, right?" Mark asks Bethany.

"Obviously."

"And what are you, Saige?"

"Fire Wielder, same as McKenna."

I was right. "How did that happen? Mom's a Fire Wielder, and Dad's human. We were taught Elemental genetics last year, but our family seems like a rare case."

Saige shrugs. "Our family history on Mom's side is extremely complicated. When we get out of here, she'll have to explain it to you."

Mark takes my hand and squeezes it gently. Bethany notices and comments, "You two seem to like each other a lot."

He laughs. "You could say that."

Saige gasps, suddenly getting it. "Oh my God! You're in love, aren't you?"

"You could say that, too," I respond.

Without warning, Saige grabs him by the collar and Bethany holds his hands behind his back. "Listen to me, punk," Saige growls. "If she sheds a tear because of something you said, or did, you'll answer to us. You hear?"

I yank at her hand, but she doesn't move. "You guys, stop it! Leave him alone!"

"It's fine, McKenna. We're making sure you don't get hurt. So do you understand us, Mark?"

"I—I understand." Mark's tongue seems to be tied in knots.

"Good," This time it's Bethany. "Because we have an amazing track record of getting revenge. And you—"

"Saige. Bethany. Let the poor guy go."

I spin around and nearly collapse with relief. It's Jacqueline. Everything is going to be okay, now that my eldest sister is here. She looks regal with her brown hair in a tight bun, pressed slacks, and perfect posture. Her sophisticated outfit is juxtaposed with her iPod with the "Different Faces of Bacon" case and Hello Kitty headphones.

The twins sigh and release their death grip on Mark.

"Sorry about that, Mark," she says. "Whenever one of us starts a relationship with a guy, the twins go all crazy."

They roll their eyes.

"How'd you get here?" Saige frowns. "I thought you were in New Exeter with Mom."

"*To vervovo,* duh." She teleported. "Mom sent me here to check up on you two. Em told her you guys were on guard duty today. You just didn't see me arrive because you were too busy harassing your little sister's boyfriend."

Ignoring the little remark, I say, "You're an Air Manipulator, too?"

"Yep."

"You're three for three so far," Mark says. I'd explained to him my theory that my sisters were all different kinds of Elementals.

I hug Jacqueline, my sister, the one who insisted we never call her Jackie. She's here. Even though they act older and are technically adults, the twins still aren't exactly responsible authorities. She looks straight into my eyes, peering into my soul, and says, "I don't know exactly what you're doing down here, but I hope it's worth it. This place is a death trap, and it's a miracle you've survived it this long by yourselves."

"Can you help us?" Bethany asks, interrupting Jacqueline's uplifting mini-speech.

"Do what?"

"We're taking them to Mom. I need you to help me *vervoy* all of us back there. It'll lessen the effects."

Jacqueline sighs. "Fine. It's not as if I have anything better to do right now."

Before I can blink, Bethany and Mark each take one of my hands and I'm ripped apart for the second time today.

The first person I see after the winds put me back together is Emma Marie. Well, three Emma Maries. I'm still dizzy from *vervoram*. My youngest sister hasn't changed a bit, which, even through my lightheadedness, is comforting. Her blond hair is tied up in a high braided ponytail, and she's wearing athletic clothes.

"McKenna?" Her worried green eyes search my face. "Are you okay?"

"I'm seeing triple, Em, so yeah, I'm great."

She sighs. "I was just trying to be nice."

Eventually, the three images morph into one, and I notice everyone else in the room … who also happen to be looking at me. The rest of my sisters are scattered around the room: Christine is sitting in a corner reading a book that probably weighs as much as Emma Marie, Kayleigh is sketching by the wall, and Mia, Shannon,

Kristen, Lauren, and Joy are huddled together, whispering intensely. And ... Mom.

"Will somebody please tell me what's going on?" Mom says, frowning. This isn't how I thought our reunion would go. I was kind of expecting tears and hugging, not crossed arms and pursed lips. "Why are McKenna and Mark in the Tunnels?"

"I can explain, Mom," I start. We are *so* in deep trouble.

"Now would be a good time to begin."

I clear my throat. "Mark and I came here with nine other people."

"Did Acerbity kill them?"

"No," Mark says. "They're busy unlocking the other Compass Doors. We got your message about an opening—is that the only one?"

Mia nods. "That is the only one."

Mom's brow furrows even more. "But why are you here? You should be safe at home in Cortlandt."

"To get you out of here! After we escape, you can explain to us why you left us, but we need to leave, pronto." I say.

"And why, may I ask, did you think this was a good idea?"

"It's safe, we swear!" I protest loudly. "But the Tunnels will cave in on themselves in a couple of days. If we don't get you out, you'll die. The thing is, we have a plan. And basically, we're going to triumph over Acerbity once and for all. But obviously, we can't do it alone. We need you."

Christine snorts. "That just might have been the stupidest thing I have ever heard."

"Dean P didn't seem to think so."

"Dean who?" Mom says, eyes wide.

"Ioanna Papadopoulos." Why is Mom so interested?

"Isabelle okayed this whole thing?"

"Who's Isabelle?"

"That's Ioanna's real name."

Mark and I nod. Dean P changed her name? Why? To protect herself from Acerbity, maybe? No, that doesn't sound right. My mom didn't change her name. So why would Dean?

There's a knock on the door. "Come on in, Olivia," Mom says loudly.

The wooden door creaks open, and an African-American woman glides into the room. "I'll have to fix that," she says. Her voice is low and raspy, but in a cool way. She's very tall and has short, curly hair, almost like a mad scientist's. Her eyes are a familiar grassy green. This woman looks exactly like Natalie.

"McKenna? Mark? Meet Olivia Wilde." Mom gestures to the woman.

"It's a pleasure to meet you both," says the woman. She sticks out a bronze hand and, dazed, Mark and I both shake it.

"Mrs. Wilde, you-you're Natalie's mother!" I sputter.

"That I am," she says. Her eyes look a little sad. "Call me Olivia. You know Natalie?"

"She's my best friend," I say. There's a lump in my throat that's the size of a TV. I try to swallow, but can't. "She's somewhere in these Tunnels."

"Natalie's here?"

"All four Keepers are," Bethany offers.

Olivia closes her eyes and takes a deep breath. "Oh good Lord."

There is a pause in the conversation before Joy pulls out a legal pad and starts scribbling in her infamous cramped scrawl. She's one of only three lefties in our family, along with Lauren and our father. "So there are two hundred fifty-six Elementals down here, counting you and Mark, McKenna. There's only one way to get in here but eleven ways to get out. So the number of Elementals divided by the exits equals … what would that be, Christine?"

"About twenty-three people per exit," she responds without hesitation. Also without looking up from her book.

"So we're leaving?" Shannon asks Mom, a hopeful smile on her face. "We're all leaving?"

Mom sighs, rubbing her eyes. "It's not like we have a choice. Olivia, would you mind relaying the message to Lawrence and Thomas?"

"Will do." And Olivia speeds out of the room.

It's a new beginning.

CHAPTER TWENTY-TWO

Everything moves surprisingly quickly after that. Mom and Olivia quickly introduce Mark and me to Emma and Samantha's dads, Lawrence and Thomas. They're both around my mom's age, and they seem like nice men. Lawrence has black hair and green eyes and a small frame and looks exactly nothing like his daughter. Thomas, on the other hand, looks like an older, male copy of Sam. We also meet the former Keepers' kids. Emma's kid sister looks like her father, and, from what I've gathered, is very shy. Natalie's two older brothers are polite and seem concerned about their baby sister. Samantha, of course, has no siblings.

I sit on Shannon's bed, swinging my legs. Since there's so much room down here, each of my sisters has her own room for the first time ever. Well, except for Saige and Bethany and Kristen and Lauren. The two pairs of twins insisted on sharing rooms.

Shannon piles her colorful clothing into a duffle bag. Destroyed materials can be turned into power, so they're collecting everyone's belongings to strengthen the sorcerers. Mark went with Saige, Bethany, Mom, Olivia, Lawrence, and Thomas to help gather everyone's things after his face was healed.

"So, what's with you and that guy?" she says, her voice smooth as silk.

"Hmm? Oh, you mean Mark?"

"Yeah."

A grin slowly spreads across my face. "He's my boyfriend. Geez, it's been so long since I last saw you, I'd forgotten that you're so nosy sometimes."

"You're so freaking in love with him. My God. I've known since the very second you guys met fifteen years ago."

My cheeks turn red, and I reach for one of her pillows and toss it at her head. "You were two years old then. You don't know what you're talking about."

Shannon sighs, blowing strands of blond hair out of her face. "You're right," she says sadly. "I don't." Then her brown eyes become bright again. "But until then, I'll just continue to date. Have you met a guy named Resland Demi? He's super nice."

I know how this will end. The guy will end up being a douche, then they'll get into the ugliest fight known to mankind. The other ten and I will console her with a ton of ice cream and a sleepover of sorts bashing guys, and then Shannon will find another guy. The cycle will repeat itself 'til infinity. Why can't she see that she's a romance-novel cliché come to life? "Don't you ever get tired?"

"Of?"

"Of dating. Let's face it, Shannon, everyone has lost track of the number of guys you've gone out, fought, and broken up with. *And* you're only eighteen years old. Don't you want to take a little break? Being single is not the end of the world."

She closes the bag forcefully. "Will you stop it, McKenna?" she cries. "Don't start acting like you're better than me just because the first guy you dated fell in love with you. I'm trying, okay? People think I'm crazy, but I don't see the problem in trying to find the right guy for me."

This time, the silence is so uncomfortable I nearly choke on the air we're breathing. My cheeks are even redder. Somehow, the flowered bed sheets have become the most interesting things in the room. I don't even bother to tell her Mark isn't my first boyfriend.

Shannon exhales heavily. "I'm sorry, okay? You found your guy without even looking. I guess I've been jealous for more than a decade."

"No, I'm sorry," I say. I always feel weird whenever I apologize. "Maybe, though I can't remember, I rubbed it in your face all these years. And by the way, I've had more than one boyfriend before Mark. Just so you know."

There's another awkward moment where my immediate older sister and I do the 'so-are-we-going-to-hug' dance. Fortunately, the intercom interrupts us before things get even stranger.

"All Elementals please report to the Lower Topeka hall. Thank you." Mom's voice rings throughout the room. Shannon and I grin at each other and, grabbing her bags, run out of her room.

"**Will we still** be able to bring our stuff?" A Fire Wielder shouts.

Mom shakes her head from her place on the podium. "We're going to strengthen the sorcerers with the destroyed remains," she explains. The man nods and Mom says, "Next question. Yes, you, Avarice."

The teenager that raised her hand starts speaking, and Mark leans over to whisper in my ear. "Doesn't Avarice mean greedy?"

I nod. "A lot of Elementals give their children peculiar names, I guess. It doesn't mean anything in Kevanese, that's for sure."

"I'll say. I thought Semper took the cake before today."

"Let's take a vote," Mom says, her loud voice making us pay attention. "All in favor of leaving? It's not like we have a choice, anyway, but ..." Everyone raises their hands, laughing and cracking jokes. Mark and I raise our hands, too.

"All in favor of staying?" Silence.

"Okay. You all have your things packed; Joy, why don't you explain the exit plan to everyone," Lawrence says.

As my younger sister starts talking, I lean over and say in a low voice, "They seem to rely on my sisters for a lot of things."

"Yeah. Christine's the brains, Joy's the planner, Jacqueline's the boss, and Saige and Bethany are the 'police officers'."

I'm proud of him for memorizing my sisters' names so fast. "And Kristen and Lauren are the town gossip." Because they're so silent, the identical twins pick up info on just about everyone here, Shannon told me. And when they do talk, they always let the cat out of the bag.

The people around us are taking things really well. They all sound pretty stoked to be leaving the Tunnels, and who can blame them? It's been nearly two years. Two years of no sunlight or fresh air or Apple products. That must have driven everybody crazy. I wouldn't be able to stand living here for one second. I honestly don't know how these Elementals did it. They should receive a medal or something.

"McKenna." It's Mark, pulling myself back down to earth. "What are you waiting for?"

I look around. Most everyone has left the hall. "Oh. Whoops. I wasn't paying attention."

He laces his fingers with mine. "This is pretty exciting."

"Yeah. No one liked it here, and now they get to leave. I'd throw a mini party."

Mark gets his *I-have-an-idea* look in his eyes. "We *should* throw the Elementals a party."

"Now?"

"Not now. When we get back to the school. We could arrange for it to be on campus. Then we could have a dance at night for everyone. It'd be the perfect welcome back."

"How come you always have the best ideas?"

He laughs. "It comes naturally, remember?"

"Is it some kind of special twin thing?"

"Nah. Liam doesn't have it."

"Whatever, Mark." I squeeze his hand and smile. Though our current mission is almost complete, we still have lots more to do upon our arrival at Lalande. And I'm not talking about partying.

Splotches of red on his left hand alert me to the fact that his hand is still wrapped up. "They weren't able to heal your hand?"

He shakes his head. "There was no time, and Olivia says that some injuries heal better when they aren't touched by magic." I must not look convinced enough, because he laughs and says, "Don't worry. It doesn't hurt that much. Your mom gave me painkillers."

I'm not really sure what it was I did to deserve a guy as great as Mark, but I sure am glad I did it. The memory of us in the side Tunnel creeps back into my brain. That, coupled with another terrible, yet wonderful thought makes me blurt out, "Mark, what happens if we get out of this alive?"

"Is that a bad thing?"

"No, I was just thinking about what you said earlier. About ... us."

Mark has a confused look on his face.

"Look, what I'm trying to say is, um ... You know in movies, when the two people say they love each other when they're about to get killed, and they end up surviving? Well, everything becomes awkward after that. I just want to make sure there isn't any awkwardness between us."

"Don't worry, McKenna. Things won't get weird."

"Promise?"

"Promise."

I sigh. "Sorry for being so paranoid. I don't know if I can handle any more unpleasant surprises. I just want everything to work."

"We'll make this work. We'll make us work."

"I like us," I say.

"So do I."

I rest my head on his shoulder, yawn loudly, and close my eyes. Maybe, since everyone has left the room, no one will notice if I take a power nap.

"Come on, guys," Mia's voice interrupts my nap. I jinxed it. "You've been here for ten minutes. We have to get moving." With her black bob, wise blue eyes, and crossed arms, she could pass for a young mother. She always acts older than her age, anyway. She should be … twenty, I think. Yeah. Twenty. Her birthday isn't until November.

"Actually," Christine cuts in, having appeared silently, "It's been eleven minutes and thirteen, fourteen, fifteen—"

"Stop it, Christine."

Christine sighs. "Fine. People are leaving already. Mom and the leaders are going to be the last ones out. Do you two want to wait with us?"

Mark and I glance at each other. "Sure," I say.

Mark shakes his head. "McKenna, we need to find the rest of the Team members."

"Right. Okay, then we have to go first."

Mia says, "We can get Thomas, Jacqueline, Bethany, or Joy to contact the Air Keeper and tell her to meet us here."

"That's perfect."

"Okay. Let's go."

Mark and I stand up, stretching, and Mia and Christine pretend not to notice when I kiss him on the cheek. Everything is going to be okay. It has to be. My mom and sisters are alive, and the rest of the Elementals are, too. We can defeat Acerbity.

As we turn another corner, I realize we don't need my sisters or the Air leader to contact Sam and the others. They're standing right there at the end of the hallway, grimy and sweaty, but smiling.

"You're alive!" Natalie rushes over to hug Mark and me in a rare display of affection. "I was worried sick!"

"You didn't respond to any of my *dimpahansi* messages." Sam says, frowning.

"I know. I'm sorry," I lie. "We were kind of occupied."

"Obviously," Liam says, eyeing my arm around his twin.

"Not like that!" Mark rolls his eyes. "We just made life easier for you. You're welcome."

"Thanks," Natalie intervenes. "How'd you do all this?"

I smile and sneak a sideways glance at Mia and Christine. "You'd never believe us if we told you."

"Try me."

Chapter Twenty-Three

It's been a while since I last thought about my dad. I wonder how he's doing. I saw him at the end of the school year, but he isn't due for another visit until the week before school starts up again. Is he holding up okay? Is he lonely? Has he changed any? Did he meet another woman?

I push that last thought out of my head.

Since Mark and I arrived here, Mom has spoken to me three times. We finally hugged it out and did all the 'I-haven't-seen-you-in-over-two-years' stuff. But those three times, she never asked how Dad was. Is that it, then? Did she leave because of marital problems? I hope not. That's a stupid reason to drag almost three hundred people into the Tunnels.

Speak of the devil. "Geez, McKenna. If you think any harder, your head will explode," Mom teases.

I smile wanly. "There are a lot of things to think about."

We're standing near one of the exits along with my sisters, the three other Elemental leaders, and the Team. The other Keepers held everyone up because they were reuniting with their parents and siblings. The entrance is two doors wide, meaning that four people can go through at a time since we need to leave quickly. Christine churned out a couple of calculations and tried to explain some other stuff to us, but no one but Natalie and her mother actually knew what she meant. She gave up after a while.

The last of the people leave. Now it's our turn to exit. I climb up the stairs next to Natalie, Emma, and Sam. "How'd you guys get here?" I ask.

"You and Mark were taking forever," Emma explains. "After a while we all met up and came to look for you. We found the hole by accident."

"You mean we fell in it by accident," Sam corrects. "I told them to be careful; I sensed something was up. It was like the rabbit hole. I had to use air to keep them from becoming the downfall of the Elemental race."

I shake my head, laughing. "I touched a rock in the wall by mistake and the floor opened up. Guess it didn't close back up."

"Yeah, that was a fault in the system," Mom says, overhearing our conversation. "Bethany, I thought I told you to go with Jacqueline and Joy so you three could go fix that."

"I forgot."

Mom sighs. "Well, it doesn't matter now, does it?"

Eventually we make it to the top, where the air is pretty stale. There's an increase in temperature now that everybody is close together, and it's affecting everyone but the Fire Wielders. The area where we've gathered is pretty open, though; I guess the Tunnels are constantly changing. I'm surprised Acerbity hasn't already found us. We've been pretty noisy.

"All right, listen up!" Thomas yells, using air to hover over everyone. "Olivia will lead everyone to the Tunnels' entrance. We're all going to follow her. We need to be as quiet as possible. If Acerbity tries to attack us … well, that's why we had those training sessions while we were in there. Everyone knows their place, everyone knows how to use their powers and weapons. Let's go!"

Being that there are two hundred plus people going from point A to point B, we are still kind of loud. But it's better than when everyone was talking. The walk back is slow, tedious, and excruciating. Olivia has to stop every couple of minutes to make sure no one got lost. Sure, it's a quick check—some random warlock uses magic to take a count—but then again, I get impatient waiting for my coffee cup to fill up each morning.

We turn corners and tread down hallways and take shortcuts. I don't know how Olivia does it. Mark and I would have been lost in a second if it hadn't been for my Sword. "This is taking forever," Emma complains. "Why can't we *vervoy* from here?"

"Because," Sam replies, "The shorter the distance, the easier the travel is on the non-Air Manips *vervoram*. Plus, something tells me it isn't that easy to get out of this place."

"Still."

"Emma, the farther away you are from your destination, the less likely it is you'll return in one piece. So if I wanted to send you from inside my house to, say, the front door, there would be no problem. You probably wouldn't even suffer any after-effects. But if I sent you from Rome to Melbourne, well, you might not arrive with a head."

Emma's eyes grow wide. "Oh."

"Yeah."

"What's this about not having a head?" Katonah asks, falling in step next to us.

"Emma wants to *vervoy* from here."

"No, I don't!" Emma frowns. "I'd like to get back to the school in possession of all my appendages, thank you very much."

The rest of us laugh.

Around two hours pass before we reach the Crossroads, stopping for a break. The open area makes me frown. We're halfway there with no sign of Acerbity. Are we going to be lucky this time?

A guy my age saunters up to me. "You look happy today."

I nod, smiling. "We're halfway there. *Wamevo* McKenna Donaldson. Nice to meet you."

"I know." Then he frowns. "I mean, I know who you are." He holds his hand out, and I shake it. "*Méi tiget nado si* Aaron Pruitte-Laive."

His strawberry-blonde hair and lopsided smirk reminds me of someone I saw earlier, although he's a boy. "Hey, you kind of look like ..."

"Me?" says the girl I was referring to, who's walking up to us. "You remember me from the meeting. I was the girl that asked the last question."

I look back and forth between them. More twins.

"Yeah, we're twins," she continues, green eyes shining. *"Féi tiget nado si* Avarice. The cooler one."

"You mean the one with the stupid name. What kind of person walks around with the name 'greedy'?"

"Whatever, Aaron. You know you wish you were me." Avarice walks away.

Aaron smirks. "Don't mind her. She—" *Bang!* A deafening gunshot pierces the air, silencing the quiet chatter. And he drops to the floor.

"Aaron?" I say. He's not moving. Then I notice the hole in his head and the blood and guts splattered on the floor and on my clothes. My ears start ringing, and I realize I'm face to face with a black clothed man holding a gun. Flames flare up in my hands in a flash, and I thrust my arms in front of me, burning out his stomach. Standing there, speechless, I watch his gun drop to the ground milliseconds before him.

"Aaron!" Avarice screams, dropping to her brother's side. She picks up his hand, checking for a pulse. But it's a waste of time. We both know there isn't going to be anything.

More footsteps. Yanking on Avarice's arm, I pull her up and say, "There's no time to mourn. More are coming."

There are noises coming from above us. I tilt my head up to figure out what's going on. A balcony of sorts is forming from what looks like dirt, wrapping around the now dome-shaped hall. The dirt rains down on the sides. More people in black clothes jog onto the new terrace. Dark figures pour into the room from the way we came, and the exits close up. Bows and arrows, guns, obsidian swords—weapons point towards us, daring us to move.

I've never been so sure that I was going to die as I am now.

Everyone is still now, waiting with bated breath for someone to make the first move. I stare at the menacing Acerbitians, looking straight into their cold, intimidating eyes.

"We don't want to fight," one says. "We just want the girl that killed our leader. Hand her over and we'll let you go. Stay quiet, and … we know the four Keepers are amongst you. We can and will silence the Elementals for good."

Me. It's me they want. Pooh Bear must have gotten back to them. My knees involuntarily begin to shake.

A silver-haired grandmotherly type yanks me behind her. "Cover your hair; it's too bright. You're not going anywhere." Heaven knows I'm not going to argue with that, so I tug my hood over my red locks and crouch down.

Then some brave Earthen takes out an Acerbitian with a rock, and all hell breaks loose.

Bullets, obsidian or otherwise, zoom into the crowd of Elementals. But we're prepared. Stones and flames and sharp ice are shot right back at them. Thin wisps of smoke fill the air. Gunshots ring through the stale air, deafening everyone here. I drop down to the ground next to Aaron's lifeless body, where Avarice is crouched next to him again, sobbing quietly. I heat my hands up, ready to shock her back into reality. When I grab her hand, she shrieks and recoils.

"What are you?" I bark. I move to the side, avoiding a huge chunk of obsidian that whizzes by.

"*Quowet?*"

"What power do you possess?" I say even louder.

"*Wame-wamevo féi wotis. Féi repsa wotis.*" *I am a witch. A regular witch.* In her grief, she's switched to our native language.

I pull her to her feet. "We have to go and fight. You're going to be killed if you stay here. Aaron would want you to fight, wouldn't he? So go."

Avarice looks dazed, but then she shakes her head. Her eyes suddenly look sharp and clear. "*Sligi saumen,*" she says, meaning *all right,* and races into the crowd.

I look back down to where her twin lies dead in a morbid pool of his own blood. Aaron's green eyes are open, but glassy. A trickle of blood runs like a river out of his mouth. And if he stays where he is, and we win this fight, we won't have a body to bury when we get back. I bend over and grab him underneath his armpits. They're slightly damp, making me gag a bit, and he's heavy, but I manage to suck it up and slowly drag him over to the side of the tomb—I mean dome. When I'm finished, I shut his eyelids.

My thoughts shift back to the battle as I turn around. Everyone seems to be holding his or her own, although I suspect Acerbity has an advantage. The people on the terrace can just look down and aim at someone—it's like shooting fish in a barrel. The Air Manipulators are using their *letetam* advantage, though, and going mano a mano on the Acerbitians at the top.

Someone's fist connects with the back of my head, nearly knocking me down. I peer through the stars dancing in front of my eyes to see who my attacker is. Great. Another soldier. He must have lost his weapons if he's resigning himself to hand-to-hand combat. A little voice in the back of my head says it's not fair of me to burn him when he can't defend himself, but I ignore it. After all, he threw the punch, not me.

The next guy I come upon is harder to fight. He seems to be extremely skilled, as he dodges my fire and lighting and nearly hacks at me with his obsidian knife. He raises his left hand and waggles his fingers. Instantly, my hands are frozen in place. I have no control over my hands. But how? He's an Acerbitian … who has dark magic.

Phantom magic.

In a split second, he has me pinned on the ground. I scream and thrash as much as I'm able to, but everyone's occupied. He raises his knife, presumably to decapitate me, and a witch's orb hits him and freezes him in place.

I look up at the face of my savior. It's Katonah. *"Grietzi,"* I breathe, wriggling out from my position on the ground.

"No problem," she says, and promptly *vervoféi*.

"Wait, don't go!" I call. But it's too late. I'm alone again.

Mark. I have to find Mark. We need to stick together through all this. He's my fighting partner. I scan the mess of people, trying to make sense of any and all of it. But I can't. It's so chaotic in here. Acerbitian leaders are shouting orders at their soldiers while Elementals are trying to communicate with one another. Out of the corner of my eye, I spot a soldier charging at me with a slick, black knife. I aim my hands at him and blast him with a jet of fire.

If I could just get in contact with Sam or Jackson ... maybe Jacqueline, Bethany, or Joy ...

Guys? Are you there? Samantha Mazer? Jackson Chrysler? Jacqueline, Bethany, and Joy Donaldson? Anyone? I think, hoping at least one of them is listening to the thoughts in my area.

McKenna? It's Jackson. I nearly cry with relief while moving out of the way to avoid being hit by a *letetam* Air Manipulator.

Jackson. It's me. Are you okay?

I'm fine. Are you?

Right now I am. Do you know where Mark is?

Yeah. He's right next to me and Emma. He's been looking all over for you.

I frown. *Is everyone mixed up?*

Kind of. Natalie and Liam disappeared into the crowd. No one knows where Katonah, Amelie, or Raven are. Sam went to go find her dad, but she wouldn't let me come with her. Chris ... Chris is injured. But he'll be okay. Natalie's mom is healing him right now.

Where are you now?

Um ... I'm ... you know what? Why don't I come to you? I'll bring you over here. Where are you?

I look around me for some noticeable landmarks, but only come up with what's behind me. *I'm next to a wall.*

Grietzi for being so helpful. Never mind, I'll find you. Then there's that feeling of his voice leaving my brain. A soldier aims for my head with a silver bullet, but this time I barely have to even think about countering the attack. I use my metal affinity to whip the ball back at the woman, and it lodges in her arm while her gun is still smoking.

Jackson materializes next to me. I'm so grateful he's here, I nearly start to laugh. But I don't because his blond hair is matted down with dried blood and his glasses are nowhere to be seen.

"How'd you find me?" I ask.

"It's an Air Manipulator secret." He takes my hands and, before I can prep myself, *vervoméi* us to where some of the others are.

The after effects aren't bad when you're only going with one person. You get a small headache, but that's it. Emma and Mark are waiting for us when we arrive seconds later. They both look like Jackson—tired and unkempt.

"What happened?" I ask, looking at them.

"Wave after wave of them" is all Emma offers. Blood trickles out of her nose and a gash on her arm.

I turn my attention to Chris, who is propped against the wall. "You okay?"

"I've been better." He gestures to his leg, which is quickly being bandaged by Mrs. Wilde. "I got nicked by an obsidian knife. Damn, those things cause a lot of damage for an igneous rock. And they hurt like a motherfu—"

"Someone needs to stay here and protect him," Olivia interrupts, brow furrowed.

"I'm fine," Chris objects. He holds his hands up, and, slowly, a barricade of rocks and dirt surrounds him, only leaving a tiny opening at the top for air. "See?"

She rolls her eyes. "Don't say I didn't warn you. If you die, it's not my fault." Before he can object any further, she runs into the pandemonium.

"Be careful, Chris," Emma warns. "You're my fighting partner." He says something back, but it's muffled.

"Guys, look," Jackson says, pointing into the crowd. Three Acerbity soldiers move towards us, weapons drawn. He, along with Mark and Emma raise their own weapons, so I do, too.

Before I fully realize what is going on, the oldest-looking one clicks a bullet—obsidian—into place. He shoots at Emma, but she's too quick for him. She catches it with ice like they're playing Little League fall ball. Contrary to her effervescent nature, Emma Richards has turned out to be one of the best fighters I've ever seen.

Mark and I move closer to each other, deciding without speaking to tackle the burliest looking one together. He snarls at us. After staring at me intently for a while, he grins. His yellowed teeth look like the unappetizing corn kernels no one wanted at the dinner table.

"The Fire Keeper," he laughs. "The Master will be so happy." He lunges at us, two knives withdrawn. For a pudgy guy, he is pretty quick on his feet. I narrowly miss the sharp edge of one of his blades by dropping to the ground and rolling to the side. Mark is surprised by the quick attack and doesn't react fast enough, but before he becomes an amputee, I hit the hulking man with a huge fireball. The obsidian blades fly out of his hand and the tip of one gets stuck in Mark's boot. Mark pulls it out gingerly, but he doesn't seem to be hurt.

Even thought the guy is on the ground, burning to death, he still tries to make one last valiant attempt, this time with a gun. He squints at me, and then fires. But I don't even flinch; I sense it's a silver bullet. I pluck it out of the air with my thumb and index finger. "Nice try, but silver doesn't work on me," I smile smugly.

"Nice try, but it's actually obsidian with a silver shell." And the flames engulf him, trying to shut him up, but it's too late. The casing flakes and my hand starts to burn. The bullet slips out of it, and I curse and grunt in pain as Mark appears next to me in a flash and takes my hand. We both watch in horror. My fingers are quickly turning a purplish color, and soon after lines starts to spread across my palm. My arm feels like it would if a piano landed on it, my hand was ripped off, and the doctors didn't give me numbing medicine when they put it back on during surgery.

Emma and Jackson have defeated the others and stand next to us, looking even worse. Jackson has acquired a gash that matches his girlfriend's, and Emma's cheek is sporting a bruise.

"McKenna," Mark says in a strangled voice. He looks like he wants to say something, anything that will make the situation better. But there's nothing he can say. And there's nothing *to* say.

I may not be able to die by a silver bullet. But I *can* die of obsidian poisoning.

Chapter Twenty-Four

The weird thing about obsidian is that when it comes in contact with an Elemental, it reflects across his or her body if it isn't healed immediately. If it struck an ear, the other ear would have the same mark. So when the fingers on my other hand get purple swirls, I'm not even the tiniest bit surprised. If only Olivia was still here … *Focus, McKenna. Priorities. You need to fight. And to fight, you need your powers.* I breathe in and out. Stretching my hand is even more painful, but I do it anyway.

"Can you still use your powers?" Emma asks.

"That's what I'm trying to figure out, Emma!" I snap, slightly irritated. I glance at her, and she looks a little hurt. *No. Stop. Do not be mad at her. It's not her fault. You were the stupid one, catching a freaking bullet with your bare hands.* "I'm sorry. I'm just angry at myself. I didn't mean to take it out on you." She waves it off, and I attempt to make a fire ball with my left hand. No luck.

I try again with my right hand. Same results. My breath comes quicker now, in short little spurts. I can't have lost my powers. I can't. I feel Fire coursing through my veins and arteries, mixing with my blood, but it's useless if I can't let it loose.

"Mark." I look in his eyes helplessly. "It's not working at all."

His eyes flash with worry. The brown in his hazel eyes stand out now. "Olivia's not here."

"And neither is Natalie."

Emma and Jackson look like they don't know what to make of the situation. I'd almost forgotten they were here. "I can try to get a lock on both of them," Jackson offers, but his expression reveals that it's not likely he'll get them. The constant barrage of everyone's loud thoughts seems to be taking a toll on him; he looks more fatigued than any of us.

"For now, I'll have to be your hands," Mark concludes, "Even though you're way more powerful than me."

I nod, unable to say anything. If I open my mouth, I might cry. Without my powers, I'm like the silver casing on that obsidian bullet. I'm a worthless, useless nobody. No one says sorry to me and I'm glad they don't. I'm not sure I could handle it if they did. They didn't cause this. "Look," Emma says. She points to the crowd of Elementals in the arena. They seem to be forming a huge circle. "We should join them."

"You two go ahead," Mark urges. "We'll be right behind you."

Emma and Jackson nod, then take off. And even though there's turmoil all around us, Mark pulls me to himself. "We're going to get you through this, and then we'll fix your hands."

I shake my head, laying my head on his chest. "I feel like I've been leaning on you like a crutch this whole time. I'm sorry I'm so dependent on you."

"If being a crutch allows me to get this close to you, then feel free to break your legs as frequently as possible," he whispers into my hair.

"Too cheesy."

"Sorry."

He frees his good hand and creates a nice, warm flame. Then he takes one of my mottled hands and, together, we hold the fire. Thank goodness the poison can't spread from person to person. "See?" he says. "You're still resistant to it. That means there's still hope for you."

His face is illuminated by the fire. His eyes say he believes everything he says. "Thanks." I pull away from his hug, though at this point in time, with all the fighting going on around us, I would gladly stay in his arms forever. "We have to go."

"Right."

We race to the growing crowd. Almost everyone is looking up at the Acerbitians on the terrace. The soldiers are still shooting into the crowd, but their numbers have halved. And the ones stupid enough to fight on the ground are all dead. Still, I have a sneaking suspicion these are only a fraction of Acerbity.

"Any ideas?" Thomas's voice rings out above everyone else's. It's not hard to do that, seeing as our numbers have depleted considerably as well. "How can we get rid of them all at once?"

There's a lot of whispering around us. Acerbity has stopped shooting, trying to figure out what is going on.

"Have you given up, then? Will you produce the girl?" a man shouts.

"Keep shooting, it's not going to happen!" somebody retorts.

I close my eyes, forcing myself not to concentrate on the pain, and think. *Really* think. How can we get rid of the Acerbitians here once and for all? An explosion? No. It'd be a taste of their own medicine, yes, but the Tunnels might collapse in on themselves prematurely. Bring down the terrace? They'll most likely survive the fall; it's not too far off the ground.

Remember your training ... What did Dean P have us do when she first taught us? I ball my fists, trying to remember.

I've got it.

"Come on," I say, pulling Mark deeper into the crowd. "I need to talk to Thomas." We push through the Elementals standing in our way before coming to a stop in front of Sam's dad.

"Yes?" Thomas says.

"I have an idea." Quickly, I relay my plan to him. His face lights up, which makes me happy. Good. Maybe I am useful after all.

"All Fire Wielders, witches, and warlocks to the front!" Thomas yells in Kevanese. Around one hundred people rush up to the middle of the circle. "We're going to set this room on fire. Witches, warlocks, we need you to protect everyone who is not a Fire Wielder."

Acerbity has given up on trying to convince my people to hand me over and is continuing to shoot at us. The Water Users, Earthens, Air Manipulators are keeping them at bay. Witches and warlocks join together for a joint protection spell on non-Fire Wielders, giving the room a purple glow for a second.

"On my count!" Thomas shouts. "*Cún ... deucé ... fasol!*"

The Fire Wielders around me create the fire that burns so hot, the Acerbitians closest to it incinerate immediately. Everything is tinted in red, orange, and yellow, and flames lick at my jumpsuit. I feel a bit better being surrounded by fire, but I'm still in pain. The fact that I can't be a part of this, can't use my powers, saddens me.

What if I can't reverse this?

The soldiers don't have a chance up there. After a couple of milliseconds, the last one dies. I guess I should feel bad. I mean, we killed people. We took lives. But then again, they were trying to kill us, too, so ...

Victory.

Cheers erupt from the huge group of Elementals. Suddenly, this feels less like a fight and more like a dance rave. The air is filled with smoke as the Fire Wielders destroy the fire. Mark grabs hold of my shoulders and, even though we can't hear each other, we scream at each other in joyful disbelief. Just for a second I can forget the monstrosity on my hands. Well ... not really. But the pain is going down.

An unidentified Earthen makes what's left of the terrace crumble with a curl of her fist. The dirt rains down like a muddy waterfall, and the rest of the Earthens go wild. Adrenaline surges along with Fire inside me, dimming the pain of obsidian poisoning and making me more alert. A group of Earthens move our room so the exit is uncovered again. The arena groans, shifts, and then returns to its former state. How did Acerbity gain control of this place? Only magic could have done what they did.

The prospect of supposedly human Acerbitians having Phantom powers sends a shudder through my body.

"Come on! The Tunnels aren't going to wait for us to leave before closing!" Lawrence yells, and we follow him out. Jackson and Emma get on either side of Chris and help him get up. I look back for a second. All the bodies have been reduced to ashes. We lost Aaron for good.

Huh. Guess I should have seen that coming.

"McKenna!" someone shouts. Natalie. I sprint towards her, disregarding everyone in my way. I squeeze her like we're going to die soon, which is kind of appropriate. We almost did.

"What's up with your hands?" she says, peering at them after I finally let her go. "Those are the marks of obsidian poisoning."

"You're telling me."

Her smile dissolves. "Are you kidding me? McKenna, you need help. Quick."

"Can you help me? I know you have healing powers."

She groans, covering her face with her hands. "You *know* I haven't had much training, Micky! I can't fix this! You need my mother."

"That wouldn't be a problem if I knew where your mother was. Unfortunately, I don't."

"She's leading everyone, remember? We can't bother her now."

"Yo, McKenna, what's up with your hands?" Katonah says, hanging back to walk with the six of us.

"Obsidian poisoning," I sigh. "You wouldn't happen to possess any healing powers, would you? I may or may not be dying."

She shakes her head. "Nope. Not my specialty, although I think I can mix up something for your pain." She unzips her jacket a bit, reaches in, and pulls out four vials: two silvery-gray, one orange-yellow, and one empty. She pours the liquids into the empty vial and shakes the mixture, holding her thumb over the opening. Smiling, Katonah holds it up to me. "Drink."

The brownish color it has taken on looks really unappetizing, but I'm not really in a position to pass things up superficially. Deep breath. I knock the vial back and immediately regret doing so. Fire Wielders, as a general rule, don't drink alcohol. Obviously. Explosions inside of your body are really uncomfortable even if they aren't technically causing damage. That being said, I imagine this mixture is what vodka tastes like: bitter, peppery taste with a hint of citrus that "burns" the back of my throat. I can't help but gag.

"Tasty, right?" Katonah laughs at my predicament.

"Totally." Despite the unappealing flavor, the tonic's already starting work. My hands feel better, my headache is going away, and I no longer have any shoulder pain from before.

Sam, Liam, and Amelie jog against the flow of people to us. Not surprisingly, Raven isn't with them. When they see my hands they all try to talk over one another about it.

"Guys!" I shout, silencing everyone. "Yes, my hands are messed up. And yes, I can't use my powers. Now can we please move on?"

"How are you going to get healed?" Amelie asks worriedly.

"I don't know, okay? Let's just focus on getting the heck out of here," I say. I look down at my hands. The purple lines are traveling up my arms, slowly but surely, but the stabbing pain is diminishing. They look hideous, but I guess I should be happy I'm still alive and not be so superficial. "How is your leg, Chris?"

He smiles, hobbling along on some crutches he made for himself. "Better, now that I have these crutches. Mrs. Wilde said it's better for it to heal on its own. Hey, what's going on up there?"

We swivel our heads to look in front of us. Everyone has stopped walking. Emma doesn't notice and bumps into someone ahead of her. "Sorry," she apologizes.

"It's okay," the man says. "Something's going on in front."

"Let's go see what's up," Sam says, and she and Jackson *vervohabet* us to the front.

After I get over the effects of *vervortade*, I notice a man arguing with the four leaders. I can sense he isn't an Elemental, but he also isn't part of Acerbity. So what is a human doing here? I raise an eyebrow at Sam, who lopes over to Emma and me. "So, apparently, he was cursed to guard the exit by the Legion of Elemental Leaders four hundred years ago for meddling in Elemental affairs. And he's insisting that we can't *vervoy* out of here without sacrificing one person."

"Sacrifice?" Emma says incredulously. "What the heck? You know what? Gather some sticks. McKenna's mom can create the bonfire."

Sam whacks Emma's arm lightly. "Not like that, silly. Some person has to stay behind to be killed while the rest of us go. It's physically impossible for people to exit these Tunnels without sacrificing someone. Felicity Caste—you know, that super-evil Phantom in the sixteen hundreds—made that a rule when she created the Tunnels so she could glean more dark magic from their deaths. No one's been able to remove it. I'm thinking that's why the Elementals couldn't leave."

I snort. "Figures the Tunnels would have a cynical rule like that. What if you went alone, hmm? How would you sacrifice someone then?"

"I didn't make the rules, McKenna. Felicity did."

"Let me at him." Emma cracks her knuckles and walks over to the man. "Excuse me! Mr. Jailor-sir?"

He grunts.

"Um … yeah, okay. The whole sacrifice thing isn't exactly going to work with us. Could you, I don't know, give us a pardon or something? It's kind of important that nobody else dies. See, we just won a battle against a group of people named Acerbity. I don't know if you've heard of them?"

"Yes, I've heard of Acerbity." He rolls his eyes, his leathery voice sounding exasperated.

"Great! Then I'm sure you're aware of how awful they are and how urgently we need to get out of here. Also, I'm not sure if you've been told? The Tunnels will collapse in less than two days—"

"Sorry, Keeper, but the rules are the rules. I didn't make them, and I can't break them. That's just how it works. And the Tunnels won't collapse. Felicity created them to last forever."

Did they trick this poor human? Or was the expiration date not disclosed to the public?

"Hey, guys," Olivia says, walking with the other leaders towards my friends. "Looks like we aren't leaving right now."

"Why not, Mom?" Natalie asks nervously from her place next to Chris.

"In order for us to leave, we have to sacrifice someone. It's impossible for us to get out if we don't do that. That's why we've spent so much time down here."

I look around at the crowd of Elementals. All are tired, grief stricken, and injured in some way.

Who is going to die?

CHAPTER TWENTY-FIVE

There's a feeling one experiences at some point in his/her life, one where the gut wrenches and a good sized TV lodges itself into his or her throat. Tears may or may not cloud the eyes. That's how I feel after Olivia shares the news with the rest of the Team. I didn't react this way when Sam told me the news, which is weird. But when the Earthen leader breaks the news, I'm like a mom of four who's just missed the holiday season sales.

"Who's going to willingly give up their lives just so a hundred other people can leave this place, even *if* the Tunnels will collapse?" asks Mark, making me realize that this is now about chivalry. "I mean, I'd do it if I didn't have anything else to lose." He glances at me from the corner of his eye, then looks at his brother.

"That's how we all feel, Mark," my mom says. "Everyone has something to lose."

"Not everybody," Amelie says darkly.

Uncomfortable silence.

"I'm going to go relay the message to everyone else," says Thomas awkwardly. "Then maybe we can go from there. We've no more time to waste."

Mom nods silently.

I look at the human man. He doesn't seem to be happy about killing any of us, even though he's been doing it for centuries. He has salt-and-pepper hair and a heavily wrinkled face. If grandfathers had a poster child, he'd be it. When he catches me staring at him, he gives me a sort of half smile. I kind of want to ask him how it feels to be alive that long.

Will we even be able to take him with us?

Thomas returns with a drained look on his face. "What?" Lawrence says. "What was the response?"

"No one wanted to do it," Thomas says irritably. "Obviously."

"So who is?"

"I don't know, okay?" Thomas growls. "I'd volunteer, but Samantha would never let me."

"You're right," Sam says immediately. "I wouldn't."

"Lawrence has two daughters. Meredith has twelve—count 'em, twelve—daughters. Olivia has two sons and a daughter. All three of you have spouses. So none of you can go." He takes a deep breath, desperately trying to calm down. "The four Keepers can't go for obvious reasons. Plus, we'd never let them. And the rest of the Team … well, they're only sixteen!"

Katonah raises her hand slightly. "Seventeen going on eighteen over here."

"Yes, but you said you have a sister to look after."

"You're right."

"I could go," Saige offers.

"Or me," Bethany adds.

"Or both of us."

"Are you girls crazy?" Mom frowns. "You two are not going. None of my daughters are going. Nor are any of your kids."

A dark though creeps into my brain. I try to push it out, but it refuses to move. If, somehow, Mom passed her Keeper responsibilities on to me, maybe I could do the same. And then I could sacrifice myself. It would eradicate the possibility of me getting too angry. It would save everyone else.

"Don't ever say that, McKenna." Natalie glares at me after I voice my idea. "There's no way we'd let you do that." Everyone gives me odd looks. Even the Jailor looks at me funny, and he doesn't even know what my deal is. Or maybe he does.

"Well, then how are we going to get out of here?" I demand.

"I'm not sure, but giving ourselves up is not the answer. Okay?" Natalie is very impatient now.

Emma twists a strand of golden-wheat hair around her finger. "Well, looks like we're up shit creek without a paddle." I laugh without humor.

Many minutes pass without a solution. The only person we haven't asked is Raven, but of course, she's nowhere to be seen. That Phantom is as unreliable as a politician. The old Jailor decides to take a catnap while we try to sort things out. But we can't. That is, until Amelie speaks up.

"Why don't I go ahead?" She looks distressed, but she still says it.

"Are you kidding me?" Chris sputters. "I thought we already agreed that none of the Team members are dying."

"Yes, but I'm the only one with nothing to lose."

"You have Alexis," I point out.

"Alexis doesn't care about me. You know that already."

"What about your parents?" Olivia says. "Won't they be opposed to the idea? I mean, you're so young."

Amelie shakes her head ruefully. "I have a deadbeat dad, and my mom's an alcoholic. Neither of them will care. That's why I go to Lalande." Something about her statement doesn't sound right. It's almost as if it's rehearsed. But why would it be?

"That doesn't matter, Amelie," Katonah says firmly. "You still shouldn't go."

"Too late," Amelie smiles, and races past us towards the Jailor. We run after her, hoping, praying she's not about to do what we think she's going to do.

It hits me right about now that Amelie is serious about all this. She actually wants to give her life up for the rest of us. But she can't.

She *can't*. Tears form in my eyes. Amelie is like another sister to me. We've been through so much crap together, and now she's just going to give it all away? She may not have her mom, or her dad, or her sister. But she has me. She has all of us. And that should be enough.

She stops in front of where the Jailor is sitting. Tapping him on the shoulder, she says, "Mr. Jailor? Sir? I'm the one you need."

He yawns, blinking rapidly. "Huh? Oh. You're the one?"

"Yes."

No. No, no, no. I reach out and grab her wrist. "Let go of me, McKenna," she barks. "I'm going."

"Think about what you're doing," I say hysterically. Hot tears create paths down my face, and I don't care. "Think about who you're leaving behind. You can't leave us. Think, Amelie. Think."

Through my tears her violet eyes flash like a kaleidoscope. Sam, Katonah, and Mom latch onto her arm. "Stop it, all of you."

"Amelie, please!" I yell. "You're not just going to some magical place, you're dying! Your life is going to be taken from you. Do you understand that? Stop trying to be brave and think straight, for God's sake!"

And suddenly, she's not there anymore. I'm grasping thin air. She *to vervoféi* to the other side of the Jailor, which I wasn't aware she was even capable of doing that.

"How'd you do that?" Jacqueline frowns. "I thought light witches couldn't *vervoy*."

"You have to learn how to do it," Amelie explains, looking at the floor. "I practiced a lot."

The Fire within grows and expands. It's angry, but I'm not. Weird. It's usually in sync with my emotions. It flares, then dies, then flares again, like a heartbeat. It rushes through my veins faster now, faster, faster, faster.

Light glows from my arms. I look down, expecting to find a break in my skin that I didn't notice. Instead, curving lines paint themselves on my skin, on top of the obsidian poison markings, making pictures that have no meaning. Now hands squeeze my heart. No, not hands. It's the icy fingers of fear. This has only happened once before.

This is the very thing I was trying to prevent.

"McKenna." Mark slips between the people surrounding me. "You can do this. Breathe. You can make them go away."

"I can't!" My breathing pattern becomes irregular.

"Yes, you can." He takes my ugly hands into his own, the bloody bandage scratching at my palm. I don't know how he can look at me when I look like this. "Breathe in and out, and just … imagine erasing them off your skin."

I shut my eyes and, through the pain of the obsidian poisoning, think of the Fire patterns on my arms disappearing bit by bit. When that doesn't work, I try mentally pushing them off of my skin. All too soon I realize the etchings are an internal problem. Great. So now I have to pull them from the inside out.

This time I have to block everything out and really, truly concentrate. *You got this, McKenna. Pull. Use your Fire to pull.* I grit my teeth and try even harder.

Pull.

Pull.

Pull.

And then, finally, the drawings start to fade. I keep pulling with the same intensity until I'm positive the patterns are completely gone. My bones seem to creak with exhaustion. I collapse against Mark. If I don't lean on something, I'll surely fall down.

I don't want to think about what would happen if I didn't pull the Fire markings out. I've heard of a previous Fire Keeper who lost control. He went on a killing spree.

Everyone cheers for me, even though some of them don't know what would have happened if I didn't succeed.

"Thanks," I whisper so only Mark can hear me. "I'm such a mess right now."

"No," he responds. "You're a fighter."

Amelie has stopped to see what the commotion is about, and she looks impressed by what I've done. I slip out of Mark's arms and dash up to her. Now she looks sad, so sad, somehow sadder than me. More tears prick the back of my eyes like needles, but this time I don't let myself.

"This isn't me being all heroic, you know. If I don't go, who will?" she says softly. "Bravery is sometimes the ability to do the right thing, even if it's really, really hard."

"I know." I don't even hesitate before giving her a huge hug. Loose strands of black hair from her ponytail adhere themselves to my tear-stained face. Cold drops of water patter onto my back—Amelie's tears. "Thank you for doing this."

When we finally pull away, she looks me in the eyes and says, firmly, "Remember what we talked about outside the van. Don't ever forget me."

"Are you nuts?" I look at her like she's crazy. "How could I forget one of my sisters?"

"*Grietzi*," Lawrence says. "I don't fully understand why you're willing to do this, but *grietzi* all the same."

Amelie nods. She exchanges hugs and handshakes and hugs from the rest of the Team members, who in turn express their gratitude. A couple of Elementals come up to her once they realize she's the one giving herself up and thank her.

She's the bravest one out of all of us.

"Ready to go now?" the Jailor grumbles impatiently.

Amelie walks over to him and gestures to an obscure pathway. "After you, sir."

And the man starts walking, and she follows him. Amelie, one of my best friends, one of my closest friends, walks away with a total stranger to her death. And I will never, ever see her again. Trying to swallow is impossible now. Of course Emma is crying, and even Lawrence and Liam are close to tears. It's some kind of

Water User obligation to shed tears when there's a sad moment in life. Everyone else looks shocked, like they can't quite comprehend what just happened.

At the worst possible moment, I remember my stupid premonition. Stupid, stupid, stupid. I wish I could take it back. With my kind of luck, I probably jinxed everything by making that prediction. I wish I wasn't right. I wish I was wrong, terribly wrong. But wishing never got anyone anywhere. Besides, it's too late. Amelie is the person who isn't coming back. And wishing isn't going to reverse her death. It's just going to make me feel worse.

So even though I feel like crying until I'm completely dry, I suck it up and attempt to smile.

Chapter Twenty-Six

There's probably nothing sweatier than Mr. Eric Wentworth's hand. It's so clammy and sticky. I think I'd rather sit in a bathtub of snakes than touch it. But I have to if I want to get out of these damned Tunnels. Natalie's on my other side, but that doesn't even matter. He's a pretty nice man, with graying hair and an impressive beard. He's just lacking in the hands category.

A deafening grinding noise stops me from spending too much time thinking about his hand. It's a crunching, grinding noise, and it's followed by what feels like a massive earthquake. Think 'attack on Lalande, circa one month ago'. Now multiply that by a thousand. My skull rattles and my teeth chatter. If I weren't holding Natalie and Mr. Wentworth's hands, I would have fallen.

"It's the Tunnels," Natalie shouts, looking scared for the first time, like, ever. "They're closing!" Before we can say anything else, the Air Manipulators—minus the one who is taking the van back—*vervoy* us back to Lalande Academy.

There are even more people being transported, so it takes me a while to even open up my eyes. My stomach is doing the cha-cha slide inside of me. There are dwarves pounding on the inside of my brain, demanding to be let out. They're making my head throb.

Blades of grass tickle my cheek as I lay on the ground. I don't want to get up ever again. Apparently Mr. Wentworth is an Air Manipulator, because he's standing up and chatting with Thomas Mazer. Mom and the other two Elemental leaders are sitting upright, but they don't look too good. I see a couple of my sisters strewn across the quad. The sun is at its zenith in the sky, but since the Tunnels were closing on us when we got out, time must have sped up.

The lighting in the Tunnels was pretty bad. Now that we're in broad daylight, I can see everyone's cuts and bruises clearly. Some people were hit by obsidian weapons; some injuries are worse than mine. I look for Mark, but he's not here. More fear pricks my heart. Hopefully he's with his brother.

"McKenna?" Samantha says, blocking the sun as she peers over me. "You okay?" Her voice sounds funny because my ears are ringing.

"Of course," I say. Dark spots appear in my eyes. "Never been better."

And then everything goes black.

Genesis trots ahead of us on his leash, his black and white tail swinging as he goes. Kayleigh scribbles furiously in her sketchbook, not bothering to lift her little red head to look where she's going. Saige has to reach a hand out to steady her when she veers off the sidewalk. Mom looks happy, whistling a familiar song. The one she said would save me if I was in trouble.

Mom always says weird things like that. Like she's not going to be there when I'm in trouble. Like she'll be standing behind a wall made of Plexiglas, wanting but unable to help me when I need her most. It worries me.

I walk closer to Mark, matching my stride to his. He is my best friend, so, as usual, he senses my fears and says, "You okay?"

"Yeah. Do you think my mom is acting weird?"

"As in, saying things that make no sense?" he asks, shoving his hands in his pockets.

I nod.

"Yeah."

I breathe a sigh. If Mark noticed it, too, then there has to be something going on. Mark and I are only twelve, not exactly English teachers. People are going to stare if I have an interpreter follow me around just because I have no idea what my own mother is saying.

A hooded figure walks down the sidewalk towards us. I think nothing of it, and Mark and I keep walking. But Mom stops. I hear her gasp.

"What's wrong?" Saige says, confused.

"Get behind me. Now. Everyone." Mom hands Mark Genesis's leash and holds out her hands.

Mark pulls Genesis back next to him. "Stay here, Genesis." The dog howls and stands at attention. Sometimes I feel like he can understand us.

I slip my hand in Mark's, growing more and more worried. I peer at the approaching figure. Cold, calculating blue eyes, dark brown hair, hands in his pockets.

"Hello, Meredith." His voice is deep and chilling. "Long time no see."

"Get away from us, Colin. Stay away from my life."

Colin laughs, and Genesis snarls. "You brought your Fire squad today, hmm? And who's that boy there? I thought you had twelve girls."

Mark stiffens, and I squeeze his hand. "Leave Mark alone!" I say. This guy doesn't know what he's dealing with, doesn't know that he could be blasted and burned to bits in a matter of seconds.

"Shh …" Saige says worriedly, but the stranger tsks.

"You brought the Fire Keeper outside?" Colin shakes his head, as if to mock Mom. "Outside where anyone can kidnap her?"

"You mean anyone like yourself." Mom steps in front of me. I don't know why this man keeps saying odd things, but Mom seems to understand what he's talking about. "And McKenna is too young for Keeper responsibilities. I'm the Keeper until she turns fourteen, so leave her out of this."

"She still is the Keeper, whether you like it or not. And her death will likely bring the end to the Element of Fire soon after, not yours. Acerbity needs her alive for now, so I don't believe she'll be continuing this stroll with you. Come with me, McKenna." Colin extends his hand toward me.

Mark hugs me to himself, protecting me from the man. It's as if my mother taught him to. "You're not going anywhere with my friend."

The villain laughs, silencing Mark. "Well, isn't that the sweetest thing I've heard. If you're not going to give her up, then I'll just have to take her from you."

He steps forward, and we step back. Genesis howls again, and Mom rushes forward, her hands ablaze. I look back down the street. It's empty. We're alone.

Colin reaches into his back pocket and pulls out a knife with a slick, black blade. Mom gasps, clearly recognizing it.

"Obsidian," she breathes.

"That's right, Meredith. Pure, black obsidian. No one knows why it's deadly to Elementals, but Acerbity doesn't care. If it does the job, use magic to make it more useful to the cause." He runs his hand along the flat side of the blade.

Saige pushes Kayleigh behind her. "Run," she says. "Run home. Don't stop until you get there. Don't pause for anybody, and if you see more bad guys, you escape as fast as you can, you hear? Go get our oldest sisters. You know, Jacqueline, Mia, Christine, Bethany, and Shannon. And don't come back."

"Okay," Kayleigh says, and bolts away at sixty miles per hour.

"They won't be able to help you. By the time they get here, all of you will be dead and there'll just be more fatalities. Besides,, they're only young girls. The oldest one is, what, eighteen?" He twirls his, sword, smirking.

Mom tries to blast him with her Fire powers, but the man— Colin—dodges her attempt by dropping to the ground.

"My God, Meredith," he says. "Clearly, taking care of your twelve daughters has made your fighting skills rusty. Maybe you can give me the little princesses, and I'll let you go retrain."

"No way," Mom says. "I wouldn't trade them for anything in the world."

I smile briefly, comforted by Mom's statement. Then I turn to Mark and say, "Want to go help my mom?"

"I thought you'd never ask."

It's battle time.

I take the leash off of Genesis's collar and whisper into his ear. "Hey, boy," I say. "See that man there?" I point to Colin. Genesis follows my finger. "He's bad. Go get 'em, Genesis."

He snarls and sprints towards Colin. Mark and I follow closely behind him.

Genesis bites Colin's leg, trying to use his paws to tear at the guy's leg. Colin shouts, kicking at the dog, and I use that distraction to train my palms at the hand holding the sword made of that deadly stuff, obsidian.

My aim is off and the Fire hits the sword. The obsidian seems to repel the heat and light, pushing me towards the ground. My breath escapes me for a second, and I pause to rest, dumbfounded.

"Yeah." Saige says, coming behind me and hoisting me to my feet. "That is some serious rock. You do not want to mess with it. Aim somewhere else next time."

I spot other hooded figures jogging towards us. "Maybe at his backup," I say. "Look!"

Saige whips her head around to look behind us, her red curls flying with the increasing winds. "Oh no," she says.

She trains her hands on the torso of a running figure and blasts Fire from them. The person falls, and my throat becomes a ladder my *stomach uses to climb into my throat. A death. Saige killed someone. Sure, the person was trying to kill us, too, but a death is a death is a death.*

You can't go back. You can't make them alive again.

Light brighter than the sun appears on my skin. It twists, turns, separates, and joins, creating patterns, shapes, all sorts of things. After a while it stops. I look at it for a minute. Saige gasps and I do, too. I know that picture. I've seen it once before.

On Mom's forearm.

Mark is sitting next to me when I open my eyes. He's holding my hand … which is lacking the purple blotches of obsidian poisoning. Instead, there's a thin white bracelet encircling my wrist. For some reason, I'm wearing a white spotted hospital gown, which means I must be in Elemental Hospital, two miles away from Lalande. Like the school, it's cloaked so normal humans can't find it. But unlike Lalande, Acerbity doesn't know it's here.

"You're awake! How are you feeling?" he says softly, brushing a lock of hair away from my face. He looks relieved. His face lacks the three garish scars and his hand is no longer bandaged.

A wave of tiredness washes over me. Placing a hand on my head, I reply, "Crappy, but I guess that can't be helped. What happened? How long have I been out?"

He tugs at a loose thread on my hospital blanket. "Two days. I landed on the other side of the school with Liam, but Samantha said you had fainted. Your injury was worse than anyone thought. The poison was spreading to your vital organs, and you almost died. Luckily, the doctors here know a thing or two about curing obsidian poisoning, so they were able to heal you." He swallows hard. "I was so worried that you'd … that after all we went through …" He can't finish his statement, but I know what he's trying to say. *That I'd died.* He looks at me helplessly, and I squeeze his hand.

"But I didn't. I'm still here. Thank goodness for that."

There's a flash of white light in front of my eyes, and the memories start flooding back. The first day of kindergarten: Liam cried and my older sisters laughed at him. My eighth birthday party: Mark and Liam were the only guys there. Our first actual party in sixth grade: I was dared by Miles Plaskey to kiss Mark and instead, I slapped him. I did hold Mark's hand, though. That was only because we were dared to go into West Cortlandt Cemetery and I was scared.

And the day our memories were erased. Suddenly, it all makes sense now. The dream I had ... that's where we first met Colin. That's when the marks showed up the first time.

That's how Mark knew what to do when they appeared.

"The memories I lost came back while you were asleep," Mark says in awe. "I remember everything now. Did that happen to you?"

"It happened to me just now." I say. "It's a bit overwhelming, though." Understatement of the millennium. Source: skull feels like it's collapsing in on itself.

"Don't worry, it'll go away in less than a minute."

"Oh," I say. I finally consider carefully what he said earlier. "I was asleep for two days?"

He nods. "Hope you had a good nap."

"Oh, stop."

"Okay," he says, sitting down on the edge of the bed. "So it *was* a good rest." He pauses, hesitating, like he wants to say something he thinks I won't like. "I'm going to have to leave soon."

"What?" I cry. "Where are you going?"

"Huh? I'm not going anywhere right now. I meant I'm leaving this room in a while. Your family wants to see you. Saige and Bethany told me to get out."

"You can stay. I'll deal with them."

"I don't think that's a good idea, Micky. Truth is, I'm kind of scared of them. I'm worried the rest of them are plotting against me like Saige and Bethany. There are only so many death threats a guy can take."

I roll my eyes. "Oh, please. Well, at least you're here now. Can you help me sit up?"

He takes hold of both of my hands. *Okay, McKenna. You can do this.* Ignoring the dwarf's drum solo in my head, I force myself to move into an upright position.

He gives me a big grin. "You're already getting better. I told you you're strong. Even an evil Phantom and her stupid Tunnels with stupid rules can't keep you down."

Stupid Tunnels with stupid rules.

Amelie.

Immediately, I start crying.

Huge, salty tears roll down my face and hang off my chin as I make sounds not humanly or Elementally possible. *Amelie. She's not here. She's gone. She's not coming back.* Mark says nothing; instead, he holds me in his arms and rubs my back. I hate that I'm an ugly crier. I hate Felicity Caste for casting the spell that put that rule there in the first place. I hate the Tunnels and its stupid rules. I hate that I'm weak after working so hard to become fearless. I hate having to depend on everybody, including Mark. I hate, I hate, I hate.

Eventually, I run out of tears and I'm left sitting there, sniffling like I've got H1N1. Mark still isn't speaking, and the fact that he's letting me get snot on his shoulder and cry all over him makes my love for him practically double.

"Sorry about that," I say sheepishly, blowing my nose with tissues from a box conveniently placed next to my hospital bed. "You didn't say anything wrong. I just can't believe Amelie's gone."

He nods sadly. "Same here." Pause. Then, "Could you pass me the box?"

"Oh, yeah. Sure. Of course. Sorry about your shirt." I feel a pang of guilt. "I'll replace it as soon as I can."

"No, no, it's fine." He swipes at the fabric until everything's gone. I'm sure I looked very hot and awesome while I was blubbering like a toddler and not at all disturbing. "Nothing's ruined." After tossing the tissues successfully into the garbage can, he pulls me back into his arms and we sit there, my chin resting on his shoulder.

"Better?" Mark asks after a while, leaning back to look at me.

"Better." I pull him in towards me. It's the Kiss of Life. With each second, I get back what I lost right when the silver bullet casing fell off. Confidence. Composure. Authority. Once again, he is helping me complete myself.

It could have gone on longer. At least, I think it could have. But I'll never know, because the door to the hospital room opens and Dad walks in. Mark and I break away from each other quickly. *He's here?*

"Dad!" I shriek, fumbling with my covers. I have to get to him. Now. Never mind the fact that I have an IV in my arm. My head protests. I've interrupted the dwarves' band practice.

"Whoa, Micky," Dad cautions. He walks over to my bedside. "You need to stay in bed until they discharge you. You seem fine, though, by the looks of it." He looks at Mark, then me, then Mark again. Saige and Bethany get their sense of humor from him. "What's up, Mark? Haven't seen you in a long time."

"Nothing much, Mr. Donaldson. It's great to see you again. How're you holding up?"

"Pretty well, now that this rascal over here is out of the house," he jokes. "I'm just kidding." He's aged a bit: his hairline has receded just a bit, gray hairs have started to pop up among the brown ones, and he has smile lines by his wise, gray eyes. *Dad's getting older.* The thought makes me a little scared.

I poke his muscled arm. "Have you seen Mom?"

"As a matter of fact, I haven't. I've been looking for her, but she's probably busy. I talked to Olivia, though. She was the one who told me to come over here."

Mark and I share a glance. Why would *Olivia* call Dad? Why not Mom? Is she avoiding him?

Dad leans down to give me a hug. "I've missed you so much, Micky." His voice is muffled because his face is buried in my hair.

"I missed you too, Dad," I say. I hold him against me tightly. I don't want to let him go.

Mark doesn't look uncomfortable when I look over at him. He looks happy. I know his parents are due for a visit this week, so his life's pretty good right now. And that makes me happy as well.

"So, you two are together, huh?" Dad says after he pulls away. When we both nod, he chuckles. "I told Meredith it was only a matter of time."

"Why is everyone talking about it?" I groan, lying back on my bed. "It's not even a big deal."

"You're right, it's not. When you two were younger, everyone thought you were going to get together when you got older. Even though Meredith got someone to wipe your memories, I still believed it could happen. And it did." He smiles at Mark. "Did Saige and Bethany harass you yet?"

Mark nods sheepishly.

"Don't let that scare you. I've tried to get them to stop doing it, but you know how stubborn they are. They're a bit overprotective of their sisters, especially the younger ones."

"That's for dang sure," I mutter.

The hospital door flies open again. This time it's Mom. She looks well rested. She's holding a tray of drinks, her crazy red hair is coaxed into a side braid, and she's actually smiling … at least until she spots Dad. The tray slips from her hands, but she doesn't seem to notice. She sprints towards Dad like an Olympian off the blocks. Dad does the same.

"Phillip!" she shrieks like a little girl. "What are you doing here?"

"Olivia called me," he says, wrapping his arms around her. "Meredith, I can't believe you're back." They're so happy, so in love, I don't know how I doubted them for a second.

Mark sits back down next to me, slinging an arm around my waist. It's kind of uncomfortable watching my parents reunite. Even though I know how they feel, it's always gross to see your parents kissing.

"I wish I could leave," I whisper to him. "Then I wouldn't have to see this."

"It's sweet," Mark differs.

"It's like they don't even know we're here."

"That's a good thing, though," Mark says into my ear. "They won't notice me doing this." His lips leave a ghost of a kiss on my cheek.

Mom breaks away and stares at us. "Nice try, guys." My family seems to have a knack for interrupting romantic moments.

"It was a cheek kiss!" I protest.

"I'm joking. Glad you're awake, McKenna. I knew you'd fight."

The door swings open for the third time, and my sisters cram themselves into the hospital room. We're breaking the two-visitor rule right now, but who cares? My family's all together.

"Who dropped these drinks?" Emma Marie shrieks. She bends over and picks up the cups. Then she waves her hand and the water dries up. "Be more careful!"

"I'm going to go," Mark whispers. "Spend some time with your family."

"Okay, bye." I give him one last hug. "Go ... smell some roses or something."

"That reminds me!" he exclaims. "I almost forgot to give you these." He reaches under the bed and pulls out a bouquet of flowers. "For you."

I recognize them as Natalie's flowers. They're sweet smelling tiger lilies. I wonder how he knew they were my favorite. "Thanks! Tiger lilies are my favorite. How'd you know?"

"I asked Natalie. She grew them on the spot."

"You are a very thoughtful person." I say in a British accent.

"Why thank you, Ms. Donaldson. Care for a spot of tea?"

"That would be lovely, Mr. O'Reilly." Mark pours me a cup of fake tea, and after clinking teacups, we pretend to take sips.

"Stop it," Joy groans. "You two are insufferably cheesy."

Mark and I crack up. I might have spilled my tea all over myself, but that's okay. I can't be burned. I think we might be going mad.

He stands up, stretching his arms. "I'll be back later. Rebecca and Patrick got out of the ICU yesterday, and I haven't had time to see them." He presses a kiss to my lips and walks out of the room.

As soon as he's gone, everyone looks at me. Mia spots the flowers and takes them from me. "If you want these to last longer, you need to put them in water." She looks around the room for a vase.

"Those were created by an Earthen," Christine comments. "They'll stay fresh for a really long time. Forty-four days on average. Not exactly *everlasting* flowers, but they're nice all the same."

Kristen and Lauren creep up to my bedside. They look surprised for some reason. Identically surprised. "I didn't know you were that kind of person, Micky," Kristen says.

"Yeah," Lauren agrees.

"What's that supposed to mean?" I say.

"The kind of person to follow stereotypes," Kristen explains. "You know, girl and boy are best friends from childhood, then they get together when they get older, then they get married later on. You don't seem like the kind of person to be a conformist."

That might have been the most she's spoken at one time. She looks exhausted by that long statement. "If you were any other person, I'd be super mad at you for saying that." Besides Emma Marie, I'm closer to Kristen and Lauren than any of my sisters, probably because they're my immediate younger sisters. Because of that, they get away with things the others can't. "I am so not a conformist."

"You're right," Lauren says. "You're not a conformist. You're the Fire Keeper. You're a hero."

"I'm not a hero, either," I frown. And it's true. I'm not a hero. I didn't even lead the mission into the Tunnels. Natalie did. Ugh. I have to stop thinking about the Tunnels. When I do, I remember Amelie, and that gets me worked up.

Wait. Lauren said Fire Keeper. Fire. The obsidian poison is out of my system. My hands are unmarked and unblocked.

Maybe I can create fire again.

I flex my fingers. The Fire in my veins pulses and flares. It's like it knows I'm about to do something big. *Okay, breathe. Then create.*

The flames dance in my palm, applauding me for my triumph.

Chapter Twenty-Seven

If I wasn't desperately trying not to burst into tears, I'd be bothered by this itchy black dress. It's not even mine. But it wasn't like I planned to go to more funerals this summer, so I didn't ask my dad to send me a dress. Plus, dresses made by witches always feel weird on me. Raven and I may be the same size, but her taste in black clothing is way different than mine. Hence the netting underneath the skirt and lace three-quarter sleeves. I drew the line at her fingerless gloves. Is she *trying* to be the Gothest Goth to have ever Gothed?

Emma is openly crying next to me, but unlike me, whose face gets all blotchy when I shed tears, she manages to look even more beautiful. Water Users are odd people.

The wooden casket in the front of the chapel obviously doesn't have Amelie in it. Instead, we filled it with pictures of her, some of her favorite things, and, of course, her video camera with her videos. I guess it's a good substitute for her actual body, but it still is burying some of our memories of her.

"And now McKenna Donaldson with the eulogy." Dean Papadopoulos nods at me. It's time. She came up to me a couple days after I was discharged and asked if I wanted to write and give the eulogy. I said yes, because why not? I was her best friend. Three days and seven crumpled papers later—God, I hate that number—I had the perfect eulogy.

I stand up and walk to the microphone stand. I clear my throat. Behind me is a PowerPoint Amek Leasy pulled together. They were friends in Mrs. Strothers's photography/videography class last year, so he was more than happy to create it. "Amelie Annabelle Avanti was the kind of person who would lend you a dollar if you needed one. In fact, that's how I met her two years ago. I was trying to do my laundry a couple days after I arrived, and I realized that I was short a dollar. Well, Amelie came in that very second, and, after introducing herself, gave me some money. It was like she was waiting for me to come in just so she could give me a buck. She was like that with everyone. Someone made a joke about her being Santa Claus. That Halloween, she dressed up as him, and for Christmas, she put on a suit and went around doing various good deeds for everyone. And she never asked for anything in return.

"Behind me is a slideshow, courtesy of Amek Leasy. Amelie took all these pictures. Photography was her passion. When she wasn't helping people out, she was taking pictures or shooting videos." I pause for a moment so people can admire her work. The photos are so good. Amelie was always talking about lighting and darkrooms and exposure and whatnot. If she was still alive, I'd bet anything she would have made a career out of it.

"A lot of people don't know how she died. There've been rumors that she was ripped apart by a monster, or that she was killed by Acerbity, or other theories. And to be honest, I can see how that could have been confusing because details about our expedition are still kind of fuzzy. So I'm just going clear things up now." I take a deep breath. "After we defeated Acerbity, we tried to get out of the Tunnels, but we couldn't. We couldn't leave unless someone sacrificed themselves, thanks to a spell that the most powerful Phantom in history, Felicity Caste, cast. No one else wanted to do it, but she volunteered. And that's what happened. She gave herself up because she knew that the Tunnels were about to collapse on us."

I open my mouth to continue speaking, but I can't. Alexis Avanti leaps up out of her seat and races out of the chapel, tears streaming down her face. She is quickly followed by Amek. Everyone watches them go, looking just as confused as I am. Alexis never gave a toe bone about her twin sister. So why is she crying now?

Clearing my throat, I look down at my notes so I can pick up where I left off. My throat tightens up, and a tear drops onto an index card. No. No. I can't cry here. Not during her eulogy. I should be a dried up husk now. I should be incapable of crying. *Hold them back. You're almost done. Just get through the last part, and then you can leave.*

But the tears keep coming.

"*Grietzi*," I whisper into the mic, and, ducking my head, I dash out of the chapel.

I don't look up even when Mom plops down on the ground in the car garage besides me. I blew it in there. I can't believe I let them see me crack. Mom clears her throat, just like I did. I don't look at her. It's her fault. All her fault. If she didn't go into those goddamned Tunnels, we wouldn't have had to go after them. And then Amelie wouldn't have had to die.

"That was a nice eulogy," Mom starts.

I don't look at her.

"She sounded like a special girl," she tries again.

Is that all she has to say? "A special girl?" I cry. "She could have had a life! She could have become a photographer. She could have gotten married, had kids, done so many things, but you just *had* to chicken out against Acerbity and drag everyone down there. Did you know Acerbity attacked the school? They detonated two bombs, one outside the girls' dorm and one outside the boys'. Five students died. Then the four of us received death letters from Acerbity. We had to go in there and persuade you to come out. Otherwise, The Tunnels would have caved in on themselves and *you would have died*. She saved your life." I stand up and kick Amelie's bike. "It's not fair! No one was supposed to die on our mission."

Frustrated, I lift the motorcycle in the air with my powers and, piece by piece, I rip it apart with my bare hands. Metal pieces fly everywhere, but I bring them together and weld them into a ball. It's not until after the whole thing's destroyed—and a tire falls on my foot—that I realize, as my heart races, that I completely freaked out.

Mom looks shocked by my outburst as well. I was holding back more than I realized. And once I got a chance to, my words became a nonstop downpour. Unfortunately, Mom was the one who got wet.

"I had my reasons for leaving." A second passes before she says, "I owe you an explanation, though."

I don't say anything.

She groans. "This location is a little unsavory, but it'll have to do. On your fourteenth birthday, while you were at the mall with Maritone and Mariah, I received a text. It was from a number I'd gotten texts from before, so I was on alert. Usually they're empty threats, but not that day. It said that they were holding you, the other Keepers, and a child of every important Elemental leader in America hostage in the Tunnels, and they were going to kill you.

"Naturally, I called your cell, but it was turned off. I tried your friends' cell phones and their parents', but they were off, too. So I called around, and everyone was getting the same results with their own children. Your father and I went to the mall, but you were nowhere to be found. We had no other choice. We contacted the Elementals officials, and together we marched down to the city. Now I know that you were accosted by Acerbitians posing as run-of-the-mill criminals on your way to Maritone's house. The other children had similar things happen to them."

I remember that robbery like it was yesterday. Some old creeps tried to take advantage of Mariah and me. Some ignored Maritone because apparently she was "only a five". Police officers arrived on scene before anything really bad happened to us, but it was still traumatizing.

"We went through the Met, just like you did. I'm not sure what we expected to find, but we went. And when we combed the Tunnels for hours, we realized we were tricked. I don't know what their trap was supposed to accomplish. All I know is that we couldn't leave. We made a life for ourselves down there. We dug out the space below the main paths and concealed it. We locked up the Compass Doors—we had the spares—and hid there. We didn't have any means to contact you, because there wasn't any reception underground. Are you happy now?"

I was wrong. I was so wrong. All this time, I thought they ran away from Acerbity, when really they ran towards them. For me. For Emma. For Natalie. For Sam. I nod, speechless.

"Good. Oh, one more thing. It's about your relationship with Mark O'Reilly. I know you don't want people to make a huge deal about you and him, but it's important."

I groan. "Mom, I already know the spiel. Say no, keep your pants on, no-no zone … I was briefed by Dad before I even came to this school."

"Glad to hear it, but that's not what I wanted to talk about. When you … when you got the Fire Marks on your arms, Mark was the person that helped you remove them. The same thing happened four years ago. The memory loss severed your link, but … It got me thinking … answer me honestly, McKenna. This is extremely important. Did you—are you in love with him? Like did you say the actual words, 'I love you' to him? My goodness, this is awkward."

She's onto me. It's so weird to talk with your mother about your love life. I kind of want to give her the wrong answer. But I know she'd call my bluff. "Yeah. I did."

"When?"

"In the Tunnels, a couple of minutes before we fell through the floor. We thought we were going to die." When she laughs, I cross my arms. "It was very movie-esque."

"But do you actually love him? Or was it a spur-of-the-moment thing?"

I can't help but smile just a little. "Yeah, I do."

Mom groans, rubbing her forehead with her hand. "That's a problem. A big, huge problem."

"Why?"

"Don't you know? When a Keeper first falls in love, the person becomes the Keeper's Guardian."

"Is that a bad thing?"

"The role of a Guardian is to protect the Keeper at all costs. The Guardian is able to sense when you're hurt, or about to be, or if something is bothering you. Then they do everything in their power to save you, whether they want to or not. So no, it's not a problem when you're twenty-seven, but when you're almost seventeen, it kind of is. Many Guardians die protecting their Keeper, and seeing as Acerbity has stooped low enough to try and exterminate sixteen-year-olds, it's not looking good for Mark."

"You're sure he's my Guardian?"

"I can see it in his eyes, and Thomas has been peeking into his thoughts. Mark is in love with you, and since you both said it out loud, he's going to be protecting you for the rest of his—or your—life."

Chapter Twenty-Eight

"I think it's a great idea," Dean Martin says. "It's a wonderful way to welcome the Elementals back to the real world."

I think we've had enough death to last a lifetime, is what he means. We've had almost one hundred funerals in two months, and to be honest, the Elemental community would probably crack if another person died. So yes. Mark's idea is a splendid one.

"Thanks for hearing me out," Mark smiles, standing up. He looks happy today. "It's going to be a great party."

He holds the door open for me as we exit Dean's office. The outside air has the bittersweet aroma of the upcoming first day of school. September starts today, and it just happens to be Labor Day. It's also Jackson's seventeenth birthday, so this party—at least for him and us, his friends—is also his birthday celebration.

"I didn't think he'd say yes," Mark exhales. "You know he's still mad at us for disobeying him. But I don't know how he'd be able to say no. Everyone needs something to take his or her mind off all this death and destruction. It'll lighten spirits."

"You bet it will. We need to start planning."

He smiles mischievously. "Already on it. I told everyone to start before we talked to him. They should have gotten a lot done by now."

"What? Why? What if he said no?"

"Then we'd take the decorations down. The party's supposed to be tonight, McKenna. We need to get as much done as possible."

A huge crack in the sidewalk pitches me forward. The pavement gets bigger for half a second … then stops. Mark has me in his arms. Adrenaline courses through my body, giving me the feeling I get when I'm about to fall down the stairs but catch myself in time. He stopped me from falling, but how did he get to me so fast? I barely even knew I was going down, so how did he?

"How'd you do that?" I ask.

He looks dazed. "I'm not sure. You were falling. You would have gotten hurt, so I grabbed you before you did."

A feeling of dread washes over me. The Guardian thing. Apparently, it applies to everyday bumps and scratches, too. Damn. I knew I'd have to tell him someday, but I wasn't expecting it to be so soon. I can't hold it from him any longer. It's been a week. And plus, he looks so confused.

But how am I supposed to tell him he's supposed to protect me for the rest of his life?

"Come with me," I say. "I need to tell you something."

"**Will you tell** me now?" Mark complains.

"We're almost there. Calm your Titusville." I sidestep a big rock. The lake should be coming up soon. It's one of the only places we can be alone today. Everybody's everywhere, prepping the entire school for the party, inside and outside, which makes no sense. The party's supposed to be outdoors.

The murky waters come into view now. I clench my jaw at the very sight of the lake. Mark picks up a small, flat rock and skips it across.

"*Now* can you tell me?"

I sigh. "Do you know what a Guardian is? Like, a *Guardian*, Guardian?"

"Yeah. Someone who protects another person. Why do you ask?" Another stone, this time round, is tossed into the lake.

I clear my throat. "Well, Mark, there's this ancient Elemental tradition. When a Keeper, um … this is so embarrassing."

"It's okay. You don't need to be embarrassed." The morning sun makes his smiling face even brighter.

"Okay. Um." I train my eyes on the rippling water. "My mom and I were talking last week, and she gave me some interesting information. And since it concerns you, I thought I should tell you. When a Keeper falls in love, er, that person becomes their Guardian. Granted, the Guardian is in love with the Keeper, too, so it's not awkward. And basically, the person's job is to protect the Keeper at all costs. Even if it means the person's death. Most of the time, the action is involuntary, like what happened when I fell. It's kind of inconvenient, but it's forever." I want to babble on and on, just so I won't have to face the silent seconds before he responds. But there's nothing else to say.

The silent seconds become a silent minute, then two. I don't look at his face. His pained expression might kill me. So when he says, "That's it?", I'm confused.

"What?"

"That's all you wanted to tell me? I thought you had bad news." My eyes flick up to his face. That is not a 'pained expression' voice. Why isn't he angry?

"Isn't it, though? Your whole life is no longer yours. You could die trying to protect me."

"Then it would be a death worth dying." He pauses for a moment, waiting for me to understand. But I don't. "McKenna, I *want* to protect you. Keeping you safe is important. I'm honored to have that job now."

Why does he not comprehend the impending danger? "Mark. Listen to me. *I* make you vulnerable. Do you understand me? I could be the cause of your death. Acerbity could capture me, then threaten to do terrible things to me, and you'd have no choice but to do whatever it is they want you to do. As a Guardian, your first instinct is to defend me. You can't fight it. This isn't like some Jiminy Cricket conscience nagging you. Your body does the action before your brain tells it to."

"That's okay." He looks frustrated. "That is fine with me. It's worth it. If I save you but end up dying, it's a job well done. And you know why? Because you have a job as well. You're the Fire Keeper. You protect the Firestone. If you die, it gets destroyed, and all the Fire Wielders die. Everyone has to work hard to keep you alive. Including you. So don't worry about me. I can take care of myself. If I die, millions of people won't perish, too. And don't worry about my life not being my own. I want to be artist—but don't tell my parents that. Or my basketball teammates. I technically don't need to go to some high-and-mighty, prestigious school for it." He tosses a medium sized rock into the lake. "Besides, I love you. Don't you realize this is the perfect job for me?"

Sparks roll down my spine as he says the scariest three-word phrase ever. He has me there. And he's right. I do have a responsibility to uphold. I need to trust that he can take care of himself. Acerbity isn't constantly trying to kill him.

"Okay. I'm sorry. Everything's changing so fast right now. I—I can't help but worry about you … about losing you, too. Especially because I feel like I'm dragging you down with all my baggage."

Mark laughs, startling me. "Why would you think that?" he says. "All this *baggage,* as you call it? It's bringing us closer together. And that vulnerability thing? I'm used to it. I think I've always been vulnerable when it comes to you, Micky D."

"You are the only guy I know who would think that way. Did you know that? Sometimes I'll anticipate your reaction to something, based on what I've seen from other guys, and you'll turn around and react in the oddest way possible. That's a good thing, don't worry."

"So first I'm thoughtful, and now I'm odd?" He laughs again, this time pulling me into his arms. "Make up your mind, McKenna."

"And you have to make up your mind about what you're going to call me. Switching between Micky and McKenna is a bit inconsistent. Most people just call me one or the other."

"Can I just call you beautiful? Or stunning? Or amazing? Or—"

"I like real names better."

"Okay," he says. "Anna Banana Fofana it is."

"You're lucky I love you."

"Why? Would you have shocked me with your enhanced, post-obsidian-poisoning Keeper powers?"

"Never. I'd never hurt the people I love. Not on purpose, anyway." I lay my head on his chest. "Besides, you're resistant to that kind of stuff, remember? You're a Fire Wielder, too."

I close my eyes and listen to the beat of his heart, trying to become familiar with it. They say two sweethearts' heartbeats will synchronize after a while. I can already feel it happening. And I hope, for Mark's sake, Liam's sake, his family's sake, his friends' sake, and mine, his heart will beat for a long, long time.

By lunchtime, most of the decorations are up. Red, blue, green, and white lanterns are hanging from the trees on the quad, bopping in the breeze. Us Fire Wielders will light them tonight. Ella Credjwell and a boy named Logan Colbenár have volunteered to DJ the event. Some tables have been set up for refreshments. Natalie is overseeing the whole thing, walking around the quad, fixing things, shouting directions to everyone.

"Testing, testing, one, two, three," Ella's voice crackles through the speakers. "One, two, three. Check, check. Logan, it works."

Natalie rushes up to me, looking triumphant. "The kitchen staff is going to finish early. I calculated everything, and if we continue like this, we'll have five hours to relax after we finish decorating."

"That's great," I smile. "Need any help?"

"No, I think we're good." she says. "We're almost done here."

I wave goodbye and start walking away. It's a beautiful afternoon. The sky is the perfect shade of blue, the leaves in the trees are a vivid green, and the atmosphere on the quad is a happy, light one. The white clouds are nice and puffy. There's an Elemental saying that the clouds are the ghosts of those who've gone before us. When things aren't going well, that's when they turn all dark and ominous. I know that's not actually how things work, but it's nice to pretend sometimes. One right above my head kind of looks like a camera. I decide that one is Amelie.

The sun shines on the school, making it look welcoming. *Ha,* I laugh to myself. If any human saw this place, they'd think it was a normal school. They'd have no idea what went on these past two months.

I decide to go wherever my feet take me, since I don't really have anywhere to go. Before I know it, I'm standing in front of the library. Shrugging, I open the door. Reading sounds good right about now.

Even though it's now September, it's still hot, which makes me happy. But this also means the library's A/C is on full blast. Shivering, I scour the fiction shelves. Tolkien, Toren, Traore … nothing interests me. My eyes wander around the shelf … then the rest of the shelves … then the whole library …

And then I see it.

I can't believe I didn't notice it before. It's in the back, way back. The wall in the rear shimmers and ripples, and if I squint hard enough, I can see the faint outline of a door. I start walking toward it. Why would they cloak a door in the library?

"Ms. Donaldson. What do you think you're doing?"

I whip around, heart pumping wildly. Mrs. Lazarus is standing right behind me with her arms crossed and lips pursed.

"Students are not allowed back here." She pauses for a moment. "How did you see the door?"

"It's easy," I say, still in shock from the scare. "It keeps rippling."

Her eyebrows rise, like she can't believe someone like her could fail at making wards. "You need to leave. You can't be back here."

"What's going on here?" Ms. Unquist comes up behind Mrs. Lazarus. "Is everything okay?"

Mrs. Lazarus uncrosses her arms. "Ms. Donaldson seems to think she is Nancy Drew. I was just sending her away. She informed me the wards were weak."

Ms. Unquist nods like she already knows. "Thank you. I'll take it from here."

Mrs. Lazarus is rendered speechless. I want to do a victory dance or something. I never liked her. She looks like she swallowed a lemon while simultaneously watching someone get mud all over her newly washed car. And on top of that, she's labeled me as a troublemaker.

"So," Ms. Unquist smiles. "You found the door to the back room."

I shrug. "Honestly, I didn't even know the library *had* a back room."

"I think it's time I showed you what's inside." She pulls out a key from her dress pocket and sticks it in the faint lock. She looks around to see if anyone's watching. Nobody. Turning the handle, she pulls the invisible door open and we go inside.

Darkness. Must. Dust. I cough, and Ms. Unquist shushes me. "Someone could hear us! I'm not supposed to let anyone in here."

I cough again. "Sorry. Maybe the next time someone comes down here, they could, I don't know, bring a duster with them or something."

"No one comes down here but me, McKenna. Not even Diane."

"Who's Diane?"

"Mrs. Lazarus."

"Oh. Right. I knew that."

I reach out for a light switch. If I try to provide a light source, the books might catch fire. Or the dust in the air. Eventually I give up after a minute of searching. All I feel are books.

The lights flick on. Ms. Unquist gives me a look while holding the cord. Whoops.

"You know you could have turned it on with your powers, right?"

I shake my head. "After everything that's been going on, I don't want to risk setting this place on fire." The room is smaller than I originally thought. Shelves cover every inch of the walls, except for the door and the peeling ceiling, of course. Old, dusty books are neatly arranged in the shelves, with titles like, *Introduction to Mistemintea, Healing 101,* and *Vervortade for Dummies.* A few are new, like the *Dummies* one, but most look like textbooks for college students who studied by candlelight.

"Many of these were written in the nineteenth century," Ms. Unquist explains. So I *was* right. "Then for some reason, in the eighties, Elementals all over the country stopped using them. We managed to snag a lot of them before they were deemed unsafe materials by the Legion and burned."

"Why were they deemed unsafe? Seems like these do more good than harm. I know I could use *The Complete Guide to Pyrokinesis,* since I'm still learning how to control power surges."

"I don't know, McKenna," Ms. Unquist sighs. "I don't know." She gazes around the room with a wistful expression before saying, "Why don't you have a quick look around? We'll need to go back soon."

"I can?" I didn't think she'd let me.

"Sure."

I finally do my little victory dance, before reaching out for the *Pyrokinesis* guide. All the books on its shelf are jammed next to each other, so I can't pull it out easily. My face contorts into a frown as I use more force. The book seems to be stuck in there, as if it's glued to the ones next to it.

I use one last tug, and everything goes wrong. The books fall out and the shelf comes crashing forward. At least I have the good sense to jump away before I'm crushed. Ms. Unquist looks on in horror.

The dust settles after a minute. Books and wood boards are all over the floor. A feeling of dread bubbles up inside me. I did it again. I messed something up.

"Omigod. Ms. Unquist, I sorry. I am *so* sorry. So sorry. Here, let me pick it up—"

"No!" she shouts. "I mean, you've done enough." She holds a hand to her forehead. "You should probably go back. I'll clean it up."

"But I was the one who knocked it over," I argue.

"It's fine, McKenna," she says with that adult tone that means *case closed*. "I will take care of it."

I leave the back room feeling dejected. What if she never lets me back in? Mrs. Lazarus would be so pleased. Fire pulses in my veins. I shouldn't be surprised I somehow exited the back room without opening a single book. It's so typical.

I know I have to find a way to get back in there, though. I have to. I saw more than just how-to books in there, which makes me suspicious. We know close to nothing about Elemental history. But in that small room, in the back of the library, a thick book caught my eye.

Fire: A History.

Chapter Twenty-Nine

The junior girls' dorm floor is a flurry of excitement. Half of us are treating it like it's prom. The other half, myself included, knows it's not a big deal. It's just a party. A "Yay, You Survived!" party. It's not about us. It's about them.

Emma stands in front of the floor-length mirror, gazing at her reflection. She's part of the fifty percent that's taking this way too seriously. She holds a necklace adorned with blue stones to her throat, turning this way and that. The light from the window hits it in all the right places, and she smiles.

"This looks good, right?"

Natalie shrugs, and I do, too. Sam glances up from her think novel and smiles. "That looks nice, but you already have a blue 'necklace' on. You want to put it on top of the Waterstone?"

"True." She fluffs her hair. "I just need him to notice me."

"Who's 'him'?" I ask, though I already know who it is. "And why does he need to notice you?"

She sighs, exasperated. "You know the answer to that question."

"And anyway," Natalie adds, "This party isn't for you. It's a 'welcome home, glad you're not dead' get-together for the Elementals we rescued."

"I know, but this is only chance I can show off until homecoming!" She clasps the necklace around her neck. "You see how this is crucial, right? I need him to ask me to junior prom. This is giving me a head start." I have to fight the urge to roll my eyes. Junior prom isn't until May. A head start would be mid-March. And she doesn't need a head start. Emma's already impossibly beautiful. Add that to the short navy dress with the tulle skirt that looks like ocean waves, and everyone else pales in comparison.

I'm dressed, too, but I don't look anywhere near as beautiful as her. My royal blue number is a cute sundress and the only I brought to Lalande. I've stopped growing, so it still fits me. Natalie refuses to wear a dress, but we forced her into a green skater skirt. Sam is wearing a floor-length pale pink dress that can only be described as dreamy.

After putting on her prized sapphire dangle earrings, Emma turns back to us. "Are you guys ready?"

"Em." Sam carefully puts a bookmark in her book and tosses it up on her bed. "We've been ready for an hour."

"Oh." She looks surprised. "You should have said something, then."

"But then you wouldn't have put enough time into your so-called 'head start'," I smirk. "We wanted to be courteous."

She flicks water at me. "Shut up. That's a nice dress, by the way."

"Um … thanks."

I can't stop thinking about the texts in the library. I need to go over them again, while there's still time. There's so much history we missed, so much knowledge to be uncovered. And all of it is locked away in the private area of a library of a private school. No one knows about it. No one has any idea of where they came from. But the info is right there. It's plain wrong.

I make my decision quickly. "I need to go check on something, guys. I'll meet you at the dance?"

"Where are you going?" Natalie looks confused.

"No time to explain." I grab my small handbag and race out the door before my face has time to get red. "Got to go!"

I don't stop sprinting until I know I'm safe in the library. I took all the back roads so no one would know where I went. I don't need them knowing about this right now. Later. That's right. I'll tell them later.

My heart won't stop racing.

It's kind of weird that no one thought to look here for ancient texts. I mean, come on. It's the freaking library. And in the movies, the books with all the answers are in the private area of the library, the one you need to be eighteen or have special permission. My guess is everyone decided they weren't going to get any answers about why they could control the elements, so they didn't bother looking.

Ms. Unquist looks up from the tabloid she's reading at her desk. The headline urges me to turn to page ten for "Seven Tricks to Keep Your Man Interested!" I'm going to pretend I didn't see that. "Back again?" she smiles. "Shouldn't you be getting ready for the party?"

"I am ready." I gesture to my dress. "My hair is behaving and I'm not wearing pants. That should be enough."

She chuckles in that pleasant grandmotherly way. "I see. But don't you want to be just a little extravagant? The party's giving you a chance to meet people you wouldn't have spoken to otherwise. You'd want to look your best, if you know what I mean."

Ugh. More people talking about my love life. I appreciate that she's looking out for me, but really. If she's trying to be subtle it sure isn't working. "Thanks for the advice, Ms. Unquist, but I'm already dating someone."

I really hope the seven people silently reading in here aren't eavesdropping.

"Oh?" She looks surprised. Why is everyone surprised I'm in a relationship? Even Raven is, with that emo guy Max, and she's, like, the most unpleasant person ever. "Who is it?"

"Um, Mark. Mark O'Reilly."

"How wonderful." And it sounds like she means it, too. Maybe entering a relationship is a Keeper responsibility. If it is, though, then it's an annoying one.

An awkward silence ensues.

"I suppose you want to check out the books in the private area." When I nod my head, she smiles impishly. "Unfortunately, Diane left early today, so I have to stay here in the front. You'll have to go by yourself. Is that okay?"

Is that okay? It's better than okay! Now I can look at the books I avoided when I came here the last time. I wonder how she knew I was holding back. Still, I smile. "That's fine." I hurry to the back before she can change her mind.

The door to the back is locked, as usual. The librarians are the only ones with the key. Agh, the key! I forgot to ask her about it. I turn around and start to head back when it appears in my hand. I look up, startled. Ms. Unquist shakes her head. "*Wamekir commen.*"

"*Grietzi.*"

The back room still has that musty dust-and-pages smell. Maybe it's permanent. The books are back in order after I messed everything up. I'm surprised she let me in here again. The tomes themselves seem to sit on the shelves in scorn.

Water Users: A History. Sounds geared towards Emma's people. *Why You Shouldn't Trust Your Keeper.* Okay, that one's plain rude. But it does have a point. I wouldn't trust me, either. *How To Control Your Powers, Volume One.* I wonder if Ms. Unquist would notice if I snuck out with that book underneath my dress. She probably would. In my defense, though, I need all the help I can get. So the last couple of days will be spent not hanging out with my friends and family, much as I'd like them to be. Nope, I'll be powering through volumes one *and* two *and* three *and* four *and* five of that series.

The lighting in here is great, probably because if it wasn't, people like me would start seeing things that aren't there even before we left the room. All this magic is making my head and teeth hurt.

See, things like Emma. God, it's already starting to happen. Lord knows she wouldn't be caught dead in this room, and my imagination wants me to believe she's walking up to me. Am I that soft? I haven't even opened a book yet!

"So this is where you went," Pretend Emma frowns, crossing my eyes. "Sam had a feeling you'd be here."

I close my eyes. If I talk to the image, I might go even crazier.

"McKenna?"

I turn back to the books. I'll start with *Fire: A History.*

"Why aren't you answering?"

Maybe I *should* tell it to go away so I can focus on blowing the dust off of this thing. Otherwise I won't be able to read it.

"I know you're just a figment of my imagination, so stop. Just go away. Leave me alone."

The image looks bewildered. "What?" She shakes her head. "No, McKenna, you're confused. I'm actually here. This is Emma in the flesh. I promise Alexis isn't messing with your vision. Here, feel." She stretches her hand out, and I touch it. It's real. She's real.

Crap.

"Why are you here?" She looks at the fat books on the table. "Why are you in the library, half an hour before the party, reading—" She dusts the cover off. "*Fire: A History?*"

I roll my eyes. "What else would I be reading? *Diary of a Wimpy Kid?*"

"You didn't answer my question. What's all this about?"

"If you must know, I got to thinking about our existence. It struck me as odd that no one knew squat about the history of the Elementals. So I decided to do a little research."

She opens the book and flips through the pages. "'Fire Wielders have been around millions of years, stretching back to the first humans.' No duh. I could have told you that."

"Give me that." I pull the book away from her. "Shouldn't you be getting a head start on you-know-who?"

"He's not out yet. Besides, this is more important."

"Well, if you're going to be here, at least get a book that applies to you," I say indignantly. "Geez. Look, there's *Water Users: A History.*"

She doesn't look in that direction. Instead, she tugs *Why You Shouldn't Trust Your Keeper* out of a nearby shelf. Scanning the pages, she snorts. "What's their beef with the Keepers? We're not bad people."

"Maybe there were some dangerous ones before us," I offer. *Like Michael, the maniac Fire Wielder.*

Emma sets the book down on the table and reaches for *Water Users: A History.* After a minute of reading, she looks up at me, beaming. "McKenna, this is great! Can you believe this? All this history ... this is important stuff! I can't believe *nobody* thought to read this. This who we are. We need to let everyone know about it."

I set my hand on her arm. "Whoa there, NASCAR driver. We need to read all this stuff first. Get a good glimpse of everything before we start spilling secrets, or whatever."

"But they need to know."

"I agree. But what if Acerbity launches another attack on the school? What if they go after the library next time? It isn't protected like the dorms. We know that we have a spy at school."

"If there *is* a next time," she argues.

"Yeah, yeah, God forbid. But it's a possibility. You and I both know no one can replace books they've never even read. We need to read them so we can tell everyone what the contents of the books were in the event that they get destroyed. Understand?"

She nods.

"Good." I shelve my book. "You said we had thirty minutes?"

She looks at her watch. "It's more like five now."

"Oh. Oops. Then we have to hurry." I help her put her selections back where they belong. I feel a sense of relief when I do, like I want them to be covered up. But that's not true. Too much of Elemental business has been covered up. It's time for us to face the music.

After saying good night to Ms. Unquist, Emma gives me a look as we exit. "Whatever we do, you need to tell Natalie and Sam about it. They deserve to know."

"Why would you think I wouldn't?" The noise is coming from the quad. The red, blue, green, and white lights are visible from our location. They lit the lanterns without me. Oh, well. This was more important. "They're Keepers."

"Just making sure." She breathes in deeply, adjusting her dress. "You wouldn't happen to know if Liam mentioned me in a conversation, would you?"

I laugh, making her huff. "Emma, take it easy. Have fun at the party. Get to know some people. Who knows? You may discover someone better."

"You're just saying that because you have nothing to worry about."

Can't really argue with that. "Fine. If you really want to know, Mark says he thinks highly of you."

"That doesn't make me feel any better. That's like giving me a crocheted sweater for Christmas when I wanted an iPhone."

"Why do you care so much? Ever since we got back from the Met, you and him have been acting weird."

Her expression turns dark. "Let's just say … something *happened* in the Tunnels."

Ella and Logan are blasting "Billie Jean" by Michael Jackson, and everyone seems to be enjoying the King of Pop. Kids and grownups alike are chatting—with people within their age groups, of course. Nobody's eating, not yet, but some of them are sipping out of red Solo cups. Through the crowd, I can barely make out Natalie, Chris, Jackson, and Samantha.

"What do you think?" Natalie asks, surveying the crowd.

"I'd say it was a success," Chris says, and he and Nat fist bump. Liam joins us shortly after.

"They're going to hand out sparklers later," Sam comments.

"Won't humans get suspicious?" Jackson says.

"Jack, it's Labor Day. They'll think we're the kind of people who use fireworks for everything."

I nudge Jackson with my elbow. "Happy birthday. I have something for you, but I'll have to give it you tomorrow."

He gives me a rare smile. "Thanks. You didn't need to get me anything."

"You rescued me back there, remember? I owe you a lot."

I excuse myself, moving towards one of the food tables. Pouring myself some fruit punch, I survey the crowd. Most of the adults I don't recognize, though I've seen all the kids at one point these past two, almost three, years. Katonah is hamming it up with her senior friends, celebrating their last year at this school. Her sister, Vianney Rose, looks just like her, only with gray eyes. She happens to be a really good dancer.

Ella and Logan seem to be having a lot of fun DJing. I walk up to their table near one of Piann's back entrances. Ella notices me and waves me closer.

"Song request?" She has to shout because the music is so loud. Her purple headphones fit awkwardly over her big brown curls.

"Nah. I just wanted to see how things were going here. You seem to be having a lot of fun."

"I am," she smiles. "Although this guy over here wants to play all the oldies to humor the adults here."

Logan hears us and says, "What? *She* only wants to play pop music. It might appease them if we give 'em some old school Prince."

"You want to play R&B at a party?"

"Why not? You think they'd appreciate Twenty One Pilots or something?"

"Dude, that's a different category and age group all together. What you're saying makes no sense."

"I know."

Ella looks confused for a moment, then shakes her head. "How about *A Sky Full Of Stars*? It works well for both groups."

Logan nods. "Sounds good. By the way, I was thinking *My Songs Know What You Did in the Dark* when they give out sparklers."

"I thought that was called *Light 'Em Up*."

"That's what everyone thinks. But no, that's not the correct title."

I slowly back away with my cup, suddenly feeling like I'm intruding. I mean, I like songs as much as the next girl. But music is so obviously their life. I search the crowd for Mark. Where is he? I can't sip this thing forever, which alarmingly tastes like Hawaiian Punch.

Trust Elementals to be frugal.

Someone taps me on the shoulder. "Looking for me?" Mark. My heart beats even faster. He looks handsomer than normal, if that's even possible. His hair is messed up in the front in that boy way that gives everyone the urge to touch it because it looks *so soft*. Not that I'm going to do that now. No, he probably put some time into doing that. But just in case, I hold my Solo cup with both hands.

"Nice party, huh?" I say. "Everyone put a lot of work into it."

"Yep."

"Nice idea, by the way."

Mark looks at me with an odd expression. "Micky, you've said that to me no less than a hundred times."

My cold punch suddenly heats up. "Oh. I guess I'm just nervous."

"What's there to be nervous about?"

I sigh. "I'm not really one for parties. What am I supposed to do? Talk to people I know I'll never speak to again?"

He raises an eyebrow. "Well, you *could* dance."

"That's the thing, though." Dang, I'm all out of my drink. Man, Hawaiian Punch is addicting. You can't have one without wanting another. "I can't dance."

"What about that day in the music hall? You danced then."

"I was just fooling around. Plus, when we danced together, well, that wasn't really dancing. That was more of me trying not to step on your toes."

"You succeeded."

"Well then." I shift my weight onto my left foot. "That's my version of dancing."

He shakes his head, smiling. Eyeing my cup, he asks, "Where'd you get that?"

I point to the table. "It tastes like Hawaiian Punch. You know, that addicting drink we had as kids. In fact, it's still addicting to this day. Want some?" My brain forgot to tell my mouth to shut up.

"Sure."

We get ourselves the juice and talk about his next art project. Chris seems to be begging Natalie to dance with him. I nearly spit the punch out with laughter. Natalie would sooner bathe with toilet water than dance. Looks like he's going to be begging all night. At least he took my advice. Emma has also taken my advice and is dancing with an attractive, preppy senior. Liam looks jealous. He doesn't seem to notice Alexis lurking near him. I really hope he doesn't say yes when she asks him. Emma would be devastated. Sam and Jackson seem to be swaying to the beat, but are still having a heated conversation about something—books, no doubt.

"You think that's going to work out?" he asks suddenly.

"What?"

He gestures to Emma and his brother. "They seem to be purposefully avoiding each other. I think something happened in NYC."

"Emma said the same thing. But you never know with her. She's very complicated."

"And Liam's a heartbreaker." Mark shrugs and finishes his drink. "Although it seems like this time, he's the one getting burned."

I nod. "I think it goes both ways, though. Being good-looking apparently doesn't mean everything is handed to you on a silver platter."

"True, true. You're gorgeous, and you've had some rough times."

Something about the way he's looking at me tells me that he's not just saying that to fulfill some boyfriend obligation. The waxing gibbous shining on us makes the whole thing even more beautiful. Mark gestures towards the dance floor, wordlessly asking me if I want to join him. This time, I say yes. What's the worst that could happen? I'll make a fool out of myself, yeah, but many of the people currently dancing, including my sister Kayleigh, aren't even keeping to the beat.

So I take his hand, and we join the Elementals, and Mark and I dance together for the second time. This particular time around, though, there's actual music, but that doesn't matter. It feels like it's just him and me anyway. And that's enough.

It's always enough.

They passed out the lit sparklers just as the opening notes of Fall Out Boy's popular song start playing. I can sense the excited energy coming from the hopping sparks. Mine seems to glow a little brighter than everyone else's. Mom smiles at me from across the dance floor, waving her sparkler around. It creates a cool pattern. I try making a heart. It works.

I never thought this summer would turn out like this. If someone told me I was going to fall in love with Mark O'Reilly, rescue the Elementals with my friends, and lose one of my closest ones in the process, I would have laughed in the person's face. But it happened. And even though most of it wasn't a cause for celebration, I wouldn't have it any other way.

I look up at the sky, gazing at the white dotted navy blanket. The stars seem to wink back at me. My sisters and I grin at each other. It's a good night, a good life, and a good year. But in the corner of my eye, I spot Raven sneaking around, as usual. She didn't bother coming to the party, but that's okay. She seems to be heading towards Maiyrn from the direction of the library. It's as if I have radar that picks up on her whenever she comes in range. I need to stop doing that. *Leave her alone.*

The old, dusty library books in her arm, however, are kind of hard to ignore.

Chapter Thirty

The day before school resumes, Olivia Wilde comes with my mom to Lalande and offers Katonah and Vianney Rose something they can't refuse: information on their birth parents. Well, to be more specific, a chance to get info on their parents on Katonah's eighteenth birthday.

"The Archives hold all Elemental birth records," Olivia says at breakfast. "Maybe they'll have yours."

I mull this over my bowl of cold cereal. All Elemental birth records? Maybe I could find out about my mother's family in there. She's been so secretive about it, like she's related to Ted Bundy or something. After taking five minutes to muster up courage, I pipe up with, "Do you think I … could I come, maybe? I want to know more about my mom's family. She won't tell me."

Almost as if she heard what I said, Mom looks over from the other side of the cafeteria and gives me a pointed look. She and the former Keepers stayed back to regroup up with the deans and the rest of the Legion members. Every other adult went home. Most of the high school-aged kids who were down in the Tunnels are starting school here, although they have a lot of catching up to do. As for my sisters: Kayleigh and Emma Marie are going to the local middle school near our house. Joy, Kristen, and Lauren will enter into the ninth grade here, but the twins will move up to tenth after Christmas, since they'll have caught up by then. Shannon,

Bethany, Saige, and Mia will start at a local community college in January. Christine is a genius, so she's done with college already, and Jacqueline is old enough to decide for herself whether she wants to continue with school. "I'm twenty-two, Mom," was her answer. "I'm done with formal education." She and Christine are applying for internships.

Katonah shrugs, and I turn my attention back to her. "Sure. Why not?"

I feel a bit guilty, like I'm encroaching on their familial space. Nonetheless, I say, "Thanks so much. I promise I won't be in your way."

Natalie has an odd expression on her face, but I'm not sure why.

The Archives is a big office building in central Cortlandt that's— you guessed it—cloaked. The Witness Protection Program could use our witches and warlocks. It's sparkling clean, there's a white and chrome theme, and the air smells like Pine Sol. The rooms have plaques on the doors. They display what records they have, alphabetically, in gold lettering.

I head to the DI-DO room while Kat and Vi go to the FO room. Each room has filing cabinets that cover all the walls. I quickly spot the DON drawer and pull it out. Since I don't know my mother's maiden name, I have to find it via my birth certificate.

Donadrian, Donahue … it's not long before I find Donaldson. Instead of my sisters' names, though, different Elemental names are in the Donaldson spot. Batoni, Cristene, Eleda Mara, Gia, Giran, Cansi, Cude, Lude, Malma, Soʒen, and Šana are there.

Are those my sisters' real names?

Gia would be Jacqueline, and Malma would be Mia. Cristene is obviously Christine, Soʒen should be Saige, and Batoni is Bethany. Šana would then be Shannon. Cude and Lude look similar, so they must be Kristen and Lauren. Giran, Cansi, and Eleda Mara are probably Joy, Kayleigh, and Emma Marie, respectively.

The name Midam⁻ela is in there, too. That must be *my* real name.

Tentatively, I pull the file out of the cabinet. It's yellowed, meaning it's been here for a while. I take a deep breath and open it.

Let it be known that on this day, December 4ᵗʰ, 1997, in the Province of Féi Conta Sa Reia (Queen's County), Kevana, Princess Midam⁻ela Blaise Donaldson (or Caste-Donaldson) was born to Philip Séamus Donaldson, human, and Princess Meredith Felicity Caste, Fire Keeper, at Exeter City Hospital in Exeter.

What?

What?

Princess?

Kevana?

Caste?

Where have I heard that name before?

A thousand trains of thought are operating in my brain right now, some of them without conductors. Alexis called me Midam⁻ela. Colin referred to us as princesses. All this time, people have been slipping up and calling me the wrong name. Referring to an old life of mine I wasn't aware I had.

Clutching my confusing birth certificate in my hand, I race out of the room.

Or, at least, I try to. Because magic is preventing me to take it outside. I slam into an imaginary wall and instantly see stars. Pain explodes in my head like a thousand glass grenades. After rubbing my head for a minute or so, I file the certificate and *then* start searching for the CA room. The protection spells cast in this place truly are impeccable.

Yanking open the CAS drawer, I study all of the Caste names inside. *Princess Florence Amelie Caste? Princess Cuerva Veronica*

Caste? King Darion Caste? Who are these people and what are they doing in my mother's family?

Amelie.

It says Florence was born in the fifteenth century, which means she and Amelie Avanti can't be the same person. But it also says that Florence and Cuerva are twins, and *cuerva* means 'raven' in Spanish.

Raven ... Amelie ...

They looked so similar. Even in the short while Raven has been at school, so many people commented on their uncanny near identical looks. Some joked that Raven was Amelie's twin, not Alexis's.

Fifteenth century?

My head wants to explode. Everything's happening all at once.

I'm a princess? My mom is a Caste? Raven and Amelie are twins born in the fifteenth century? Felicity Caste, the Middle Ages' version of the Big Bad Wolf, is their mother?

The door flies open. Olivia stands in the doorway, looking terrified. "Oh, good," she says, seemingly relieved. "You're here. I need you to come with me."

Numbly, I put the papers back where they belong and follow her out of the room. We make a left, then a right, then a right again, and then we're finally at the FO room. Tears are streaming down Vianney Rose's cheeks. Katonah looks boiling mad. When she sees me, she thrusts the certificates into my hands. "Look," she growls.

I examine what she's given me. *Let it be known that on this day, September 9th, 1980, in the Province of Terite, Kevana, Katonah Ivanka Fordham was born to Paul William Fordham, warlock, and Isabella Ioanna Papadopoulos, witch, at Koele Hospital in Alimony.*

Let it be known that on this day, January 27th, 1982, in the Province of Hodemra, Kevana, Vianney Rose Petrakova Fordham was born to Paul William Fordham, warlock, and Isabella Ioanna Papadopoulos, witch, at Disena Medical Hospital in Disena.

Dean Papadopoulos. She's their mother?

My eyes flit up to Katonah's, asking so many questions without opening my mouth. She just crosses her arms tighter while her fifteen-year-old sister—no, sorry, make that *thirty-something-year old* sister—continues to sob hysterically.

What the hell is going on?

The car ride back is uncomfortably quiet. Katonah and Vianney Rose sit in the back seat, giving me no choice but to ride shotgun. I study Mrs. Wilde's profile, still surprised by how much she looks like an older version of Natalie. She seems tired, though, like she's worked herself too hard. That's understandable, considering she's been extremely busy ever since she got back.

Desperate to break the silence and get answers, I say, "Did you know?"

She doesn't take her eyes off the road. "About your royal blood? Absolutely."

One beat. Two. "How come I'm not in a castle now or something like that? Not that I want to be, but ..."

Olivia sighs. "It's not my place to say. Meredith will have to tell you, but only when she's ready."

After a minute of pause, Vianney Rose squeaks from the back, "How is it possible that we're in our thirties? We don't *look* like it." Judging by her lack of tears, I'm guessing she's come to terms with it.

"My guess is a time bubble," Olivia says, "but I'm not totally sure. It could also be a time travel spell. Both are near impossible and have serious repercussions for the spell casters. The bubble seems more likely."

"A time what?"

"Bubble. It's an extremely complicated spell. It holds a person—or two, I suppose, in your case—and puts him or her in a sleep-like state. The aging process is all but stopped. It's kind of like an extreme form of hibernation. The caster of the spell sets an amount of time the person will stay in it, say, ten years, and it keeps the person invisible. After the time is up, it pops, leaving the person on the surface of wherever they are. I think that's what happened to you two."

"But who put us there?" Katonah mumbles, still sulking.

Olivia slows for a red light and looks at the sisters in the rearview mirror. "Isabella Fordham. Your mother."

Olivia barely has time to put the car in park before I leap out of it and sprint toward the dorms. Natalie is usually in our room at this time. She'd better be there. I take the Maiyrn steps two at a time, clutching my phone so hard it might break. Natalie is blasting Whitney Houston's greatest hits while doing schoolwork—ugh— when I barge in the room. "Natalie!" I yell, but she doesn't hear me. I walk over to her desk and slam my hands on top of her textbook.

"Hey!" She frowns, but reluctantly turns off her music. "What was that for?"

"I'm a princess!" I don't bother to apologize. "My sisters and I are princesses. We have Elemental names. My mother was some sort of queen!"

Natalie gnaws at her lip, looking uncomfortable. Why is she … I gasp. She knew. "You *knew*?"

"A lot of people did, I guess."

"You *guess*? How many?" *And why does everybody know but me?* She winces. "Um … everybody?"

"Everybody?" I lay eagle spread on my bed. "Great. Just great. That must have been the best kept secret on campus, huh."

"It was harder than you think. I kept reminding myself not to spill the beans, and it was even harder to make sure other people didn't tell you accidentally." She tugs at the lace of her tall brown boots. "I wanted to tell you, but Dean Martins specifically instructed me to protect you."

Protect me? "But why? I don't need protecting!"

Natalie sighs. "You want the full story?"

"Please. I've heard enough lies to last me two lifetimes."

She sits down on her bed. "We had a country in Europe. I was born there, you were, most everyone old enough at this school was born there. In fact, the only person I know who wasn't born there is Chris. It was called Kevana, and it was situated between France, Germany, Switzerland, Austria, and Liechtenstein. Since it was closed off from the human world and you needed to go through a portal to get in, we managed to stay out of most of the European wars. But then came the nineties. You already know how Eastern Europe was pretty much a mess then. Acerbity used that distraction to infiltrate Kevana. They had self-hating turncoats on their side. We weren't expecting it, and the country was torn apart."

"That's horrible," I say, shocked.

"Your mom was queen regnant, and many people were superstitious back then. They claimed that her marrying a human tainted the Caste name. She was a good queen, but people couldn't let that go. And when traitors from Ordena Province let Acerbity through the portals, people blamed her even though she couldn't have done anything to stop it. Your mom got pregnant with you before everything started going wrong, and as soon as you were born, your family fled. People want you dead. They want all the Keepers' kids dead, particularly because our parents married humans out of defiance."

"You couldn't even tell me about my own country?"

She shakes her head, rubbing her thumb against the nervous pebble forming in her hand. "Nope." She opens her dresser drawer and fishes out something. A map. "See here? This is Kevana." I take the political map in my hands. This is my country. My people lived here. A sinking feeling makes my chest feel all heavy. *So many things I don't know.* Looking at it closer, I smirk. The outline makes it look kind of like a chicken nugget. The country's divided into different parts: Hodemra, Faverly, Nasitet, Ordena, Gartesci, Norlot, Serdow, Leyón, Drable, Stepes-Gir, Teca, Caséi, Aitar, Féi Conta sa Reia, Pacméi, Terite, and Sulot. Seventeen provinces. Faverly is the biggest by far, gigantic compared to the tiny Teca. Féi Conta sa Reia is shaped like a star, and Terite resembles Idaho. The Rhine River flows through the western part of the country.

This is where I belong.

"Does anyone still live there?"

"Barely." She shrugs. "At least no one with sense. The place is in ruins. I think some of your older family members are there, though. No one's heard from them since the Destruction." Her green eyes light up all of a sudden. "McKenna!"

I narrow my eyes. "What?" Natalie only gets excited when she has a radical idea.

"This could be the beginning of your revolution! Unite the Continental Keepers, defeat Acerbity, and reclaim your throne!"

"Whoa, whoa, whoa. Wait just a second, science fiction novelist. My throne? It isn't mine. It would be Jacqueline's." *Gia.* Natalie must've taken crazy pills this morning. "And ... the *Continental Keepers*? We haven't spoken with them since freshman year. The last one we talked to was Alexei Romanov, and he hung up on us because I pissed him off. Remember?"

She shakes her head. "Never mind all that. We can all discuss this later, but it would make sense for a Keeper to be the reigning monarch. We can bring Elementals from all over the world to help defeat Acerbity once and for all, and go back to Kevana."

"You're starting to sound like Emma."

"Please?" She ignores my comment. "All you have to say is yes. We'll figure things out."

Less than two months ago, I was a normal Elemental. I didn't know who Emma and Samantha were, most of my family was still missing … but I was still normal. Somewhat. This? This could change my life forever. Become queen? Am I ready for all that? I'm only sixteen. Sure, I'd get training for that, but this isn't *The Princess Diaries*. This is real life. This is who I am now.

This is my chance to vanquish Acerbity.

"Yes."

"Good." She grins. "Now let's start fighting back."

ABOUT THE AUTHOR

Ndidi Aguwa is a high school junior. *Fearless* is her first novel. When she isn't writing or studying, she loves watching soccer, listening to music, and reading. She dreams of going to Stamford Bridge and meeting the players of her favorite soccer team. She lives with her parents and two younger siblings in New York.